# Joyful, Sorrowful,

## AND

# Ordinary Mysteries

## RAYMOND FORTUNATO

CENTRAL PARK SOUTH PUBLISHING

# JoyFul,
# SorrowFul,
### AND
# Ordinary Mysteries

Michelle,

Thank you for bringing Nothing's Plenty For me to life and sharing it with an enthusiastic audience. Your dedication was amazing. All the best.

Raymond Fortunato
Feb 13 2022

# CONTENTS

# DEDICATION

To my writing teachers and mentors, who have encouraged me and guided me over the years: Tony Conniff, Shela Xoregos and Jacqueline Gay Walley. I'd like to thank the writing group I am a member of for enthusiastically enjoying what they began to call "Ray" stories. Here is a whole book of them. I hope the reader enjoys the stories at least half as much as I did writing them.

# THE ZONE OF THE TRAIN

Bess charges, her one red eye blazing, looming larger every second. Is she a bull? Am I a toreador? No. Bess is an oncoming train and I'm running over a trestle towards her. Am I crazy? I'm beginning to think so but I hope not...

What's going on? Simple, I'm a modern American writer trying to write like Papa, Ernest Hemingway. Everything else I've tried has failed, maybe this will work.

I'm being impolite. I haven't introduced myself. My name is Thomas Sand, better known as TS. I have an engaging wife, Lorretta; I like to think we have a good relationship. Two teenagers, Billy and Adele. We love each other but make each other crazy.

I'm the very junior partner in my brother's lawn service business, spending my days cutting other people's lawns. It pays the bills but it's as emotionally satisfying as deflated party balloons. I crave a life of mastery, like being the first person to hit the ball clear out of Yankee Stadium. No one has ever come close, not even the Mick or the Babe. I'm no athlete but what of it? Facts don't change the size of your dreams.

Instead, I cut immense, perfectly planted lawns. No crabgrass.

No bumps. No multitudinous greens like the shimmering Irish ones, dimpled by the ever-changing weather. I've often wanted to cut a figure eight or maybe a checkerboard pattern into their lawns and leave. Then they'd have something interesting to look at.

I'd love to know rich people's secrets. Did they steal their money? Does it make them happy? Do they hate or love to excess? But rich people don't talk to strangers sitting on a riding mower. Instead, I began to imagine stories about these people and jot my ideas in a notebook.

One day, I was cutting the lawn of the comic who specializes in making fun of people's foibles. You know him; he hosted the Academy Awards three times. One blistering July day, I got sunstroke and almost fell off my mower. A shaggy man came out and introduced himself as the comic's elder brother Adam. He said the smell of freshly cut grass tickled his imagination. He offered me what he called the comic's elixir that helped him write his brother's jokes. I drank and immediately felt better. Adam explained that he'd started in comedy first but his brother was the better performer so Adam wrote the material and his brother performed it. First rich person's secret I learned. Adam lamented how hard it is to make it in standup and said most people drop out in less than six months.

My fortieth birthday rolled around. I looked in the mirror and saw tired, sad eyes. My wife wrote in my birthday card, "For your present, why don't you take me to Spain?" The actual present was a copy of Hemingway's *The Sun Also Rises*.

Like you, I'd read it in High School, you know where you have to write a book report to prove you can actually read and, if the book report is too good, you get hammered by your classmates as a pathetic nerd.

Then I was more interested in impressing the girls than trying to figure out why I liked it. Now I read it for pleasure. I am in Spain, watching bullfights, drinking a bottle of brandy followed by two of wine, struggling to get the girl I love away from her toreador. I cared.

I had a notebook full of ideas and I wanted to write them up, as Papa would have. I knew it wouldn't be easy but I was sure I could do it. I hoped that, a thousand years from now, people would compare Sand to Hemingway and not laugh at me.

I signed up for a writing workshop. There were lectures and each student got to write two stories, which were critiqued by the others. My first story was about an imagined set of brothers in comedy, like Adam and his brother, whom I gave the fictional name of "Wrecking Ball." People loved the story.

By the end of the course, I realized that every story was highly praised. I wasn't special. I took three more classes, writing more and more stories. I didn't try to get them published. I was waiting until I thought they were excellent.

One day, as I sat writing for hours, Lorretta interrupted me saying, "Let's go out and do something."

I repeated the line used by Hemingway in Paris to his wife Hadley, "I need to write one good sentence first, even if it takes all day."

"Try again tomorrow. Let's go now," demanded Lorretta. I don't blame her. My sentences were nothing like Papa's. Why should she let me have a whole day to write just one?

I found a writing tutor, Juliet, who read my short stories saying some were fascinating but others felt as unappetizing as a cup of tea brewed without the tea bag. Ouch. Then I thought what a wonderful turn of phrase that was and I liked her honesty. I had a lot to learn from her. We'd discuss the failures. Some stories could be fixed, others only abandoned.

I joined Juliet's writing group. By my third story, people said, "I'd know a Sand story, even if your name wasn't on it. "

Fifteen months later, I had a short story collection which both Juliet and I thought was of publishable quality. I queried fifty-three literary agents. Nothing. I was discouraged but Juliet said, "You have a gift don't give up." I queried another twenty-one agents and wrote new stories.

I now entered every writing contest I could. Most contests cost between twenty and forty dollars and they make it so simple to enter, using a credit card on an online service called Submittable. When Lorretta opened our Visa bill, she asked, "Who is this Submittable? We could have taken that trip to Spain."

It was hard to explain why I wrote. It definitely wasn't the money. Even if I sold a short story, I'd make less than fifty cents an hour. "It's not worth it," said Lorretta. "You could spend more time with me and the kids." We came to a compromise. I'd write a bit less and spend more time with them.

I began to send stories to literary journals, many online and so small that they boasted to having a circulation of 500. I suspected the circulation was probably about 50 but I didn't care, I had to get published. In seven months I sent to ninety-seven journals. I got a few polite rejections saying my work wasn't suited to their magazine.

I was discouraged. My ideas started to peter out. I'd cross off one idea because it was too bizarre, the next was too commonplace or it had been done before. I'd talk to my kids to get story ideas but they wouldn't tell me much. Why did I think they would? I had kept my secrets from my parents. I talked to my friends and their lives had the liveliness of a mute, singing.

I doubted my abilities. I thought of Adam's six-months rule. I'd made it several years but wasn't sure I could get any further. Papa'd been published when he was more than twenty years younger than me. I complained to Juliet, who urged me to keep going.

What was I missing? I studied *The Sun Also Rises*. I knew I could never write sentences like Hemingway but wondered if it was my style that held me back? Suddenly, I thought no, it isn't that. It's the intensity at which Hemingway's favorite characters lived.

In the novel, there were two toreadors. One never let the bull get close to him. The spectators detested him. The other continually entered "the zone of the bull," risking all and at the last instant stepped aside to thunderous applause. Women loved him. This character was alive.

I looked at my writing and my life. I was that first toreador. Maybe I didn't have the passion to be a great writer. Hemingway had been to war. Maybe I should go fight in Afghanistan. Went to a recruiting station and was told I was too old. Good thing. I don't really want to be a soldier.

It was October and the lawn season was winding down. I could spend time pursuing my own interests. How could I get into the zone of the bull? They no longer fight bulls in Spain. How could I simulate that danger and adrenalin? I could furiously drive my car, swerve around corners, cut in and out of traffic but I might hurt someone else and I didn't want that to happen. Then I thought of the perfect idea, a duel with a train. I could enter the zone of the train just like that toreador had entered the zone of the bull. I knew my family wouldn't approve but I didn't intend to get hurt. I'd be like the second toreador and at the last second slip from danger.

There is a railroad straight away ten miles from me with a two hundred yard trestle a few yards above a slow moving river. A train passed regularly at 3:30 PM. Why not start running towards the oncoming train, on the far side and jump off on the land, on the train side before the train got to me? That's the zone of the train. The area was in deep woods and deserted. No one would notice me. Just to make sure I wouldn't create any suspicion, I parked my car about a mile away and walked there.

How long would it take me to run across? One afternoon, after the 3:30 had passed, I got on the track, ten yards on my side and ran across. It took me 41 seconds. The next day I watched how far the train traveled in 50 seconds. I wanted to give myself a healthy cushion.

It took me over a week to figure out exactly where the train would be 50 seconds before it got to the trestle. It turns out that there's a towering pine there, easy to spot. Each time, I'd stand about ten feet off the track and watch the train get closer and then pass. My imagination of the worst outcome with the train reminded me of a mouse crushed under an elephant's foot. If I was going to do this, I'd have to lasso and tie up my emotions. Easier said then done.

I decided that the first time I ran on the track, I'd run only on my side of the bridge and jump off before getting to the trestle. This would assure I got my calculations right and be safe. I wouldn't yet be in the zone of the train yet but was moving in that direction. Even if I miscalculated slightly, I could still safely jump off the track on land. I figured I had more than a 99.99 percent chance of success.

It was 3:29. I could see the train in the distance. The expression "Bess' eye's bulging" popped into my mind. Why was I calling the train a she?  No idea. I saw Bess get to the towering pine and took off. I had run well on the school track but here, on the railroad ties, under pressure, I stumbled. Why hadn't I practiced here? Idiot, I thought. I got up and ran again. You have to have the right length stride to land on the ties. When you hit between the ties, you could slip. I wasn't terrified but the pounding of my heart could have powered a small village.

I looked up, Bess was moving faster than I remembered. When Bess got to the far side of the bridge, I was about ten strides from my end point. Too close. I chickened out or wised up and immediately jumped off to the right, fell to the ground and rolled over. By the time I was able to look up, Bess had passed. I wondered if anyone in the train had noticed me?

I was elated. My breath shallow and quick. I thought I should get up and walk away but I counted over a hundred fast breaths before I could feel secure enough to get to my feet and walk. I drove home alternating between stupor and euphoria. This is going to work.

When I got home, I kissed Lorretta and said we'd be going to dinner at Momma Rosa's. I had chicken scarpariello made extra spicy. It was wonderful. Was it my imagination or were Lorretta and the kids enjoying this more than they usually did? For the first time, Billy talked about his dream of playing football. Adele said she'd tried out for the upcoming school play. She'd never mentioned that interest before.

I tried to write the next day but still had writer's block. I knew I had to, at least once, enter the zone of the train. For the next week, I practiced running on the train tracks, improving my stride and balance, getting better times. I decided to guarantee I'd make it all the way over the trestle by starting ten yards onto the trestle giving myself extra time.

On Monday, 3:25 PM, I was ten yards into the trestle. The weather was in the low sixties and cloudy. I waited, leaning forward when I saw the train about two minutes from the tall pine. Time slows down sometimes. It felt like Bess would never even get close to the tall pine.

When Bess got to the pine, I took off. My feet hit the ties evenly. My breathing was steady. Bess' single menacing red eye bulged and grew larger but I was going to make it. I was two thirds across when the train's whistle blasted and the driver slammed on the breaks. I must have been seen. I panicked. I didn't want to be caught, be in the news or arrested. I jumped into the river, which was a few yards below the trestle. I was lucky. I didn't hit the side of the trestle or the bank of the river. I'm no Olympic diver. I'm sure there was a huge splash. I wondered why I hadn't worn a life preserver while running. Idiot. How could I forget?

The river flowed faster than I had thought. Luckily, it was a clear channel with no rocks but the banks were steep and rocky. I couldn't grab on to anything. I was being dragged along.

I'm not a religious man. I tell people there is no God who orders all of life for the good. To ask for help there was absurd. But perhaps there are some friendly spirits, someone to help us when we're in a bad way and really need help. So I called out, "Please help. I've learned my lesson. I have more to contribute. Help me please."

I tried to relax and float on my back. If the water hadn't been cold enough to give me hypothermia, I might have enjoyed it.

Finally, the river entered a large lake. The current pushed me quite a way from shore. I saw an old man in a small boat fishing. I waved. He saw me, motored over and threw me a rope, pulled me towards the boat and carefully helped me get aboard.

"What the heck are you doing? You could have drowned," he asked.

"I really don't know," I replied.

We introduced ourselves. His name was Stanley. He made a joke saying that I was the biggest and dumbest fish he'd ever caught. He took me to his mobile home, gave me some dry but far too large clothes. He turned on his oven, opened the door and had me stand in front. He made me hot tea and had me drink four cups. Neither of us said much.

When I'd recovered, I started to tell him of my life, my burning ambition to write well and my life successes and failures. He asked me what I wrote about. I told him all about *The Sun Also Rises* and how I wanted to add passion to my writing.

"That's Hemingway's book," he said. "Don't write like him. People want something new. You know what I'd like to read?"

"No idea," I said.

"About people who are in trouble but still remember the sheer joy of getting up in the morning knowing they're lucky to be alive."

It was getting dark. He drove me to my car. I thanked him again and again. "One sincere thank you is enough," he said. "Glad we met. If you do write that story, I'd love to read it."

I drove home. Lorretta asked what happened and I said I'd met an old man who took me fishing. I tripped and fell in. Lorretta looked suspicious but didn't say anything.

It took a month to write Stanley's story. I took it to him. We drank a beer while he read it. "Enjoyed it," he said. "Are you going to publish it?" I assured him that I'd try.

That was five months ago. I've sent the story to thirty-nine journals. None have decided to publish it but there are plenty more journals to try.

I've felt cheerful since I entered the zone of the train. Please don't try it. I was a complete dumbbell. I still want to write like Papa but realize I never will. Now, if I like the stories I write, that's enough for me.

There's been another advantage to having once been in the zone of the train. Sometimes, people say they have a secret that they can't tell me because it's too strange or embarrassing, I tell them I have an outlandish secret too. I say, "I'll tell you my secret, if you tell me yours." We promise never to repeat what we're going to hear.

I didn't think it would work but it did with Lorretta. She was embarrassed to show me the one oil painting she'd kept from the time she'd dropped out of college to couch surf and study painting for three months in the East Village. "I didn't eat for three days to buy the paints. It's pretty awful, isn't it?"

I would never have guessed her secret. The painting wasn't a Rembrandt but it had life. "Let's put it up," I said. Lorretta demurred. I got it framed and hung it in the living room. Now whenever someone new comes to the house, Lorretta takes them into the living room and regales them with her story of creating her masterpiece.

I've told my secret many times. Secrets, told privately but never shared publicly are, well I can't say what they are … maybe coins plucked from a wishing well. Sort of like turning on my living room light and noticing that Lorretta's painting has the Mona Lisa next to it. You know no one will ever believe your fortune.

Some people say that I'm just pulling their leg; no one would be as stupid as that. My only reply is that human stupidity is like a rubber band; it expands effortlessly. So is human joy, or at least it can be.

So far, I haven't heard a single secret more outrageous than mine. Someday, I'll work what I learned from these conversations into my stories. Not the actual events, mind you, I'm going to keep my promise of silence, but the feelings that these secrets produce.

I really enjoy writing now. That's all that counts.

# JOYFUL, SORROWFUL AND ORDINARY MYSTERIES

"So long since laid, forget what feel like."

This was the third time Mona, my Russian cubicle mate, had made this pronouncement in the past two weeks, each time in a very plaintive tone of voice. She was a petite, thin, black haired woman, who seemed to be in her mid-twenties with a svelte yet luscious body. We were both contract computer programmers.

I was twenty-two, just out of college and this was my first real job, my first assignment. Our cubicle had five-foot tall walls and was barely large enough for two computers on one desk and two chairs. We were cramped. Our cubicle was situated in a large, dilapidated room crammed full of such cubicles. The carpet was bare, the lighting dim, and the walls had peeling paint. There was a faint smell of spices and perspiration coming from the fifty or so almost exclusively male consultant programmers packed into that one room. Most of the rest of the building had been renovated a few years before and there existed large comfortable cubicles and offices in other areas but, for some reason, our area had not been updated and looked like it hadn't been maintained in decades. We heard no rumors of updates coming to our neglected area. Our comfort and pride seemed to be or were considered to be extremely unimportant to management.

I was proud that my first job was for one of the founding members of the New York Stock Exchange, the firm O'Brian, Halston, and Irving. They were listed on the stock exchange with the symbol "OH" but we consultants always called the firm Often Honest Investments, because they seemed to take advantage of us whenever they wouldn't be caught.

Mona's repetitive laments about missing having a sex life disturbed me. At least she'd had one. I hadn't yet. I, like many other male computer programmers, was awkward around women. Having grown up in a large Italian extended family, which was almost exclusively male, I had little understanding of women. Mona was one of only three female contract computer programmers at "OH." I wasn't sure how to respond to her talk of not being laid. No woman had ever said anything remotely like that to me. It didn't seem like she wanted me to do anything about it but I wasn't sure.

"Tell me how is your cat Euler doing? " I asked to change the subject.

"Still sick, make stairway get on bed."

Mona had only been in America for about a year. She and her mother had been expelled from the Soviet Union for being Jewish. Her father was still waiting to be able to come to America. If I wanted to agitate her, all I needed to do was ask about her father and his struggles to leave the Soviet Union. I had accidently done this once and tried hard never to repeat this folly.

When I started at Often Honest, I had a hard time understanding many of the other contract programmers. You might think me a bigot but I grew up in an almost entirely English-speaking suburb. My experience was limited and I was now enjoying an enlarged view of the world.

At "OH", native English speakers were a distinct minority. I had landed in a sea of different languages, accents and foods; Chinese, various languages from the Indian sub-continent, Russian, Polish, Spanish, Japanese and many others. At first, the accents grated but, after a few weeks, they sounded natural, interesting. Communication seemed to become easier.

Male programmers wore suits to work except on Fridays, which was a casual dress day. I had grown up in an extremely frugal family. When I got the job, I bought one blue polyester suit, which had two pairs of pants, one blue and one black. I'd switch the pants off, wearing each pair twice a week.

Mona normally wore a black skirt and a variety of different colored and styled blouses with two and occasionally three buttons unbuttoned and she never wore a bra. If you looked closely, and I, at first, seriously tried to stop doing so, there was often a heavenly view. On casual Fridays, she wore a colorful, loose fitting dress with a plunging neckline that, when one stood close and talked to her, made it difficult not to see what I always thought of as Mona's amazingly beautiful living sculptures.

At college, besides studying programming, I had studied art history. My favorite period was the High Renaissance. I thought Michelangelo would have been proud to create a painting of someone as beautiful as I thought Mona was in the flesh. No, that is wrong. She wasn't a Michelangelo. The longer I knew her the more she seemed to be more like Botticelli's Venus Rising.

I wasn't the only one to think this way. Many other male programmers came over to talk and stare at Mona. She didn't like it. She'd bear down on her work while making chitchat for exactly one minute. Then she'd look the man in the eyes, smile, turn towards her computer screen and fall completely silent. It worked every time. They'd be gone by the end of the second minute. Only once did a man stay beyond that. She looked at him malevolently, directly in the eyes, pointed a finger away from her and said fiercely, "Go now." He obeyed.

Our programming team, which numbered fourteen people, had a 9:30 meeting with our manager, Susan, who was the only employee of "OH" on the team, all the rest of us were consultants. She had a richly decorated office on a renovated floor far from the team she managed. We always met on Susan's floor in a large, well appointed, conference room with extremely comfortable chairs and a picture of the President of Often Honest on the wall.

Susan had grown up in Queens. Besides Mona, she was the only other woman on our team. She was about thirty-five, black haired, attractive. She was extremely formal with us, always emphasizing that she was THE BOSS. She didn't interact with us either socially or intellectually because we were lowly consultants.

Susan talked to me first. As always, the volume of her voice changed continually from a near shout to an almost inaudible whisper and back again. I'll try to use capitalization, non-capitalization, and empty space to indicate what it was like to hear her.

"FIRST, I'D LIKE .......to talk ... ERIC, about the partition program. The user wants .... the interface ... TWO DAYS .... you'll be IN TROUBLE .... ."

"What does the user want?" I asked.

"I TOLD YOU. ... Don't you understand?" She looked at me as if I were a recalcitrant, unintelligent child.

I tried a third time and failed to find out more. It was time to admit defeat. I intoned, "You're right, as always, Susan." She didn't notice the sarcasm.

"And you, MONA, ... looking at the ... THEY ARE COMPLETELY .... I want YOU to ..."

Susan's whispering moments usually lasted four to six words and occasionally several sentences but this time, when speaking to Mona, she was inaudible for almost a minute. Yes, her mouth was moving and there was a hint of a sound but what she said remained a mystery. I whispered to Mona to ask Susan to repeat what she had said in a louder voice but Mona wouldn't ask. I've noticed that consultants, especially foreign born consultants, tend to follow direction and not make waves.

I asked Susan to repeat what she said about the problem. She gave me an even more demeaning look and repeated in a mostly moderate tone, "Mona, you have one week to do this or you are in trouble," before she again was almost inaudible.

"I understand," said Mona, and I think she definitely understood the threat, even though neither of us knew what she was supposed to be doing.

A half hour later, I went to bring Susan the results of a test she had wanted completed. As I walked down the corridor, I heard Susan's voice coming from the office of her boss Ryland. I stopped and stood outside, to the side of the corridor, making sure they didn't see or hear me. Ryland was in his early forties. He had four managers like Susan working for him. I'd entered his office once when he wasn't in it to look at what appeared to be a small mace, that medieval ball weapon with spikes on it, on his wall. I wondered why this weapon was on his wall?

Susan said, "I liked it back in the old days when we were all employees. We have far too many of these consultants. Most are no better than pond scum and that Mona is the worst of the lot. We'd do far better if we got rid of them." She continued on in this vein for another minute or two.

Ryland made no comment. Maybe he'd heard this speech before. What shocked me was that Susan's volume and tone were moderate and easily understandable the entire time she spoke to Ryland. Why did she speak so differently to us than to him?

I decided to retreat to our floor and return to talk to Susan later. I kept thinking of what she had said, "Pond scum" and "Mona is the worst of the lot." What was Susan's motivation in specifically targeting Mona? Was it jealousy because Mona was the only other woman in the department and definitely prettier or was it rivalry among the consulting companies at "OH." Perhaps one of the rival consulting companies would pay Susan to replace Mona with a consultant from their company. Susan's motivation could be any, all or none of these reasons and I had little chance of finding out what her reasoning actually was.

I had been observing our working environment carefully and thought I knew the two unstated "laws" for contract programmers at Often Honest.

Law One was that no consultant is ever on the level of an employee. We were pond scum to more people than just Susan.

Law Two was that each consulting company was the bitter rival of every other consulting company and each company would try to replace the other company's consultants with consultants of their own.

I was hoping that there was a third law, as yet unobserved by me that said, "If someone has common humanity or is deeply in love, they would violate rules one and two." I didn't think so. That idea seemed naïve.

There were three consulting companies at our site. My consulting company, "Spectrum Consulting," had twenty consultants; our chief rival, "Intuitive Consulting," had twenty-three. Mona's company, "Halcion Consulting," was disorganized and had slowly lost programmers, going from six consultants a year ago to now having only Mona on the account.

I talked to the head of my consulting company and tried to convince him to help Mona. He refused and said that he was determined to replace Mona with one of our own.

I was sure that Bruce, the head of Intuitive Consulting, our main rival, thought the same. By my reckoning of the laws, Mona had Susan and more than forty other people against her. Right then, I decided to see what I could do to make sure she didn't lose her position.

Why wasn't I also against Mona? It's related to my beliefs. I don't always follow them, of course, and some of them contradict each other but I had thought a lot about them and found them to be sound.

I don't want to bore or try to convince you of their verity but here they are. I was raised a Catholic. To me, there are three core beliefs in Catholicism.

One is that God loves us. I'll let you decide whether or not you agree with that.

The second is the dignity of human life; all people have an inherent, God given, and profoundly important right to exist and flourish and we should love them and do good by them, without regard to what we think is their apparent worth.

The third core belief of Catholicism is that this world and many aspects of the divine are mysteries.

I think that most people, even if they disagreed with the first core belief, would agree with the second and third.

Mysteries are all around us. Catholics meditate on the ten Joyous and the ten Sorrowful Mysteries. There's no need to get into the details, because if you're interested, you can look them up, but you don't have to think very hard to see that life does consist of many joyous and many sorrowful mysteries.

I had personally come up with an extension to the Joyful and Sorrowful mysteries. I called them the "Ordinary Mysteries." The world is filled with "Ordinary Mysteries," among the most prominent for me, were the questions "why," women and love.

How did all this apply to Mona? She had great dignity and I wondered why the Soviets kicked her out. It didn't make sense to me that being Jewish was reason enough for people to hate her and her people. She was brilliant and pleasant, when not annoyed, where she could show a well controlled but sharp temper. Did a sharp temper matter? No. Thinking of the injustices she'd already suffered, I determined that I would figure some way to keep Mona in her job and, if possible, help her get laid, which is what she said she was missing. The getting laid part certainly wasn't a stated Catholic priority but I thought if I could find her love, it would also get her what she said she wanted. Two birds with one stone.

Were these my real motivations or did I really just enjoy looking at Mona and her living sculptures? Probably both. And here I have to say that I was embarrassed for myself because the more effort I put into not looking at Mona's breasts, the more I wanted to look. The only way I could not spend the whole day obsessed was to talk to Mona in the morning from a place with a clear view, and slowly count down from ten down to zero and then look away.

But I did not want to stop looking. Sometimes, I had to do this more than once in a day. Mona seemed oblivious to my looking and I began to relax a bit. I started to not only count down from ten to one but to continue the count by adding fractions before I got to zero, one half, one quarter, one eighth, eventually getting to one four thousandth ninety sixth and then zero. I hoped that Mona never noticed but I was unsure and unsettled. This disturbed me and I thought of my conduct as something I couldn't control which was one of the Sorrowful mysteries. The fact that such beauty existed, in this world, was one of the Joyful mysteries.

After the meeting with Susan, the first order of business was to find out what Susan wanted Mona to do. I went to the business analyst who wanted the changes. For some reason, contract programmers were kept away from the business analysts but I was desperate. Eventually I found him. He was an employee and worked on another well-decorated, richly appointed floor. It was a typical conversation between programmer and business analyst.

"So in all cases we are supposed to do what you just said?" I asked.

"Of course," he replied.

"Are you sure there are no exceptions."

"Absolutely positive."

"What about when the markets are closed in Hong Kong?"

"It's different then."

"Can you tell me what to do then?"

"I'll need to think about that but go ahead and work on what I told you."

"Are there any other exceptions?"

"No."

"What if the stock price goes below a dollar?"

"I never thought of that."

"What should we do in that case?"

"I have no idea but you should do the right thing."

Business analysts seemed to think that there was a programming command that said, "If we can't tell you what to do, do the right thing anyway." Unfortunately, there's no such command in any programming language. Definitely a Sorrowful mystery.

It was a frustrating conversation but at least I gained some knowledge of what Mona needed to do and she could make a start on her assignment.

On my way back to my cubicle, I was introduced to Isaac, a new programmer working for our main rival, Intuitive Consulting. He was a rather tall American born Jew with dark brown hair, piercing brown eyes and prominent ears. Today, he wore his grey Armani suit. I was trying to find an ally in the fight to save Mona, so I invited him to lunch.

We went to a Chinese buffet and started talking about nothing in particular. I learned that Isaac had gone to college with Bruce, the leader of his consulting team, and that Bruce sometimes got together with friends to play poker. I filed that information away, as a possible future means to help Mona. Then I asked Isaac about his attempts to go out with girls. First we traded pick up lines that neither of us would ever have the nerve to try and, then trusting each other a bit more, I said, "The first time I tried to kiss a girl, we were walking along the shore letting the waves hit our feet. When

I turned to kiss her, she screamed out 'Don't you dare!' and pushed me into the water."

Isaac tried but could not hold back a chuckle. I chuckled too. This occurrence was no longer the great tragedy I had originally thought it was but I was still sensitive about it.

Isaac topped that: "I could only get a distant cousin to go with me to my high school prom and I really tried to impress her. She had a flask and got drunk and then shouted at the top of her lungs that I was boring and she left with someone else halfway through the night."

I tried but could not hold back a chuckle. Isaac didn't join in.

Isaac was funny, nice, Jewish and also had a cat. I thought it would be worthwhile introducing him to Mona to see what would happen. If Isaac went out with Mona, then maybe he could convince Bruce to protect her, which might validate the theoretical Third Law of the Contract Programmers that love or common humanity can overrule Laws One and Two.

I brought Isaac over to our cubicle and introduced him to Mona. He looked at the back of her head as she was trying to work and tried to make small talk. She talked for exactly one minute, looked him in the face, smiled, went back to work and was completely silent. This was not going to be as easy as I thought it might be.

Mona was obviously worried about her job and whether she could do what Susan wanted her to do. I told Isaac I'd see him later and sat down to help Mona.

Mona showed me why she was so frustrated. A programmer in Bruce's company had written the program she had to modify and he had used every trick he could think of to make what was already a complex program, unintelligible. This is often done to provide job security because only the person who wrote the program could understand it. One way to do this is to use slight variations of the same word to mean entirely different things. In this program the names "Money," "mOney," "money," MoneY," and "MOny" were used to signify five entirely different things. If Susan wanted to get rid of Mona, she certainly picked a real puzzler of a program to give her.

I explained to Mona what, from a business point of view, needed to be done and Mona and I worked through the day trying to understand the program, taking extensive notes. I noticed that her attention to detail was better than mine. She then helped me with my work by explaining a few of the more arcane technical considerations of my program. I could tell that we would make a good team, me figuring out what needed to be done and she figuring out the best way to do it. Mona had to stay.

Wednesday started with Mona again complaining she hadn't been laid for so long. I invited Isaac to join Mona and me for lunch. It was pleasant. They talked about their cats but that didn't seem to light a spark.

I had been reading the Jeeves stories by P.G. Woodhouse. Jeeves is Bertie Wooster's butler. Bertie and his crazy friends got into all kinds of problems and miraculously, at the last second, with no apparent effort, Jeeves, who is intelligent because he eats a great deal of fish, gets them out of their difficulties and saves the day. I craved finding my Jeeves.

I first thought of talking to my mother. Then I recalled the time when I was ten and we were in line at the bank. The man behind us said to my mom, "Do you know who I am, I'm Mario Puzzo, the author of *The Godfather*," and my mother replied, "Big deal, that's nothing." I was afraid that she'd think my problem too trivial for her to give me any advice. Besides, if she were going to teach me about girls, wouldn't she have done so already?

I couldn't think of anyone who could help me until I remembered that there was a woman in my building, Veronika, who writes a lovelorn column for a local weekly paper. I bought some cake as a gift and rang her doorbell. I explained the situation to her.

"It's a hard case. You tried getting them together and nothing happened?" asked Veronika.

"Yes," I replied.

"Then you'll have to set up a situation where she's bound to notice him, a situation which will show her his heroic side."

"I don't know if Isaac has a heroic side."

"If put in the correct situation, all men can be heroic. Figure it out."

I wasn't sure this was good advice but I began to think how I might implement it. I thought about what Mona and Isaac had in common. I didn't know but I would try harder to find out.

As a second way to help Mona, I thought that maybe I could outplay Bruce and his friends at poker. If I could win enough money, I could trade it for them making sure that Mona kept her job. But I didn't have enough money to make the stakes high enough so they'd have to help her. Plus I was worried that I might actually lose.

I'd been playing cards since I was three years old at my grandfather Andrew's house but we never played poker. My grandparents had nine children. I knew eight of his children. The ninth, Robert, had moved to the Boston area and never visited my grandparents. Robert and his wife, whose family was from China, had a son, named Luigi, whom I also never met. He was born on the same day as I was. Quite a coincidence.

Grandfather Andrew's passion was playing cards. He was by far the best card player in our extended family. People would vie to be on his team. It almost guaranteed victory.

Andrew started the grandchildren off with a simple card game, called Seven and a Half, which is the Italian version of Black Jack and then, in succession, moved on to Canasta, Bolivia and finally combo-Bolivia. Combo-Bolivia is played with four decks of cards. It has complex rules and dwarfed all the other games in complexity and interest. Playing with four decks, each person could end up with an enormous number of cards in their hands.

Andrew, his wife and two of his children, still lived in the old house that had been their home for fifty-five years. At the center of the house was a large dining room, which had an ornate mahogany table that could seat eighteen people. There were paintings of our ancestors on the wall. This was the room where the two great passions of the family, eating and playing cards, were enacted.

On Thursday night, I went to visit Andrew. He was playing cards with seven relatives including my parents. When the game ended, Andrew insisted that he put the cards away himself. All hugged and my parents and the visitors left. My aunt and uncle went to watch TV, soon to be going to bed. Only Andrew and I were left at the table.

Let me describe Andrew. He is a mid-sized man, who looks to be larger than his five foot four height. He has a well kept mustache, black hair with a few steel colored hairs, large biceps, a face that can be very animated depending on what he is doing and he smokes a hand carved pipe whose smoke smells wonderful. He is the head of the household and plays in every card game that goes on. I'll write what we said in modern grammatical English because Andrew doesn't speak English well and I speak appallingly bad Italian but we have been talking to each other since I was three years old and I have no difficulties in understanding him.

I asked Andrew if he knew how to play poker.

"I'm an expert but I warn you, many people go too far playing poker. It's very dangerous. I won't teach you." He looked stern and added, "We only play for chips, not for money here and turn them in at the end of every game. That's the only safe way to play."

I told him of my problem with Mona. He laughed because he was said to be very popular with women. My mother said that, when he was young, women threw their keys at him as he walked by, hoping he'd come to see them. I wish I'd inherited that gift.

When he understood why I wanted to learn he said, "That's a good reason to learn but I'm not sure you wouldn't abuse what I teach for evil purposes."

"What evil did you experience?" I asked.

"You're too naive and inexperienced for me to tell you. Live a little and we can talk. You're a pretty good card player but there's a lot you don't know. I'll teach you something. This will be our personal secret. Don't tell anyone else." With his eyes he pointed to the table, where everyone had left the cards they had at the end of the game.

"Let's look at the cards," he said.

"Why?" I asked.

"You can learn a lot from looking at how people arrange the cards in their hands." Without turning the cards face side up, he told me that my father would have more aces than anyone else and that he ordered his cards with diamonds always on the left side, followed by hearts, spades and clubs. We looked at my father's hand and Andrew was correct.

He asked me if I had any idea how Mary arranged her hand. Of course I had none. "Everyone else puts the highest cards of a suit to the left and the low cards to the right. She does exactly the opposite." We looked and of course he was right. "Knowing the order helps you figure out what other cards they have in their hand. When they pick up a card or the deck, they'll put the cards in a particular place. If you know how they arrange their hands you get an indication of what it is and what they've got. On the discard, you can see that they threw out the ten of diamonds and you can see exactly where they took the card you have an advantage. But don't let anyone catch you watching."

"Isn't that cheating?" I asked.

"If you don't cheat a little, you don't want it enough." I was dumbstruck that he might cheat.

"They've all played thousands of games of cards. Do you think it's easy to beat someone consistently who has had that kind of experience?" He paused and answered his own question. "Nope. But it isn't cheating, it's just knowing your opponent. I call it bending the odds in your favor. What about you? Do you know what order you put your cards in?"

"Not exactly."

"The order of your hand will be spades, diamonds, hearts and clubs, starting from the left to right with the high cards on the left and low cards to the right."

We looked at my cards and of course he was right.

"Now take a look at my hand."

I picked up his cards and looked at them. "I don't see a pattern," I said.

"So no one can tell what cards I'm holding from my discards or pickups. Big advantage. Having my hand in no order makes me pay much more attention to the game, an even bigger advantage."

"So you'll teach me poker?"

"You'd be better off if you start to really observe."

"Are you going to teach me?"

"I've already told you some secrets. Practice them. Learn how you play better and how to vary how your play. I'll only teach you poker if there's a good reason, one I can believe in."

"What do you believe in?"

"I don't know if it is a belief or an observation."

'What have you observed then?"

"Jesus said he'd make us as cunning as a serpent and as innocent as a dove. I've observed that unless you're both, you run into big trouble in this world. You, Eric, only have the innocence of a dove and that's as dangerous as only being a cunning snake."

"So you won't teach me?"

"I said that if you really need to learn, I'd teach you." With that promise I left.

I started to observe Mona and to notice the books she brought to work. I thought I'd learn something that might help Isaac but what she read was in Russian. When she went to the lady's room, I opened one of the volumes and saw that it must be poetry. I xeroxed the cover and showed it to another Russian speaker who said she was reading the poems of Anna Akhmatova.

I went to the library and found an English edition of some of her poetry. I was impressed by its simplicity and depth. Was Mona yearning for a better world? Anna's poem said yes.

> Somewhere there is a simple life and a world,
> Transparent, warm and joyful. . .
> There at evening a neighbor talks with a girl
> Across the fence, and only the bees can hear
> This most tender murmuring of all.

I lent the book to Isaac.

About a week later, I told Isaac that I had thought of a sure-fire way to get Mona to love him. "We can do it on Friday, because Mona comes to work early that day and that way, we'll have the place to ourselves. I'll set up a situation where you will be the hero. All you have to do is to come into my cubicle after Mona gets in and pay attention to what I signal you to do. Be ready to act and save her. I'll take care of the rest," I said.

The first thing Mona said to me, early on Friday morning was, "So long since laid."

She really looked down in the dumps. She talked about her father and the continued difficulties of getting him out of the Soviet Union. It felt like a bad day to try what I had in mind but I thought this might be the best day. If Eric saved her when she was depressed, it might be more powerful than if he saved her when she was happy.

A few minutes later, Mona left the cubicle and I called Isaac over. About five minutes later, Mona returned. Isaac and I were standing near Mona's chair and she began to slowly sit down. I gave Isaac a signal to be ready to catch her and I pulled Mona's chair away. Isaac had an easy chance to save Mona from falling to the ground and being the hero.

Isaac saw that Mona was going to fall and that he could easily catch her. He knew what he should do but he wasn't moving. I thought I could save her but I didn't have an angle to catch her. As Mona fell, she had a major wardrobe malfunction and Isaac couldn't take his eyes off her treasures. He was frozen in place, eyes bulging. Mona hit the floor and began to sob. She pulled up the top of her dress, mumbled something in Russian and then screamed at me in English, "Why do this me? Why do this?"

Then Isaac yelled, "How could you pull Mona's chair out like that?" and he punched me hard in the right eye. I fell to the ground. Isaac knelt down and comforted Mona. He did something extraordinary. He recited a poem to her. The pain of my eye did not stop me from hearing it.

Candle Light vigils amid the deep snow
Snow drifts and blowing amid fire glow
I hate the vast cold that keeps us apart
I've never told you, you've stolen my heart

Mona responded "my darling" and continued with some sweet sounding Russian words. Neither paid me the slightest attention.

I got up, left them and went to the bathroom to bathe my eye in cold water. I was hurting but rejoicing. I had done a good deed for my neighbor. I'd paid a price but it was worth it. Later, when asked about my black eye, I told the other programmers I had got it the night before in a fight at a bar. The black eye enhanced my status with most of them.

I asked Isaac where he had got the poem. Turns out he wrote it himself, his first ever. It was corny but very effective.

That day, I went home early to celebrate, raising a glass of wine in praise of Veronica, who had given advice that I realized, after having finished my second glass, was of no help at all. I was still on my own, without Jeeves.

I went into work on Monday early before anyone else arrived. Mona came in smiling, and I knew I had done something heroic, not for my own glory.

Mona said, "Isaac and I good time Friday night. All fixed. I laid. No more complain. Proof in bag."

I had no idea what was she going to pull out of her pocketbook and show me. I didn't need to know how she got laid. I wanted to make some excuse to end the conversation but I couldn't think of anything. I'm ashamed to say that I was more than a bit curious. Mona dug into her bag and pulled out an envelope with a piece of paper in it. I wondered how it related to her getting laid?

"Look," she demanded and handed me the paper.

I looked and, wonder of wonders; it was a check for about a year's pay from her consulting company.

"What's this?" I asked.

Mona said, "Men never listen. I say not laid forget what feels like?"

"I heard that," I replied, not understanding her.

"Finally, my company laid me."

And I understood it all and what a complete idiot I'd been.

Isaac arrived.

Mona said to Isaac, " Can't get laid too much."

I smiled and agreed, "You can't get laid too much" and chuckled.

Isaac smiled and looked confused. Maybe he was already day dreaming of an exciting night. I didn't want to interfere. I decided to wait till later to tell Mona of her language error. I'd never tell Isaac about it. No need to discourage a man with high hopes.

Later that day, I explained to Mona her mistake in usage and she was hot. She couldn't understand why I had not told her sooner. She didn't believe me when I said I had honestly made a mistake.

"It mistake look my breasts count ten to one and say fractions?"

"How do you know I count down including fractions?"

"You count loud. Neighbors ask what count. I tell you crazy. Angry at you."

I apologized and was embarrassed for what I had done and

amazed that I had actually counted down out loud. I had no idea I did that.

Isaac came by and Mona calmed down. After Isaac left she said, "You my friend. Friday's dress please me." She looked down towards her breasts and smiled. "Pretty. You look once, count ten to one but no fractions or I kick you."

It was an agreement I could live with.

Isaac and Mona went out day after day. Finally Mona said, "I give Isaac little kiss. No, didn't get paid."

She looked into my eyes and smiled. This was the first joke she ever told me. I laughed.

On the Monday, I had doubts that I had succeeded. Isaac talked to his boss, Bruce, pleading that he help Mona keep her job but to no avail. Bruce confirmed that they still planned to oust Mona. "She'll find another position somewhere," said Bruce. Laws one and two of contract programming were the only ones Bruce acknowledged. He would get rid of Mona and replace her.

I determined to do one more thing for Mona. I'd win her job by beating Bruce at poker.

That night, I played Canasta with my grandfather. I did not put my cards in a definite order and I really concentrated. I beat him in the first round and he looked surprised. During the second game, he smoked, blowing the sweet smelling smoke towards my face. It was something he used to take his opponent's minds off their games. It didn't work, I won again. The third game he asked me to talk about my black eye. Few people can chat and play well but I won the third hand.

We played one last hand. While we played he spent a lot of time telling me, "There's a lot more to you than meets the eye. You really are a wonderful player." I won again. He threw down his hand and said, "That was my final test. Few can think of themselves as wonderful and concentrate on cards at the same time. You are a fine player."

He went and got us both a glass of Anisette to celebrate my victory. I told him all about my adventure with Mona and Isaac and he genuinely laughed and enjoyed every second of it.

"That was heroic. Maybe you're learning something about life."

"But they're still going to get rid of her. It isn't fair."

"And you can help how?" asked Andrew.

I explained my plan to play poker for her job.

"It's a dangerous game. You can make eternal enemies if you win."

I had never thought about that. I asked, "Are you going to teach me?"

He thought for a while. Looked at me closely. Poured us another glass and looked at me again. "I'm going to take a chance on you. What will you do to make sure you don't create a permanent enemy by winning?"

"Why is that important?" I asked.

'Once you make an enemy of a man, he can be of no further use to you," Andrew said.

"What do you suggest?"

"Beat a man hard then make a deal and give back a good deal of his money."

"Then I won't make that much."

"Poker can make a man greedy. Dangerous. Better to make less and part as friends."

"How can I be sure to beat him?"

"You can't be sure but you're good and there are other things that can help. Play poorly at first. Don't tip your hand. When they think they'll easily beat you then really start to use all I taught you and start to bet high."

"Is that all?"

"No. There are other tricks. Have much more money than they do. That way you can afford to lose for a while."

"I don't have much money."

"I'll help you."

"Why?"

"I've made a lot of bets in my life and I usually win. I'm betting on you and hoping you won't be stupid."

He went to a certain place in the room, did something I didn't expect and a panel moved. He put his hand in and pulled out a bag that had what looked to be a small fortune in fifty-dollar bills. "My winnings," he said. He gave me a year's pay in cash. "Only use it if you need it and I expect you to win and add a little of your winnings to my winnings."

"What if I lose?"

"This is my bet on you. If you lose, you owe me nothing but I'll know I can't help you. Don't worry about the money. I'm an old man. I won't miss it. Worry about your play."

We then played hand after hand of poker. It is a far simpler game than combo-Bolivia. As we played each hand, my grandfather told me all the things I was doing well and where I was failing.

When we finished he said, "I've taught you a little about being as wise as a serpent. Don't become a serpent. Poker can ruin a man."

The next week, I played poker with Bruce and his friends. Though they were good, they obviously did not have a Grandfather who had made a lifetime study of playing cards. I followed Andrew's advice and first lost quite a bit and then started to win. As soon as I started to win and bet a lot more money, only Bruce had enough money to beat me.

I won over a year's salary from Bruce. He didn't have that much in cash so he wrote me an IOU for about three quarters of it. I had thought Mona was angry when I pulled her chair out but that was nothing compared to what I saw in Bruce's eyes. I asked to talk to him alone.

I offered to rip up his IOU if he could make sure that Mona kept her job.

"How could I possibly do that?" he asked.

"I'm sure you can. You have a huge incentive to do so."

The next afternoon, Mona told me that her contract had been extended for two more years. I congratulated her, went to see Bruce and gave him back his IOU.

"Are you sure I can have it back?"

"Yes. Tear it up."

He smiled as he tore it up. He asked if I wanted to play poker on his team.

"Not now. Maybe another time."

"Yes, another time."

I had done what Andrew had wanted, won and not made an enemy.

Two nights later, I visited Andrew, thanked him, and gave back his money plus half of my winnings. He only took an eighth of my winnings. He put his original loan back in the safe place. A few minutes later, an uncle and aunt rang the doorbell and came in. They were talking about my cousin Luigi, from Boston, the one I had never met. All of grandfather's children always got together except for some reason Luigi's family never visited Andrew. My aunt was excited that Luigi had just got a job on Wall Street at one of the investment houses.

"Which one do you work at? I always forget, " asked my aunt.

"Often Honest," I said. Then I remembered the real name. "I mean O'Brian, Halston and Irving," I said.

"He got a job at Smyth, Symington and Harrison. Are the two companies friendly?"

"No. Deadly rivals."

"Make sure you look him up and show him a good time when you see him," said Andrew and he gave me a significant look.

"What's he like?" I asked Andrew.

"I haven't seen him in ages."

"I've had a bit of luck. Let me take all of you out to dinner," I said.

My aunt and uncle argued as our family was frugal and almost never ate out but Andrew said, "We have so much to celebrate. A job for Luigi, some victories for Eric. Let's do it," and we all went to the only Italian restaurant in town.

I ordered two bottles of Chianti. Andrew raised a toast to me and my cousin Luigi. "May the two of you be fast friends." My aunt said the wine wasn't nearly as good as the wine Andrew made. My uncle didn't enjoy his meal but both Andrew and I were in a triumphant mood and enjoyed the meal, the wine and each other's company.

I went to pay the bill and Andrew insisted on paying.

"You've become a man," Andrew said to me on the way out. "Maybe now I can teach you something about women."

"I can't wait," I said.

"The first thing I suggest is that you buy better clothes."

"You don't wear fine clothes," I argued.

"Every person is different. I don't need to. You do. Just do it. You have the money."

"I thought I'd save my winnings."

"Spend some on clothes. You wear the same suit day after day. You look like a miser. Women don't like misers. You do want to learn, don't you?"

"Yes. I'll buy another suit. "

"Buy two; fine designer wool suits not polyester. They have good sales at Barney's. And make a friend of Luigi and bring him to see me."

"I will."

"Is that a promise?" he asked.

"A solemn promise," I said.

Had I found my Jeeves? I had no idea but I think so. I was ecstatic.

# ENDING IN DEATH

"James, I'm betting it's murder, but it could have been an accident. I think I know who did it and probably why. You're often called as an expert witness. Let me tell you what I found out."

Tom Averdal looked around the small, quiet bar near the office of James Carforno, a psychiatrist in his mid-forties, whom he had chosen to help him. Tom, who was thirty-nine, medium height with a crew cut, was not smiling. He seldom smiled when he was talking business. He'd used James on several occasions to offer advice involving odd employee behavior and possible drug problems when Tom was the owner of the Hardwired Technical Consulting Services. Tom had sold the Consulting Services to a large multinational about a year ago for thirty-five million dollars.

"I need your advice on the emotional and medical issues in the murder. Just let me know what I owe you for this session. Tell me exactly what you think, no sugar coating anything. Do you agree?"

James liked Tom's directness. He replied, "I can't help without information. Start at the beginning. What's this murder you're talking about and what do you want me to do?"

"I only said it could be murder. It started two months ago. I was supposed to stay on for a year after the sale but the new tech owners forced me out in June. Thought I was too opinionated and not deferential enough. That's true. They could, it's their company now. I don't feel sorry for myself but I miss the excitement, beating the competition.

"I took up golf and I'm terrible at it and it doesn't get the adrenaline moving. Tried skydiving once. Not for me. You've met my wife Elvira, she teaches high school. She's off for the summer and, with us being home together so much, we were getting on each other's nerves. She said to me 'Tom, you're becoming impossible. You've got to get your mind off being fired and find some hobby that will mean something to you.'

"I like looking at paintings and Elvira was dying to go to France. The best way for impatient people, like me, to see the world is to go on a good tour with an expert. Saves so much time, so we booked a two week art tour to Southern France with a stop in Spain and that's where it happened."

"Where what happened?" asked James.

"The murder of course. You seem to have the same problem I do, not being able to concentrate and really listen." James winced and thought that what Tom called "straight talking" wasn't always pleasant talking.

"I first meet Thane Angus MacThubur and Lady Shelly on the tour. They were both from Ohio and don't really have titles but that's what I called them, behind their back, anyway. Even started calling them that to their face later in the tour.

"A long time ago, the local rulers in Scotland were called Thanes and Angus was the descendant of one of these Thanes. Lady Shelly's ancestors were upper class, snobby English.

"We'd all just arrived at the small airport in southern France;

the damn airline lost one of my bags in Paris. They're always doing something like that, idiots, so inefficient. Our tour guide, Phyllis, told us the airline would deliver our luggage that night. She didn't strike me as very reliable but she was right about the luggage but, since the tour, I've checked some of the stories she told about the artists and she messed up lots of details. Have to give her credit, though, if you were looking to capture the atmosphere of an event or place and didn't care about all the little details, she's a good guide.

"The hotel was over an hour's drive from the airport. Phyllis put the four of us into a mini-van with a driver. We started chatting. Angus mentioned that he was a lawyer and loved his job. He called himself an "honest ambulance chaser" but his real passion was pro-bono legal work, working on appeals of poor people's convictions. He looked to be early fifties, over six feet two and had, for a lawyer, longish, dark brown hair, swept back over his head. Had the hint of an actor in him. Damned useful for a lawyer to be an actor. He seemed to be on all the time, as if he believed Shakespeare that all the world's a stage and he was the one bright shining star of that stage. He talked with a subtle smile in his eyes as if he was charming you and I got the distinct feeling he'd charm most of the people on the tour."

"Interesting how the Thane, what did you say was his name? irritated you so much yet you liked him. Probably could charm a jury too. Hope you're not going to accuse him of murder," said James.

"We'll get back to him later. His wife, Shelly was younger, maybe mid-forties and she emanated a much more complex feeling. She had stringy blonde hair and what I'd call a willowy smile. She was medium height and very thin. She had magnificent breasts for such a thin body. I thought that she must have kept the Thane warm at night.

"Shelly said they had plenty of money and it was time for him to retire so they could spend more time together while they were young and healthy. It was the second marriage for both of them and

Angus' first wife had died. 'Doesn't that just prove one should enjoy oneself when one can?' she asked.

"Angus frowned and said he was enjoying his life and work and he wanted to continue to serve all his clients. Emphasizing the word "all" which I took to mean especially his pro-bono work on appeals.

'I agree with Angus,' I said. 'Retirement is boring.'

"'Life's never boring for me,' Shelly said and she started talking about how charming the town they lived in was and how many talented people lived there. As she spoke, she got more and more excited and began to talk faster and faster. I became bored, looked out the window, and stopped paying attention. I became engrossed watching the scenery and figuring out how different or similar everything here was compared to what you see in New York State.

"After a few minutes, Shelly tapped me on the shoulder and said that she was sure I'd be interested in her next story. She began telling us, at a slower tempo, of how she and Angus had gone to Scotland trying to find Angus's ancestral home. "If Angus's family had stayed, we'd be Lord and Lady of a gigantic estate," she said. Elvira and I were blessed with a long description from Shelly, Angus never saying a word, about how they found the ruins of the MacThurbur manor house.

"The manor house was abandoned, in the 1700s when Scottish Highland small farmers were pushed off the land and sheep grazing became the norm. Shelly went through all the adventures they had trying to find this ancestral home.

"Shelly's voice got louder and faster as she described the manor ruins they had finally found. She said the foundations were prominent and were about 120 feet by 90 feet.

"Thane Angus, a more practical man, or maybe just more observant, said quietly that the foundation of the manor house was barely visible and appeared to be about 30 by 50 feet."

"Classic marriage and their differing vision," said James.

"You're right. Those disagreements between spouses can be explosive. Lady Shelly glared at Thane Angus as if she might hit him but he continued quietly saying he was glad his family had left Scotland because he preferred being a lawyer in America to being a poor Lord in a dime sized, deserted, destitute place in Scotland.

"After the adventure of finding the manor house, Shelly said she was dying for a few drinks but there was no pub nearby. Angus said quietly, seemingly to himself 'I don't drink and I don't chew and I don't go with girls who do.'

"'I drink every day and it's totally natural,' Shelly almost yelled and the Thane whispered quite audibly, 'Except for you, dear. Except for you.'

"I had to stop myself from laughing and I started to respect the Thane even more. He could speak truth to power, even if under his breath, and get away with it. He must be an awesome lawyer.

"So you heard all that?" asked James. "I thought you weren't paying attention."

"I heard most of it. Some I picked up later. In the four days she had to live, Shelly told that same story, to various people, at least three more times.

"The hotel we stayed at was a converted early nineteenth century school, in a very old small town. There was a tall, cream-colored stone clock tower, falling apart from the sixteenth century and many stone houses from around that time. Shelly insisted on taking a selfie with Angus, with the hotel in the background, and posted it on Facebook.

"At dinner, all 14 people on the tour sat at the same table. Shelly's mood continued to soar upward saying to Phyllis, the tour guide, that she was a High School art teacher and that all her students were madly in love with her as both a teacher and an artist.

"Phyllis smiled and said how wonderful she thought that was. Guides have to put up with so much. I often wonder what they really think. I thought Shelly was bragging and said that, by the law of averages, it was impossible for all her students to love her. Shelly snapped at me. Elvira, whom I should have known would object to my cutting but true observation, kicked my shins under the table, our not so subtle sign that tells me to just shut up, and so I started talking to the people to my right.

"After dinner, we walked around the town. Elvira said she hoped I'd be more tolerant of the foibles of others during the tour. She reminded me that people, like myself, who studied mathematics, tend to argue and that most people don't enjoy being argued with.

"They sure don't," said James. "I could tell you --"

"'Yes, Yes. Anyway, I told Elvira that we seem to get along, even when we argue."

"'Dream on, dear,' Elvira said. I laughed. Didn't know if she was joking or serious.

"The next morning, Elvira and I were at breakfast early and Shelly and Angus came in when we were almost finished. Shelly complained of having the worst nightmare of her life saying that it terrified her. A mad dragon was following her car, trying to land on the roof. She couldn't drive fast enough to get away from it. Extremely vivid dreams can be the result of taking some anxiety medications, I thought. That's correct, isn't it James?"

"Yes, there are many medications that cause vivid dreams such as --."

Tom cut James off. "I know, I looked it up. After the nightmare, she couldn't sleep. She looked tired and morose. She opened the small purse that hung loosely on her shoulder, took out a prescription pill bottle, removed a pill and took it. I couldn't see clearly what was written on the bottle. Angus made a show of being concerned about Shelly but to me it seemed overblown. I said nothing, not wanting to get kicked by Elvira again.

"That day the tour went to Albi, which is best known as the home of Henri de Toulouse-Lautrec. The bishop's palace was turned into a museum to house many of his work. The huge high ceilings and often-austere rooms really complimented the bright vivid drama of his works.

"Shelly was morose all day. Several times, I heard Angus try to cheer her up, telling her stories but nothing worked. The only time she smiled was when Angus insisted that they take a selfie of both of them on the bridge over the river that ran through the oldest part of town. At dinner, she seemed a bit better but still quite down. Angus looked tired.

"Before I went to bed, I continued reading Agatha Christie's, The Caribbean Mystery, where a husband and wife run a hotel and the wife has searing dreams and becomes emotionally unstable. I wondered what was causing the wife's in the book's odd behavior and it made me think of Shelly. Was Shelly unstable or merely changeable?  Was she taking drugs to calm her mood changes? I had no idea.

"Was reading a mystery making me think of Angus and Shelly as a mystery that might end in death? Why would Angus want to do away with her? They seemed to have plenty of money. I thought that possibly she had manic and depressed periods and that must be tiring for Angus."

"Yes, I'd have to say that Shelly might be on a very quick changing cycle,". That's just speculation, on my part. However, living with a manic-depressive spouse can be exasperating and exhausting but there are ways of coping," said James.

"But why try to bring it on?" Tom continued. "I went to bed pondering this problem and was woken about 4 AM by mosquitoes flying around my head. They don't have screens on windows in Europe, idiots all. The mosquitoes were swarming around my head and Shelly and Angus started to swarm around my mind.

"We didn't see the Thane and his Lady at breakfast, the next day. That day, we were heading for a town near the Mediterranean, going towards the Spanish border. We stopped at Carcassonne, which once had been an important frontier fortress town.

"At the center of the town is the restored fortress with the original, must be thirty foot high battlements. Our guide said she never goes up on the battlements because she's afraid of heights and you have to crawl in certain places. Shelly said she was petrified of heights. I asked Angus if he wanted to go up with me but Shelly insisted that he stay with her. Alvira and I went up and they were high and exposed and you had to crawl around a bit. Loved them.

"Except for the mention of this dread of heights, Shelly, for the first time on the trip, seemed perfectly ordinary. When we got down, she was chatting amicably with Phyllis, without being in any way manic or depressed. They discussed aspects of late medieval architecture and art. Elvira and I listened to Shelly and learned a great deal.

"'Shelly could be a tour guide. She has an interesting take on the period and was more informed than Phyllis,' Elvira said to me later.

"'If she could only stay in a single mood,' I replied.

"At lunch, Elvira and I were sitting with a middle aged gay couple on our tour, who lived in D.C. Andrew, a salesman, was rather short, turning gray; Charles was mid-height and rather on the heavy side. I tried to bring the conversation around to the Thane and his Lady. To my surprise Elvira didn't kick me under the table. Elvira had also become somewhat interested in what I kept thinking was our Caribbean Mystery.

"They didn't want to talk about it. 'I never gossip about other travelers, at least not until after the trip,' said Charles, with a wink of the eye. 'Right now I'd say that the two of them are a lovely couple,' said Andrew. He winked back at his partner and they both laughed.

"I said, 'Don't you find couples who are so very publically affectionate, like Shelly and Angus, nauseating, especially if they always take selfies together?' Elvira kicked me under the table and later asked me if I had noticed that Andrew and Charles constantly were taking selfies together? Sometimes, I thank God for Elvira, at other times my shin hurts and I'm not fond of that."

"Later, I asked Elvira how she knew Andrew and Charles took so many selfies together. She smiled at me and said in her most endearing voice, what to me seemed an unpleasantly true fact, 'I'm actually interested in people and their welfare. Often, you're only interested in confirming your thoughts about them.'

"'Ouch. How so often true,' I thought and changed the topic.

"There are some useful techniques to learn to be more empathetic," said James.

Tom ignored James' comment and continued, "That night at dinner, Elvira and I sat at a group table with Angus and Shelly. Shelly was still relatively sedate and smiling. Angus was more relaxed; less tired looking. Before the appetizer was served, Shelly, taking her handbag, excused herself and went to the lady's room. When she came back, she drank three glasses of wine with her meal. As she drank, her mood began to change. She began bragging 'My daughter, Gwen is the most beautiful girl in our town. She's very top of the senior class at University and a champion gymnast as well.'

"The next day, was partly cloudy, with just a breath of wind. We went to the Salvador Dali museum. Dali transformed an abandoned theatre into an elaborate museum in which Salvador and his wife Gala are portrayed, as the restorers of Christianity, heroes and she as a goddess. I started out loving the museum but by the time I left, it gave me a very shallow, depressing feeling. Dali's early paintings of his sister, for example, had heart but overall the edifice was a cathedral to Dali's incredible egoism, not to anything real or human. When I mentioned this to Elvira,, she said, 'Egoism, egoism. Never seen that before.' I started to laugh but it hurt a bit.

James said, "It's almost impossible to recognize one's own egoism. I try to get my patients..."

Tom cut James off and continued. "As one enters the first floor of the museum, there is an immense painting, which looked to 25 feet high and 50 feet wide, depicting Dali and Gala saving humanity. Our guide said this was a reproduction of the original work. Shelly, with pride, said that she had seen the original and made a study of it. 'The original is more impressive and the colors more alive than the reproduction here,' Shelly said.

"Shelly said she was feeling sick to her stomach. Except for her stomachache, she was on top of the world. All people notice that Dali's paintings look completely different depending on what perspective one took to them but Shelly was seeing far more images buried in the artworks than anyone else, indeed most of us couldn't see any of the things Shelly claimed to be seeing.

"I was unsure Shelly was really seeing what she said she was seeing or was just trying to show off or maybe she was hallucinating. The museum is packed with illusions. Looking around at all the objects that turned into something else, when seen from a different angle, I began to think that maybe the museum was designed to blur the distinction between reality, illusion and hallucination. I wondered if I was hallucinating too.

"I mentioned this to Elvira who told me, 'Don't worry, you never hallucinate. I wish sometimes you did.' I gave her a kiss and said, 'I'm glad I'm not hallucinating you.' She laughed and said, 'Thank you.'

"Curious that you couldn't see what Shelly said she saw, even after she explained it. Very unusual."

"When we were on the third floor, Shelly said she had to rush to the bathroom. The only bathroom was on the first floor. She began to turn away from the painting she was looking at and tried to cover her mouth but it was too late. A small quantity of projectile vomit hit the wall eight or so inches below the left corner of the painting. Why was I not surprised when the vomit seemed to blend naturally into the wall?

"Before Shelly vomited, the painting looked, to me, like a human head when viewed from one direction and to be a fish when I looked at it from another direction. With the vomit, I was convinced that the painting was of an angel's face. I said to Elvira, 'amazing how one simple observation changes everything.'

"'Yes dear,' she whispered back. 'I'm worried about Shelly's health.'

"After the museum, everyone had time to do some touring and eat lunch on their own. It was now warm, mostly cloudy. Elvira and I found a small street café that specialized in tapas and salads. After we ordered, Shelly and Angus sat down at the next table. We greeted them, talked of how much we enjoyed the museum for a minute or two. Shelly was at the peak of her enthusiasm, as I might call it."

"She went off to the bathroom taking her small purse. She came back and said very quickly 'There's something subtly wrong with the colors."

"I immediately thought of what she said about the giant Dali painting on the ground floor. 'I'm not an art expert, and I haven't seen the original painting so I don't have direct evidence but, whenever I took a photograph of a painting, the colors in the photograph are always slightly off.' Shelly heard me and shook her head "No.""

"I agree,' said Angus. "Subtle differences in color aren't important.""

"After about ten minutes, Shelly became much calmer. Her whole countenance had changed, once again."

"When the tour bus drove into Spain, it took the inland superhighway. Because of the European Union's open border policy, crossing into Spain was easy. There were no guards, no police, no wait, nor any cameras.

"Going back to France, we went via the small, two lane coastal road. This road went way up over low mountains and then plunged down towards the Mediterranean and then back towards the sky making extremely sharp turns to the left and right. The bus had to slow down to almost a crawl at some points. The wind had picked up and there was a steady breeze with gusts of stronger wind.

"The road was often only a few feet from the edge of the cliff. I pointed out to Elvira that, of course, this being Europe, they don't have guardrails. Idiots."

"Not as bad as a roller coaster," Elvira said with a smile.

"The road was barely large enough for two cars, going in opposite directions, to pass each other. Our bus was very wide. To make the turns, the bus had to go into the lane of the oncoming traffic. We did this often, going into the oncoming lane just before or after a car came from the other direction.

"Elvira and I were sitting in the second seat from the front. Shelly and Angus were in the same seats across the aisle. Shelly was saying that she was deathly afraid of the road's elevation changes and the sharp turns the bus had to make into the other lane. She worried the bus would go off the road or hit another car. She looked terrified and started to clutch Angus' arm.

"We came to a portion of the road, quite near the French border where the road became even wilder. Shelly held tightly onto Angus' arm, who urged her to close her eyes and relax. Shelly said she had to look because it was even scarier when she closed her eyes.

"We came to a very sharp turn. The bus would have had to go completely into the other lane to make the turn but there was already a car in that lane. The car could not pass our bus and the bus could not pass the car. Both stopped short. Shortly later, additional cars stopped behind the car in front of the bus and there soon were also cars and a motorcycle behind our bus.

Now we're finally getting somewhere, James thought.

"The only way for the bus to continue on was for the cars in front of the bus to back up, giving the bus room to turn. Our bus couldn't back up, without taking a chance it would go over the cliff. The two lanes were only about eight feet wide and there was only two feet from the road to the edge of the cliff and at this point there was no guardrail. Our driver got out of the bus and started to shout in French at the cars in front of us demanding that they back up. The drivers of the first two cars got out of their cars.

"Shelly gave a cry, got up from her seat and hopped off the bus. She waved and shouted for the cars to back up. I got up and stood on the steps in the front of the bus, watching everything. Elvira asked me to come back to our seat but I ignored her.

"Shelly was screaming in English. Our driver was screaming in French. The first driver screamed back in what, to me, sounded like German and the driver of the second car was shouting in Spanish. I looked behind the bus and there were two cars, followed by a motorcycle.

"Shelly, our bus driver and the front car drivers continued to scream at each other in different languages. No driver moved his or her car back.

"The driver of the first car was standing furthest from the cliff, our bus driver was on the road, about six feet from the cliff. Shelly was about 2 feet from the cliff; she had one foot on the road and one foot on the rocky surface between the road and the edge of the cliff.

"I turned my head and saw the Thane beginning to get up, probably wanting to go out and help Shelly but he'd need to get past me to get off the bus so I stepped off the bus standing immediately to the side of the exit. I looked back at the side of the bus and a slightly built person, whom I took to be a woman in a motorcycle jacket, leather pants and wearing a helmet was walking her motorcycle, awkwardly because she had bowed legs, towards the front of the bus where the car drivers, bus driver and Shelly were shouting. When the woman with the motorcycle was between Shelly and the bus driver, touching neither, she hopped on her bike and gunned it. The motorcycle backfired, and then made a loud roaring noise, accelerated and the driver skillfully went around the cars in front of the bus and then took off.

"The motorcycle had touched neither Shelly, nor the driver, nor the car drivers nor any of the cars but Shelly was startled, probably by the noise, and took one more step, tripped and over the cliff she tumbled, a hundred feet into the Mediterranean. We wanted to help but there was no way for anyone to get down the cliff safely. Shelly floated, face down, unmoving.

"We were all shocked. Phyllis used her mobile to call the police, who came in about ten minutes. There was a traffic jam by this time.

The police got the bus moving to a place where it could safely pull off the road and stop. We were eventually told that a police boat recovered Shelly's body from the sea. She was dead of course.

"The police took brief statements and let us go. I thought that if there were anything unusual, the police would find it.

"I told the policeman that Shelly had said that she was afraid of heights and seemed to be excited and scared by the ride on the mountainous road. I said she could be moody and changeable. I tried to describe the person on the motorcycle that I thought was a woman but said the person had a helmet on and I hadn't seen her face. I didn't, at that time remember anything about how they walked. Perhaps it was a man.

"Elvira told the police that Shelly was a wonderful person, full of life and knowledge and that she'd miss her.

"Angus stayed on in Spain to make arrangements and our trip continued on to Arles, in France, and other places associated with Van Gogh and then on to Aix where we saw Degas' art studio.

"Of course, everyone on the tour talked that night. One other person said they also told the police that Shelly was moody but the police didn't ask them for details. No one besides me said that they told the police that they'd seen a person on the motorcycle.

"The trip went on and we heard almost nothing of the accident. I finished "The Caribbean Mystery." Miss Marple discovered the secret. I won't say what she found out but I wondered if the Thane wanted to do away with Shelly, could he give her drugs to make her psychologically unstable and prepare for her murder?"

"It's a definite possibility," said James. "There have been many cases but you usually need some motive and opportunity to prove it."

"That's what I thought. I wrote down some of the mysteries I'd have to solve to know if it was murder. How could Angus have arranged for the bus to get stuck at the top of the hill? Maybe he'd been on the trip before and knew this happened or read about it.

That had to be unlikely, I thought. Shelly would have known if Angus had been on this trip before. How would Angus know Shelly would get out of the bus? It wasn't likely but was possible but not something Angus could be sure would happen.

"How could he have arranged for the motorcyclist to be at that exact spot? I had no idea unless the person was following us on the whole tour, looking for an opportunity. It was unlikely but certainly possible. Could Angus have known and pretended not to? Yes, he seemed to be acting most of the time but were his acting skills that great? Maybe.

"Had Angus drugged and killed his first wife? I could investigate. Was he drugging Shelly to make her crazy or was her changing behavior a result of her natural moodiness combined with whatever prescription drug I'd seen her take? Could she have been taking these drugs and would they be compounded by her daily drinking? Everything pointed to an accident but I felt it to be a mystery."

"Like I was trying to say earlier, before you interrupted me, yes, you're right, psychoactive drugs like Prozac don't mix well with alcohol and some people stop taking their medicine when they drink. That's not recommended. For some people this can cause additional anxiety," said James.

"That's what I thought. After the trip, I got to know more about both Angus and Shelly by buying public record profiles of them. I confirmed that both Shelly and Angus had been married before, he had two children and she had one. Angus' children had graduated from college and Shelly's was going to be a freshman. Angus and Shelly had said as much on the trip but they might have been lying. I found the obituary of Angus' first wife, which said that she had died of breast cancer. That's hard to fake; nothing suspicious there.

"I wanted to know if Angus had insured Shelly, whether they had a prenuptial agreement, whether Angus had a girl on the side? The police would be able to find out all this information, but I couldn't. But maybe at this point I didn't need to know any of these things.

The problem was that I had absolutely no evidence that it wasn't an accident.

"I decided to assume that there was some motive for murder and started looking for some evidence. If I had some tangible evidence, then I might be able to get some official interest in the case.

"I had to make a trip to DC, so I decided to call on Andrew and Charles to see if they had thought of anything. Charles refused to see me but Andrew said he'd have a drink with me. He started telling me about his latest sales campaign. I wasn't really interested even though I tried to hide it and then I started talking about the accident and the two unfortunates, as I called them. I asked exactly what he had seen and he described the bus stopping and, significantly, he had noticed someone walk their motorcycle next to the bus but didn't see anything of the accident. He'd turned his head towards the bus driver and missed Shelly going over the cliff. I asked if he had noticed anything that would identify the motorcyclist?

"'Only that the person had a labored walk.'

"'Did you notice if it was a man or woman?'

"'I didn't notice but the person had a slight build.'

"'Did you mention the person to the Spanish police?'

"'They never asked.'

"'Did you notice how oddly Shelly was behaving all trip?'

"He had noticed some changes in emotions but wouldn't call it odd. 'We've travelled all over the world. Perfectly ordinary people behave very oddly when they travel. Away from home, in different time zones, away from their routines and the food they normally eat. Sleeping on strange beds, meeting all sorts of new people. It's natural that they're on edge and cranky sometimes.'

"I asked if that described Shelly and he said that they hadn't spent much time with Angus and Shelly. So besides confirming that the person with the motorcycle had some kind of problem walking and had a slight build, I had learned little. On the way out, I overheard Andrew saying to the barkeep, 'Strange man. He certainly has no interest in me; he only cares about himself. Well, to each his own.' I watched through the window for a few minutes and they talked together like old friends. I was sure the barkeeper could have gotten a lot more information out of Andrew than I could. I was jealous of the barkeep's ability to make friends."

"If I didn't know how obstinate you can be, I'd suspect you of being involved in this so called murder. Boredom usually isn't so driving," said James.

"Suspect me if you want. Let me go on. Next, I decided to tackle Angus, so I called to say I would be in Ohio and asked if I could come by to see him, have dinner and chat. He didn't have time for dinner, but he could see me at his office at 1:30 PM.

"I got there early and there was a motorcycle parked outside. I introduced myself to Lizza, Angus' assistant, who said Angus should be back soon. She had a slight build with short black hair, a very pleasant smile, looking to be about the same age as Angus. I asked her about Angus, 'Good lawyer is he?'

"'I've worked for him for almost nineteen years and he's is the most wonderful lawyer, so kind, understanding and talented and he really cares about his clients and helping people.'

"I asked her about Shelly.

"'Wonderful woman. It's such a tragedy.' She said this with what seemed to be a lack of enthusiasm.

"The office itself was decorated in a gaudy manner. I thought bright blue and orange clashed a bit. I told Lizza how much I liked the decorations.

"'Shelly decorated it.'

"'So wonderful,' I said.

"'Some of the clients find it a bit loud and not quite suitable for a personal injury lawyer.'

"'Is that what the Thane' and I stopped. 'I mean, is that what Angus said?'

"'No, he was very pleased that Shelly had designed the changes.'

"I looked around Lizza's desk, she had five Van Gogh reproductions on the desk and wall behind her. 'You like art?' I asked.

"She nodded appreciatively. 'Used to paint when I was in college. Never got back to it. Would love to find the time.'

"Angus came in, greeted me in a friendly professional manner, asking me to come into his office. I got up slowly and meandered towards Angus' office. As I was walking, I heard Lizza tell Angus that she'd put his refills into his desk drawer.

"Angus escorted me into his office, which also was gaudy. On the wall were his diplomas and professional certificates and a large photo of Angus receiving a Martin Luther King Award for service.

"We both sat down. I said how sorry I was about his loss, how much I liked the two of them and missed them.

"He thanked me for my concern and friendship and then smiled and asked, 'So you didn't call us Thane and Lady to put us down?'

"No, it was a compliment. I thought of you from the first as a natural leader and Shelly was definitely a Lady.'

"'Thank you for saying so. I thought you were putting us down on the trip or maybe just teasing but thank you for the kind words now. I like to know where I stand. There's so much lying, I try to avoid it.'

"'Don't your clients lie or stretch the truth when they sue people?'

"'I'm sworn to tell their side of the story but if I think a client is lying or even exaggerating a great deal, I pass them on to other lawyers saying I can't help them as I'm overbooked at present. They don't like it but it usually works out best for everyone involved.'

"'So you lie to some of your would be clients about your availability? Very interesting.'

"'I wouldn't call it lying, just helping them find a more suitable lawyer. Why are you questioning me like this?'

"Where was I going? I wasn't sure but I've conducted many negotiations when I ran my company and usually knew when the other party was telling the truth. So far, everything Angus said rang true. I decided to go for it and bring up my suspicion that he was medicating his wife.

"'I suppose you told the Spanish police how strangely emotionally unbalanced Shelly was during the trip.'

"'What are you talking about?' he asked.

"'I saw her take her medication at breakfast one day. Her emotions were constantly changing during the trip.'

"Angus said, 'You never met Shelly before. How could you know if she was unbalanced or acting oddly? Haven't you noticed that people react differently to travel? Shelly never slept on planes and was very tired when we arrived in France. Eating different kinds of food that you aren't used to can also wreak havoc on sleep and emotions. It happens all the time. Haven't you ever noticed that?'

"Tom turned to James, "What do you think of that explanation, Doc?"

"Could be true but he it's also possible that he knows she was acting oddly but was ashamed and didn't want anyone to know. People can be very protective of their spouse. That's not necessarily suspicious though. What did you say to Angus?" asked James.

"'Travel and tiredness can cause some changes of emotions but I don't believe it can possibly explain constant mood changes, especially when she was manic. It seemed obvious to me that her mood were being manipulated by someone.'

"'Shelly could get excited but so can anyone. You say she was manipulated. Absurd.'

"'Look's clear to me that you are the person who could most easily manipulate her moods.'

"'I wouldn't normally speak to someone so directly but you aren't a client and you're accusing me. You obviously know little of Shelly and even less of the law. What you say is a false statement, a slander and if you repeat that as fact, I'll sue you.'

"'I can afford to pay a settlement. I've got to know the truth. Was she on medication for her moods?'

"'That's none of your business. I'll show you the only thing you should be concerned about.'

"He buzzed Lizza and asked her to bring copies of the accident report, in both Spanish and English. As she brought the reports, I could swear I saw her looking at Angus with love. As Lizza walked out, I noted that she walked with bowed legs, similar to the person on the motorcycle. Similar build, similar legs; I thought it could easily have been her.

"I sat and read the English version of the report wondering if it was indeed a translation of the Spanish. I asked if I could make copies of both and the Thane gladly agreed. That meant that the translation had to be accurate. I checked and it was."

"The report was relatively short and to the point. It described what the people on the bus, the tour guide and the passengers remembered. The report described the place where the bus stopped, the cars in front of the bus, the shouting of the bus driver and car drivers and the confusion. That was pretty much what everyone said.

"I was the only person who the report said saw a motorcyclist walk past Shelly. I had said that the motorcyclist had touched neither of them. Only one other person had seen Shelly go over the cliff. He hadn't seen what precipitated the fall. I was thinking just how little information made it to the Spanish police.

"The report concluded that Shelly's fall and death were an accident and that no one was at fault. An addendum noted that two other people had plunged to their death on that section of the highway in the past four years and suggested that the authorities look into improving its safety. A separate page listed what was found with the body and I noted that her handbag had not been recovered. If she had any drugs on her, they would have been in the handbag.

"I asked Angus if there had been an autopsy. The Thane explained to me that in the case of an accident, an autopsy would only be performed with the request of the next of kin. He saw no reason to do so.

"I said to Angus that Shelly's purse wasn't among the items found on the body and asked if it was on the bus and did he have it? Angus said no, he didn't know what happened to the purse.

"'Did you hide it?'

"'Of course not.'

"'Would you ask for an autopsy now?'

"'Absolutely not. I wouldn't disturb Shelly's rest without a good reason and there is none.'

"I sat and thought. The police never found the purse, nor was it in the bus. If Angus had hid it, he could easily have disposed of it and we'd never be able to find it. No recovery of the pill bottle, no autopsy, no details of Shelly's mental state, besides that I said she was moody in the report.

"I wished Angus had told me about her medications but could understand why he didn't do so. I agree with you, James, Angus seemed to be telling as much of the truth as he could without saying anything negative about Shelly. He seemed to be concerned about her welfare during the trip. I thought he was overdoing it but I'm not an expert on people. It might have been difficult at times being married to her but he didn't want to say that. I wondered whether it was simply an accident or if it was the perfect murder?

"'I'm going to keep looking into this," I said to Angus.

"He smiled and said that I was wrong to suspect him but that he admired my stubbornness. We shook hands. I was surprised he was still so friendly after what I'd accused him of doing.

"I thought more about Lizza. She drives a motorcycle, had bowed legs and appeared to be about the same height and weight as the driver at the scene of the accident. If I pushed, would she tell me if she was there?

"On the way out, I chatted with her. 'I'll bet at one time or other, you went to see the sites associated with Van Gogh in France.'

'I went once.'

"'I bet that driving a motorcycle on a small road over the mountains in a foreign country is very difficult.'

"She hesitated and then said, 'I wouldn't know about that.'

"'Can I ask one more question?' If I thought that Lizza answered truthfully I might drop the whole thing.

"I told a flat out lie. 'I'm going to have the police check the airline records. Would they find that you were near the French and Spanish border at the time of the accident?'

'You won't tell Angus?' she asked.

'Not, if you tell me the truth.'

'Yes, I was in France.'

'I thought so. Why did you go?'

"'The office was closed. I've wanted to see that part of France. I decided to go and have a vacation myself. I had their itinerary and thought it would be interesting to see some of the same places they were going to but I stayed out of their way.'

'I recognized you at the scene of the accident.'

'Impossible.'

'I say I recognize you.'

'I wasn't there.'

'One other person on the trip noticed you.'

"'What proof do you have it was me? The police confirmed it was an accident. Leave us alone.'

"'Leave us alone.' That seemed very significant to me.

"'I'm not going to give up on this. I'll find out what happened and why.'

"'What are you going to do?'

"'I don't know yet.' I smiled and left.

"I went back to my hotel to think. If it were murder, how could the circumstances possibly have been arranged? Lizza was in the area but didn't admit to being on the scene. Even if she were on the scene, would getting on the motorcycle and starting it constitute a crime? Could she have known that this might cause Shelly to go over the cliff? Lizza just might have been afraid of being recognized by Angus and driven off so he wouldn't see her. Or maybe it wasn't her at all. What could I do to actually find some evidence?

"That's when I decided to consult you James. What do you think?"

James looked at Tom and said," Give me your final opinion before I say what I think."

"As I told you all this," said Tom, "I've been trying to think about what I've missed and there seems to be only one thing. I've been thinking of what Shelly said to Angus over lunch. 'There's something subtly wrong with the color.' I was sure that she meant of the original Dali painting she'd seen before and the giant copy in the museum were slightly different colors. That would make sense but now I'm not so sure. When I mentioned that photos of pictures never have the correct colors, Shelly shook her head. Maybe she was saying that I didn't understand her at all.

"She had just come back from the bathroom with her purse. She could have taken one of her pills there. Suppose she poured a bunch of pills into her hand and she noticed that the colors of some of the pills were slightly different from each other? What if she began to suspect that some of her mood swings were unnatural and caused by taking different medicine at different times or what if some of the pills were merely sugar pills of the correct size and almost the same color? In that case, there would be either a different drug or no drug at all in her body and she would be getting the entirely wrong pills, or no relief from some of her pills, when she needed it most.

"Shelly must have known she had mood swings and that she probably shouldn't drink but she did. But she was used to the mood swings and the alcohol, they were almost predictable, mostly controlled by her medication.

"My hypothesis is that it was Lizza, who figured out that she could find sugar or real pills that look very similar to whatever Shelly was taking and put some of the false pills and some of the real pills into her pill bottle.

"I saw that Lizza got Angus' medicine. Why couldn't she have also gotten Shelly's before the trip and modified it. I would think that if one gave Shelly a pillbox with similar looking but divergent medication, her ability to control her emotions would be lost. That seems to be what I observed. It must have been extremely scary for Shelly. And Lizza's motive was that she loved Angus and wanted him to continue doing what she would have thought of as good works. Lizza didn't think Shelly was good for Angus and was protecting him. Maybe Angus knew absolutely nothing about the plot and was just as mystified as I was. Lizza called the two of them "us." Tell me. You're an expert. Is what I'm saying psychologically and psychiatrically possible?"

James answered slowly, "Shelly wasn't my patient and I haven't seen her medical records so I'm reluctant to make any professional judgment. You knew Shelly for a few days and couldn't judge if what you saw was typical. Your theory is clever and could explain what you observed about Shelly but getting other pills that would look like the real ones and had very different properties would take a lot of knowledge. Shelly might notice, especially if she was extremely observant. You didn't get a good look at the motorcyclist and what that person did, let's call her a she, gunning her motorcycle when, she was next to Shelly. I'm not sure that's serious enough to be a crime. She couldn't have known Shelly would panic and trip."

"But gunning it made it very likely Shelly would trip."

"I agree," said James, " If Shelly was taking an unknown medication and drinking, the interactions could be erratic. I think you should pat yourself on the back for coming up with a clever, possible but impossible to prove solution and just give this one up and look for a real crime to solve."

"But unofficially would you say that my theory is possible?"

"It's very imaginative. More likely a delusion of yours than true."

"Are you judging me now?"

"No, but I know you better than I know Shelly. "

"Tell me in as clear a manner as you can what you think."

"You said how often you are distracted and influenced by the mysteries you read. I might say you have too much time on your hands and that you're being an interfering busybody but maybe you're on to something. You need proof beyond a reasonable doubt. All you have is all doubt, all the time."

"But is what I said a possibility? Could it be murder?"

"Sure. But Angus' statement that she was just a bad traveler who got tired and moody probably has a much greater chance of being true. You don't even know what medication she was supposed to be taking nor spoken to her physician."

"Would you find her physician and speak to him or her privately about what medication Shelly was taking?"

"Nope. That would violate the HIPPA medical privacy laws and I could be fined or go to prison. You don't have any evidence. I don't see how you can continue this investigation. I suggest you drop it."

"What could convince you that I found something tangible to go on?" I asked.

"Find the pill bottle and if it contains two different kinds of pills, the police might become interested. If the symptoms you observed are completely different from what the actual medication suggests would happen, you'd have some basis for further investigation. But even if you found the pill bottle, it might have been in nature or maybe the sea for over a month and it probably could be contaminated. The odds are astronomically against you. I wish there was something I could help you with."

"There is."

"What?"

"It's damn obvious. I've decided I want to be a detective and I have poor people skills. I'm arrogant, pushy, short-tempered, often bored by people. What would you diagnose me as having."

"We don't diagnose that way."

"Come on, say it. What's the official term for "asshole and busybody?"

"Just the fact that you've noticed that you need improvements shows you have potential. Most people have no idea of what they're bad at. If you really want to talk, come to my office and I'll see what I can recommend to help you but I suggest you drop this case; it's hopeless. "

Tom didn't take James' advice. The accident had been near the French and Spanish border and he liked French food better than Spanish food and could babble a bit in French, so it just seemed easier for him to start in France. He found a detective agency on the French side of the border run by Henri LeClerk who said that he sometimes worked with the police in both Spain and France and had a Spanish colleague, just over the border.

When they spoke, Henri didn't encourage Tom to come, saying it was unlikely they'd find anything and, if they did, it probably wouldn't matter considering the circumstances but if he wanted to waste his money, he was quite welcome to come and try to find something.

Tom liked what Henri said about the unlikeliness of success. Tom didn't want to work with a con man, who would have encouraged him to come, telling him he could work a miracle and find some evidence. Tom knew he probably wouldn't find anything but he decided to give it a try.

Henri and Tom meet with Henri's Spanish colleague Jose and drove to the place on the highway where the accident had taken place. It wasn't hard to find, as Tom had taken some pictures and they had the accident report. They had to find a place to pull over safely nearby and walk back.

There was nothing in the road of much interest. The spot was at the very top, at the steepest part of the slope, with a sharp, short turn in the road. The road was obviously easy for a small car to maneuver but hard for a large bus. There were many footprints, they didn't know from when or which was Shelly's. They didn't see her bag or pillbox when they looked over the slope. They had harnesses and could go over and look but they found nothing. They then thought that maybe they'd see more with a boat. They put a marker on the correct spot that they could see from the sea.

The next day was too stormy. They came back the day after that, on a calm, sunny day, in a sturdy motor launch. They had binoculars to gaze at the cliff. Jose had brought along a drone equipped with video. Tom had paid for a scuba diver to search the sea. If they found anything, they'd leave it in place and get the police to retrieve it. Henri and Jose maneuvered the drone all over the entire cliff face. The water was clear. Neither the diver nor the drone nor the three of them using binoculars found anything of interest.

The last possibility was to find out if they could sample Shelly's vomit on the wall of the Dali museum. Maybe it could be analyzed. Henri, as usual quite honest, told Tom it was useless to try but Tom insisted. Even though it wouldn't be admitted in evidence, Tom was curious if they'd even find the vomit and if they could collect it.

The painting was there but the wall had been washed. Someone official must have noticed the vomit and cleaned it up. Tom wondered how often odd things happened in that very odd museum.

On the last night, Henri and Tom had dinner at a very small, crowded restaurant. Over two bottles of 2010, Chateau Lafitte Rothschild, Henri introduced Tom to a custom of his. When a project failed, he asked his client to eat something they'd never had, which they thought would be horrible. Doing so would take the client's mind off of their failure. Tom chose frog legs. The legs were served with elaborate presentation. Tom saw Henri look at the legs with great affection as if he wished they were for him. Tom, hating the looks of them, cut a small morsel and popped it into his mouth. Heavenly. Tom was glad of Henri's custom; eating the frog's legs did take his mind off his failure.

The whole trip cost more than Tom's first tour and he didn't like wasting money but this wasn't a waste of money. He learned something valuable about himself. In his professional life, he hadn't failed often. He had thought his intense drive was caused by a deep fear of failure. But this trip had been a failure and he learned that he was not afraid or angry because of it. He wasn't afraid of thinking himself unintelligent; not afraid of not finding the answer. He was simply enjoying the hunt.

On the plane ride home, he thought about giving up. What right did he have of accusing Angus and Lizza with no evidence? If he were on a jury and had been presented with the evidence he'd found so far, he would have voted "not guilty." Perhaps a few years from now, a pill bottle with Shelly MacThurbur's name on it would show up on some beach and there might then be some evidence but it seemed he would have to wait for that near impossibility to occur.

He came back and had dinner with Elvira. It was so pleasant to return from a trip to someone who was happy to see him. He told her of their failure. Elvira asked if he minded failure. He replied that failure was just a change of pace and he'd pick a more likely mystery next time.

Elvira surprised Tom. "Maybe you've tried a few ways," she said, "that have failed. Why not try one? What would another failure cost you?"

"Nothing, except I'd have to eat something I've never had before that I don't think I'd like."

"If you fail, I'll eat it too," said Elvira. "If you have another idea, go for it."

Tom had to remember more about their trip. He hired a hypnotist who took him through the trip until he remembered what he needed to remember.

He contacted a private detective in Angus' town, Asher Zeitener, who was a former policeman, who had had some dealings with Angus. He had always found that Angus was scrupulously honest and he'd heard no rumors about him. It wasn't a big town and rumors spread easily. When Tom explained his plan to him, Asher agreed to invite Angus and Lizza to dinner with Elvira and Tom and to neutrally observe what happened.

They met them at Angus' favorite Chinese restaurant. Many Chinese restaurants have low lighting, much red on the walls and have a vague calm, spiritual atmosphere. This one was quite different, being plain, having a modern utilitarian feeling. They sat at a table for six, by the windows in the front, where there was as much natural light as possible. It was late afternoon, when there would be few others in the restaurant. After they sat down, Tom explained to Angus and Lizza that he had gone to the scene of the accident to see if he could find any evidence of what really happened and he wanted to tell them about what he found.

The waiter came over and they ordered drinks while they looked at the menu. Elvira and Tom had wine, Lizza had a Cosmopolitan and Asher and Angus had Chinese tea. Lizza was tense but tried to look unconcerned and Angus looked relaxed but interested.

"Let me describe to you what started me on this investigation." Tom described Shelly's sharp turns in moods during the trip, watching her take her medicine, her talk about the worst nightmare ever and her intense fear of heights.

Elvira then talked about how much she enjoyed meeting Shelly, about how she saw how much Shelly loved life and had real talent. She described the talk between Shelly and our tour guide and how much Shelly knew about art and then Tom's comment that Shelly could be a tour guide, if only she had one mood. Elvira said how sad it made her to watch Shelly's constant change of moods and the pain these changing emotions must have caused her.

Tom described the visit to the Dali museum and how Shelly had seen that huge copy painting and compared it, in her mind, to the original and said that the colors of the original was more impressive and alive.

Tom then described how Elvira and he were sitting at a table and that Shelly and Angus had sat down and they started to discuss the museum. Shelly had gone to the lady's room, with her purse, which contained her medication and had come back and sat down again. As Tom talked, he pulled out a pill bottle that looked just like the pill bottle he had remembered under hypnosis, and held it in his hand. He opened the bottle and poured out into his palm about ten pills, some with the exact color he had also remembered under hypnosis, and some with a very slightly different color. Both Lizza and Angus were paying full attention now; any pretense of not being concerned had vanished.

Then Tom described how Shelly had said, "There's something subtly wrong with the color." Lizza gave a quiet moan. Tom said that he had thought Shelly meant that the original painting and the copy had slightly different colors and he had said that photos never had the same colors as the original. Shelly had shaken her head, as if to say that was not what she meant at all.

"Angus, you told her that differences in color weren't important. What did you mean by that?"

Angus didn't say anything.

Tom pointed to his palm "Look at them, they aren't all exactly alike, are they?" He held them closer to the window so that there was more natural light on them.

Lizza breathed hard and asked. "Where did you get them?" She almost began to weep.

Tom was silent.

"Where did you get them?" Lizza said even more softly.

"Do you have anything to say?" Tom asked.

"Absolutely not," said Angus and he shook his head sending his longish hair back over his ear. "I told you that some of my clients lie to me and I send them elsewhere. You're lying to me now. Let me see that container. I bet the pill container isn't Shelly's."

"That is what I was about to tell you," Tom said. "We found nothing at the site of the accident. I've suffered from anxiety since the trip and asked my psychiatrist for a prescription. These are my pills. Lizza can you tell me which pill I should take?"

One tear fell from Lizza's eyes.

"I've seen these kinds of stunts many times in my profession," said Angus. "Lizza, we're going to leave this liar to himself. Tom, I applaud your interest in finding the truth but am very disappointed you tried to make us believe a lie. Elvira, it was wonderful to see you again. I'm so glad you had so much sympathy for Shelly." Lizza followed Angus as he left the restaurant.

Asher, Elvira and Tom just sat there for a second.

"It always works in the books," Tom said.

"What does?" asked Asher.

"In the books, when you tell the guilty party how they did it, they always confess."

"Did you really think it would work?" asked Asher.

"It seemed to be the only possibility. He's a damn fine lawyer. If I ever need a lawyer in Ohio, I'll definitely use him," Tom said.

They ordered another round of drinks. This time Asher had a Scotch. Asher asked Elvira what she thought.

Elvira said, "I'm sure Lizza messed with the medicine and felt guilty. You could see it in her face but I'm not sure she'd have verbally confessed, even if Angus hadn't dragged her off. And Angus is too experienced. You didn't have a chance, Tom, not without any real evidence."

"I wish we could dig up the body," said Asher.

"I'm sure we wouldn't find anything. It's hard to prove that someone died because they didn't get enough medicine. I don't even know if Lizza really had any definite plan," Tom said.

"We failed but I'm proud of you, Tom, for your concern for Shelly. Maybe I was wrong about you," said Elvira. "Maybe you are changing and now actually care about people and not just your ideas about them."

"I have really begun to care about Shelly. Lets have a toast. Shelly, may she rest in peace and all the best to Angus and Lizza."

"I don't know if I can drink to that," said Asher. "Lets just drink to Shelly."

And they did. After the drink, Asher left them.

"We've failed; we need to eat something we'd never think of eating and think would taste awful."

They looked at the extensive menu, with page after page of exotic Chinese dishes. Tom ordered Hunan Chicken extra spicy, Elvira ordered Moo Shu pork. But for an appetizer they picked something that both Elvira and he thought would taste awful, two portions of cold jellyfish.

They stared into each other's eyes as they took their first bites, both trying hard not to show any emotion. First Elvira laughed at him then Tom laughed at her. They made a contest of who could finish their jellyfish first. Elvira won. Before they ordered it, Tom wondered why it was on the menu and it was still a mystery to him after he ate it. He made a joke that next time he'd order warm jellyfish.

That night, Elvira and Tom kept each other warm, and Tom thought that perhaps cold jellyfish was eaten for other purposes other than mere taste. Or was he just hallucinating about the cause of a wonderful evening.

About three months later, Elvira and Tom got a post card from Spain that showed the large painting from the Dali museum. The back had computerized printing, with no signature or identifying information. It said, "The colors are slightly different. Finally painting again. I swear I will get the colors right one day."

"A remarkable woman," Tom said to Elvira. "Lizza might create something worth seeing. We've all thought about making someone disappear. At least I have. But to actually do and get away with it, moves you into an intriguing category."

"That's a horrible thing to say. We still don't have proof," said Elvira.

"True but irrelevant. Fascinating. I'm going to contact the Thane and tell him I heard Lizza was painting and I'd like to buy a painting. I'll put it up in my office."

Tom looked up and saw that Elvira was shaking her head "no" and frowning. "What's the matter?" asked Tom.

"If we ever run across a painting of hers, fine, we'll buy it but let's not contact either of them. I liked her. Let's let sleeping dogs lie."

"Maybe you're right."

Elvira looked directly into Tom's eyes. "You know I am."

Tom looked back, smiled and laughed, "Yes, I know." He hesitated and continued, "remember how our neighbor said his daughter moved to Michigan? I'm not so sure."

"You're not going to investigate are you?"

"Maybe a little."

"You never do only just a little."

"How well you know me."

"Let me know if I can help."

"I was thinking that maybe –"

# THE TORAH SCROLLS

"There are two Torah scrolls in this synagogue," explained Max, our Israeli tour guide. "This one, on the altar, is read every day. The second, in the Arc on this side of the synagogue, is only read once a year, by the head rabbi, on Yom Kippur. Every time the Arc has been opened and that Torah read on another day, the reader has died within a year."

Max, a short, medium weight man in his fifties, with the beginnings of grey in his dark hair, had been giving tours in Israel for almost thirty years. He had led many hundreds of visitors to this historic, stone synagogue. A few synagogue members, who knew Max well, nodded their heads and acknowledged his presence. They were proud of their place of worship and enjoyed having Max show it off.

Max picked up the Torah scroll from the main altar and read a few lines in his sonorous voice. Hebrew, to most of the Americans in the tour group, who had never or infrequently heard it, seemed both exotic and vaguely familiar as if the sounds themselves were ancient and powerful; sounds that they had heard in dreams and should hear more often in life.

After reading from the Torah on the altar, Max led the nineteen members of the Awakening Tour Group to where the second Torah scroll was housed. It was in an enclosed niche with a silver metal gate in front. "As I said, this scroll is only read once a year by the chief rabbi and all those who read it on other days have died within a year." He smiled and asked, "Would anyone like to read from the second scroll?" Max asked this rhetorical question every time he gave this tour, in hopes of a quiet laugh. No one had ever shown the slightest desire to read from the second Torah scroll.

Today was different. Giovanni Turin, a big man, with a thick neck, who often had to wipe sweat off his face, was in his late 50s. He owned a chain of restaurants on Long Island and was known to everyone on the tour as Gino, now looked directly into Daniel Espi-nosa's eyes and asked, "What about you, Daniel? You've been trying to convince everyone on the tour that there is no God. You've told us you can read Hebrew. Take the Torah out and read it. That will convince us all that you really don't believe in God." Gino paused, looked at the others in the tour and continued, "You're not afraid, are you?"

Gino's wife, Gina, who wore more make up than was necessary and had five long rows of fresh water pearls around her neck, added, "Go ahead. Prove to us you're not a coward."

Daniel, who was tall and in his late twenties, was startled by Gina's words. He looked around at Max and the other people in the tour group. He looked up at the expansive windows high up the white stonewalls of this sixteenth century synagogue and at the bright streaming mid-day sun, which strongly illuminated the members of the tour.

Three synagogue members, standing to the side, were observing the tour group and it looked to them that the tour group was on a stage, in the spotlight, waiting for something dramatic to happen.

After the challenge, the rest of the tour group looked at Daniel waiting to see what he would do. Some of them, including Daniel's wife, Adelaide, were convinced that God was also watching them. What was He thinking? she wondered.

Dan swallowed, scratched his chin, took out a handkerchief to wipe his forehead and asked quietly, "What are you asking me to do?'

Gino said, "Act like a man. You say there is no God. Take out the Torah scroll and prove you mean it." Gina smiled and nodded her head in agreement.

Was he a man, a mouse or a fool? A year ago, Daniel would have proclaimed that he was a man. Now he wasn't so sure. Gino's question sent his mind scurrying on a journey backward to understand what was happening to him. He thought, "How did I get myself in this mess? I know Gino's hostile but I never expected anything like this could happen. What am I to do?"

The big change in Daniel's opinion of himself started about a year ago when his boss, Oscar, the hard driving, former Ohio State linebacker, the amazingly rich, founder and director of Forward Progress Now, a small merger and acquisition firm, had called Daniel to his office and severely berated him. Daniel's main job was to investigate the companies Oscar planned to buy. "You never stand up for what you believe in. You wrote in your report that there was a problem in the Henderson takeover but when we met and I told you there wasn't any problem, you backed down. Why did you just roll over and not try to convince me of the facts you knew?"

Daniel tried to think of an answer that wouldn't start what he thought would be a job ending confrontation. "After you spoke, I thought you were right."

"Bull. Don't lie to me. You knew the facts were on your side and you just backed down. That's incompetence." Oscar paused, smiled broadly and continued, "Are you a coward? It's about time you stood up for yourself and your analysis. Tell me when I'm wrong. I'm going to send you to assertiveness training. If you don't learn, I'll fire you."

Daniel and Adelaide had just had their first child, Gallia, and the economy wasn't doing well so they couldn't afford for Daniel to lose his job. Daniel agreed but was disheartened.

Adelaide, her usually cheerful self, when told of this encounter with Oscar said, "God loves us and is sending you a blessing. Let's write it into my blessings book."

Adelaide constantly wrote in her blessings book. Adelaide had started keeping the blessings notebook, a birthday gift from her father, when she was eleven years old. She wrote of her experiences with the Lord and all that He bestowed upon her. After they were married, Daniel occasionally wrote in it too. On their wedding day he wrote, "I am so thankful for Adelaide and her love and Your blessings."

Both were believers and devout Roman Catholics. In college, Daniel had thought he might study for the priesthood, majoring in history and taking a year of Hebrew in college. He learned enough Hebrew to sound out words and read simple texts but not enough to understand the language's complexities, but his study made him dream of visiting Israel.

In his sophomore year, he met Adelaide, a tall blonde freshman Education major who was comfortable with herself and assured around others. They fell in love. Daniel abandoned the idea of becoming a priest and began studying finance and investing. They were married after he graduated. Adelaide's parents helped the couple and he got an MBA, and soon got a job with Oscar.

About two years later, when their daughter was born. Daniel wrote, "I am blessed with the love of my lovely, wonderful wife, Adelaide, and our incredible daughter, Gallia."

Now, to commemorate Daniel's assertiveness training, Adelaide opened the blessings book and wrote, "Jesus is so generous that He is offering Daniel training in becoming a better employee and a better man." She said, "It's so wonderful. Why don't you write something in the book too?"

Daniel said he'd write in the book when the training was successfully completed.

Daniel had difficulty with the training. At first, he did not feel comfortable in putting forward and defending important personal views when they were vigorously challenged. It was easy for him, for example, to insist that the New York Yankees were the best baseball team, even to a Red Sox fan, which to Daniel's mind, they obviously were, but when it came to his personal views about life, love, politics and religion, he had a much harder time. He would have preferred to say nothing but the training required him to stand up for his beliefs.

In the assertiveness training, they discussed the distinction between assertiveness and aggression. One possible set of definitions is that to be assertive is to stand up for one's beliefs, not back down, but to state one's beliefs clearly. To be aggressive is to attack other people's beliefs. The distinction, on an intellectual level, sounded simple and easy to understand but, when Daniel tried to apply it practically, it was much more difficult, especially when he had to deal with his boss, Oscar.

About two thirds of the way through the training, Oscar had insisted that Daniel's analysis of the Heritage Mountain Company takeover was incorrect.

Daniel asserted himself, even though he felt fear. "My analysis is correct. You may have misunderstood what I wrote."

Oscar countered, "You made a huge mistake in the handling of line twenty-seven of page two. You really don't understand what the terms of the contract mean. You've been soft in your thinking."

"No I haven't. I am sure I am right," said Daniel.

Oscar started to laugh humorously. "Obviously you're a numbskull to say that. Do you even know the definition of the terms involved?"

Daniel asserted that he did know the meaning of the terms. The next day, he got into another disagreement with Oscar, who said with a quick smile, "You got that wrong, Dumbo." The funny thing was that when Oscar said "Dumbo," the smile on his face got brighter and his tone even lighter.

For the first time, Daniel snapped back, "Of course I'm right, blockhead, the facts back me up." He was immediately sorry; convinced that was the end of his job. To his surprise, Oscar laughed heartily and replied, "Now I see your point; very well done. Glad we cleared that up"

From that day forward, almost every disagreement with Oscar ended this way. Unless and until Daniel got personal, Oscar did not take him seriously. Dan began to feel they were like two men debating in a swimming pool. Unless one of them playfully splashed water directly in the other person's face, they didn't know the other person seriously believed they had the facts on their side.

Daniel was confused and said to his assertiveness instructor, "The difference between assertiveness and aggression isn't always clear. Isn't it different when dealing with different people and doesn't it depend on the tone of voice they used?"

"It shouldn't," the instructor said. "There is an objective difference between assertiveness and aggression."

"You've obviously never met my boss, Oscar. With him it's different. I really don't think you know what you are talking about," replied Daniel.

"That's an aggressive statement," said the instructor.

"To me, that's just a statement of fact. Your experience is very limited."

"I think you should think more on this topic," said the instructor.

"Which is another way of you saying you don't think I know what I'm talking about," said Daniel.

"That's not what I said."

"It's clearly what you implied," said Daniel.

After this, the two men agreed to disagree on the finer points of aggression versus assertiveness.

To Dan's surprise, work, although it became louder and seemingly more confrontational, also became more enjoyable. The relationship between Oscar and Daniel became much more equal and Daniel began to enjoy what he sometimes considered a game of "friendly confrontation" that almost bordered on play. "Now that we understand and are honest with each other, I can give you more important work," said Oscar. He began to let Daniel help find new deals and have more decision making power in the evaluating of and pursuit of the company's objectives.

Oscar was married and he and his wife often had dinner parties to which they began to invite Daniel and Adelaide.

"Oscar's not at all like you describe him," said Adelaide as they drove home after the first one. "He didn't argue with me once and he was so friendly and attentive."

"Maybe he didn't argue because there was no money involved."

"I like him. He's much easier to get along with than my principal."

Meanwhile, at home, Adelaide and Daniel were conscientious parents. Gallia's crib was in their room and each night they made sure that she slept on her back and that she didn't get caught in her blankets. Almost every night, Gallia would wake crying and they took turns taking care of her.

One morning Adelaide and Daniel woke up; surprised that Gallia had slept through the night. They were quiet, trying to make sure she got the sleep she needed. It was only about five minutes later that Adelaide began to realize that something unusual was happening. She raced to Gallia's crib, picked her up but Gallia was cold. She had died suddenly in the night. They called an ambulance but it was too late. Adelaide cried for hours. Daniel held back his tears.

Both Adelaide and Daniel were devastated but over time they reacted very differently.

Five days later, Adelaide said to Daniel, "God always has a reason for what he does. He is doing this for His grand purpose, which we don't know."

Daniel said nothing. He felt as lost as he did when his parents had died in a car crash when he was eight years old and he had to live with his maternal grandparents. He had felt abandoned then and now he felt that deep sense of abandonment again. He would never see his parents again and now he would never see Gallia.

A week later, when Adelaide said for the third time that God had a purpose for Gallia's death, Daniel replied, "We did everything we could. It's usually boys who die suddenly and they die on their stomachs. We made sure Gallia slept on her back. She shouldn't have died. What grand reason could God have in taking Gallia from us? It doesn't make any sense. I can't believe it."

Adelaide was shocked and cried and Daniel held her. Before his training, he probably would have taken back what he had said but now he did not retract his statement.

Daniel tried to make sense of his loss. From an intellectual point of view, he knew that life is precarious but to actually experience the instability of life is a very different experience from just thinking about it. And this was his second major loss. Intellectually, he should not blame God but somewhere in his confused emotions he did blame Him.

Daniel noticed that once doubts got hold of him, they began to grow. Faith and gratefulness, he told his wife, often look entirely different from the vantage point of deep suffering than from joy.

Daniel's doubts began to impact his marriage. He would pretend to be happy because he did not want Adelaide to see his pain. He believed that to show pain was to show weakness and he didn't want to be weak, plus he didn't want Adelaide to worry about him.

Adelaide knew that Daniel was suffering and she tried to soothe his pain. Daniel misinterpreted Adelaide's attempts to soothe as actually seeing him as being too weak to deal with his own problems. The little, easy times of joyful communications that had characterized their early marriage became less frequent. Neither knew how to deal with their different reactions to the tragedy and their communication grew less frequent with many awkward silences. Adelaide suggested they see a therapist but Daniel was against the idea. He walked away from her, saying he wanted to go for a walk alone. There seemed to be no easy way out of their difficulties.

Daniel and Adelaide had expressed over the years a strong desire to go to Israel. Adelaide's parents noticed their emotional difficulties and thought a long-desired trip might help them. They bought them tickets for a fifteen-day Israeli tour.

Adelaide took out her blessings book and said out loud and wrote, "I have such wonderful parents and a loving husband and we're going to Israel. Thank you Lord." She asked, "What would you like to write Daniel?"

"Nothing."

"Why not write something, it will make you feel better?"

"I don't feel grateful and I don't want to write anything."

"We both have so much to be thankful for."

"I don't feel that," he said and he stopped himself from saying, "My parents and child died for no reason."

Daniel left the room so that he wouldn't say more. He wanted to protect Adelaide from his despair. I'll get over it eventually, he thought. Adelaide began to feel pushed beyond her limit of easy compassion. She brooded, thinking that she was trying hard but making no progress. Why wasn't it working? Would God figure out how to get them over these problems? She believed He would but did not see how this would happen.

Two week before the trip, Daniel got a promotion and a large raise. Oscar called him into his office and said, "You haven't smiled much lately but I've noticed what a remarkable talent you have for business."

"You didn't call me a block head. How do I know you're sincere?" asked Daniel.

"Just check your next paycheck. Besides, I'll say it. You're one of my best blockheads. Feel better now?"

"Not really but work takes my mind off my problems."

"Mine too," smiled Oscar.

When Daniel told Adelaide of his raise, she said, "We have to thank the Lord for your promotion, let me write it in the book."

For the first time, Daniel said what he really felt. "God had nothing to do with it. I made lots of money for Oscar and he's rewarding me. It is all cause and effect in the here and now world. I don't want to write in the blessings book. Sometimes life's intolerable."

Adelaide knew Daniel well enough to realize she had no solution to his problem. He sounded depressed and abandoned. She had faith that God would deal with the problem during their trip to Israel but she was honest enough with herself to realize that her own faith had become a little less firm. Had she been treating God as a magician who would, for her sake, automatically make everything right? She was, for the first time, a bit ashamed of her lack of faith and her non-critical assurance that all her problems would be fixed without any serious efforts on her part.

Light from the synagogue window hit Daniel in the eye and he was suddenly back in the present moment. He saw Gina smiling wickedly saying to Gino, "I told you he wouldn't do it. All his arguments that there is no God are false; he doesn't even believe them himself. "

Daniel winced; the challenge was real, not just a dream but he couldn't move, he just stood there.

Gino watched carefully and said to Gina, "He looks like he just woke up. Maybe he didn't hear what Max said," and to Daniel, "You've been saying God is nonsense, so why don't you take the scroll out and read it?"

How did Gino and Gina get so aggressive with me? Daniel wondered and quickly started reviewing what had happened during the tour. The first few days had been so enjoyable. In Tel Aviv, their hotel room was on the twelfth floor overlooking the sea. They saw little sailboats race up and down the coast. The Mediterranean changed colors from azure to purple, sometimes bordering on black depending on the light.

Their tour guide, Max, during a walking tour of Tel Aviv, pointed out a few of the cafes that had been bombed and where buses had been blown up but he was an optimist that the political situation could improve. He wanted peace and was willing to make compromises. He praised the Palestinians and urged the tour members to buy from their shops, as they needed financial support. He also gave tours to Palestinian groups. "They want to go to most of the same places that the Jews visit. They just tell different stories about them."

To see that the situation in Israel was tense, one only had to look around. There were soldiers on guard and young Israeli men walked around with machine guns over their shoulders. The tour members became used to the situation and the tension slipped into the background.

Once out of Tel Aviv, many of the sites the tour visited were religious sites associated with Judaism, Christianity and Islam. Max tried to keep the discussions of religion light but it was not always easy. At dinner one night, there were eight people eating together; Max, the couple Gino and Gina, another couple in their late forties, very nicely dressed, with an air of professional educators', Adelaide and Daniel and the only single woman on the tour, Svetlana. Svetlana was in her twenties, was short and thin and had long black naturally curly hair. She had a wonderful smile and a lovely figure, which she, in a very modest manner sought to enhance. She was a very secular daughter of Russian Jews who had been expelled from the Soviet Union in the 1980s. She had just passed the New York State bar examination and her parents had given her this trip as a present.

At dinner, Max observed that Jews believe in God and that He has a special relationship with them.

"How can you believe in such a God? You say the Jews are His people, how could He abandon them in the holocaust?" asked Daniel.

Svetlana joined in. "If God loves us Jews so much, why is everyone, through all of history always discriminating and attacking us? Why were my parents expelled from the Soviet Union? How did they deserve that? Why didn't God stop it?"

Max was used to this. "Of course I understand your point of view. I have sometimes thought that way myself but the way I see it is that sometimes our people have turned away from their Creator and His ways. Plus men often decide to do horrible things to each other and, when they do, God won't always stop them. God gave man free will. It's man's fault, not God's."

"I don't think there is a God," replied Daniel. Adelaide winced. This was the first time Daniel had said this.

"I respect your views and won't argue with you about them," replied Max, ever the conciliator.

As Max and Daniel had this conversation, Gino and Gina frowned and spoke to each other. After Max finished, Gino spoke up. "The existence of God is obvious. As Saint Paul wrote to the Romans. 'For since the creation of the world, God's invisible qualities – his eternal power and divine nature – have been clearly seen, being understood from what He has made, so that people have no excuse.'"

Daniel countered with talk of the materiality of the world. "Man is such an insignificant creature in an immense universe which perhaps never ends. It is absurd that we should think we are so important to the universe or that there is a God who cares about us."

One of the couples suggested that the two men have a series of debates, "It will be fun." Gino and Daniel agreed. Max and Adelaide objected suggesting that the debates would create hostility but the others were for them, so the debates began.

During the debates, the whole tour group ate together and listened picking a winner after each meal.

The first debate was close. Daniel closed by pointing out that from a historical point of view, almost all the gods and goddesses, that have ever been worshipped, are no longer believed in. "This proves that almost all people in history have been fooled and believed something that wasn't true."

"A very good point," said Svetlana, who looked admiringly into Daniel's eyes. Adelaide was so upset that she barely noticed the look. A slight majority judged that Daniel had won the first debate. Gino was incensed and was determined to win the next one.

Before each debate, Max urged the two men to respect each other's beliefs and keep the tone friendly but, with each debate, the tension grew stronger.

As far as the individual debates went, there is no need to go into the details. Suffice it to say that Daniel was the more highly educated individual who had taken part in many debates in college and he was taking the easy side of the argument, that there is no God and that religious people often do absurd things. Daniel, having studied theology, knew all the arguments that Gino would make and knew how to parry these familiar arguments.

Gino was quite new to debating or he might have pointed out that all people, not just religious people, frequently do absurd things. He had never been to college and still less had he read any works on divinity. He was unaware of most of the arguments that Daniel made. This lack of experience hurt Gino's arguments and doomed his chances of winning. Besides this disadvantage, debate is an intellectual endeavor and, since the best arguments for the existence of God are more emotional than intellectual, Daniel had a natural advantage.

At the second debate all but Gina gave the victory to Daniel, which enraged Gino. Max and Adelaide who didn't vote. In the third de-bate, Gino made his attacks much more personal. Daniel at first tried not to imitate but he soon also became more personal. Neither one actually called the other "blockhead" nor "Dumbo" but these words came across in their tone of voice. It was a completely differ-ent atmosphere than when Daniel called Oscar a blockhead. With Gino and Daniel, there was no element of play in it. They were both deadly serious. Neither Daniel nor Gino smiled. Adelaide watched the debates with growing despair.

This was not her idea of an en-joyable vacation. Daniel enjoyed the debates and the glory of "win-ning" and he noticed and was flattered that Svetlana was constantly smiling at him and offering him encouragement and her congratu-lations.

"Are you asleep or something? Tell us whether you 're going to take out the scroll?" said Gino.

Again, Daniel was back in the present moment. It had only been a short time but Daniel felt that he had been thinking about whether to pick up the scroll for several hours. He was still not sure what to do. He was in an ancient place. Many, even atheistic people con-sidered it to be important, historical and beautiful. Did he want to make a scene here? One part of Dan's brain said, "It's one thing to say there is no God, it is another to step forward and desecrate a historic site." The other part of his brain said, "All you'd be doing is picking up a Torah scroll. The scrolls are made to be read. Who could object to that? Live your life and assert what you believe. BS is BS." He hesitated. The light shone around him and everyone was looking at him wondering what he would do.

"This is absolutely delicious but I'm sure he won't do it. He isn't a fool," said one husband to his wife. Another husband, with a huge grin, bet another man that Daniel wouldn't take the Torah scroll out. "I know people like him. They never do anything bold. I'll buy you and your wife dinner if he does."

"You're on. He'll take it out. He has no sense at all." The two men shook hands on the bet as if this was a bet on a football game. They were enjoying the show.

Daniel saw Svetlana shake her head yes and smile, as if to en-courage him.

Adelaide was in disbelief and passionately shook her head no. Daniel ignored her. Adelaide didn't know what else she could do but she desperately wanted to help Daniel. She said, "Gino, how dare you ask my husband to do something like that? It's very ungenerous of you. He wouldn't think of doing it."

Adelaide's plea pushed Daniel over the edge. He did not want to feel protected by his wife. I'm not weak, he thought. I can speak for myself; I know what I want to do. I said there is no God and there is none. There are no curses, only our thoughts. He took a step towards the scroll.

The grate, in front of the second scroll, looked like it had been polished that morning. Daniel reached out and immediately began sweating and wishing he'd listened to his wife. She loves me and is looking out for me, I should listen to her when she's right, and then he thought, But she always thinks she's right. I have to stand up for what I believe. I can't back down now. Gino will call me a coward the whole trip. He made a firm decision to go forward and take out the scroll. He reached out to open the grill, which opened very reluctantly.

I hope that Max was making this curse up, was his next thought. He really knows what he's talking about, I'm sure he didn't make it up. Bastard. No need showing any fear. He finally opened the grate, plunged his hands in and took out the scroll. It didn't seem to be as heavy as he expected.

As he pulled out the Torah scroll, a very old, squat, synagogue member, with long grey hair, wearing Orthodox dress, walked up close to Daniel and shouted at him in Hebrew.

Perspiration rolled down Dan's neck as he loudly declared, "All that exists is material, subject only to the laws of physics. There is nothing spiritual." He held the scroll in his hands, looked at it and began to try to raise it over his head. As he raised the scroll, it felt heavier and heavier and he couldn't get it above eye level. One of the married couples looked at each other, their eyes saying, "What the heck is he doing? Should we help him?"

No one helped Daniel.

The old Hebrew man shouted again. Another member of the congregation came up and joined in the shouting. He took out a video camera and began to record the scene. Max said, "You've made your point Daniel, please put the scroll back. Immediately."

Daniel couldn't hear Max over the two shouting men. His mind was caught in two, totally opposite thoughts: The scroll's valuable, someone worked a long time creating it, was one thought and the other was, If fools want to believe in God, how can I stop them?

Straining all his energy, Daniel got the scroll over his head. "I did it, I've stood up for my beliefs and I've beaten Gino again."

Daniel stepped backward, tripped over his own feet and dropped the scroll to the ground, falling directly on top of it. Another Hebrew man went to get a security guard from the street. Daniel slowly began to get up, the scroll still on the ground, his head pointed to the ground when he tried to shout something at the Hebrew man. Spit flowed out of Daniel's mouth, hitting the scroll.

The Hebrew man, with long grey hair, put his face close to Daniel's face and continued to scream.

Daniel asked Max to tell the man, "I don't want to destroy anything here." Daniel got up, tripped again, and by accident kicked the Torah scroll for a second time. "What is he saying?" Daniel asked Max.

"I don't think you really want to know, just pick up the scroll and put it back," replied Max, even more loudly than before.

"Why don't you help me?" asked Daniel.

"I didn't make up that story of the curse," said Max.

"Are you afraid, Max?"

"Yes. For many reasons," Max said in a voice that was much more reasonable and restrained than he felt. Daniel just sat there waiting for help. With Daniel's continued inaction, Max lost his composure and shouted, "Get up and put it back NOW."

Daniel heard the capital letters in Max's shout. He looked at Max. His heart was pounding and his hands sweating. He was trembling.

Finally Daniel got up and put the scroll back into its resting place and closed the grate. He said to Max, "I want to know what that man said."

"Later," said Max. He loudly addressed the entire tour group, "Go back to our tour bus immediately. I'll deal with this." The tour members left talking excitedly among themselves.

Max spoke in Hebrew to the first member saying how sorry he was about the incident, "But what do you expect, they're Americans."

The second member answered Max in English, "Yes, Americans. They're our friends but often so stupid. Let's forget about it."

"Never," shouted the first man, in Hebrew, "it was an intentional insult and desecration."

Max tried to reason with the first man, saying in Hebrew, "He's been under incredible strain lately. His daughter died suddenly. Do try to forgive him. Yes he was stupid, but please forgive."

"I will never forgive his desecration. It is more than an insult."

As Max left the synagogue, a security guard demanded to see his guide license and to know where the tour was spending the night. Max said they were staying at the King Solomon hotel in Tiberius.

About a minute after Daniel got onto the bus, Adelaide entered. She was visibly shaking and said to him, "What the hell got into you. I'll pray and try to seek a way out of this." She did not sit next to Daniel.

After they sat down, far from Daniel, Gino said quietly to Gina, "I hope the curse is true."

At this, Gina began to weep. "Why are you weeping?" Gino demanded. "Our enemy has been defeated."

"He isn't our enemy," mumbled Gina and continued in an almost inaudible voice. "He never was. We made him our enemy. I should have stopped you. It's my fault. Jesus please forgive me. How can I make this right?" Gina continued to weep. Gino was dumbfounded.

Svetlana, as she went by, smiled at Daniel and said, 'Congratulations, you showed them."

Daniel was in a mood he had not experienced before. It reminded him of what Winston Churchill said when he was a war correspondent in the Transvaal and came under fire for the first time. "There is nothing as exhilarating as to be shot at and be completely unscathed." Daniel felt justified in himself. He had shown his courage and, even if he had also shown that he was clumsy, he didn't care. It was a triumph of will.

Max got back to the tour bus but he said nothing to the passengers about his talk with the security guard. He hoped nothing further would occur because of the incident; Max sat next to Daniel and asked if he really wanted to know what the man in the synagogue had shouted in his face.

"Yes," said Daniel.

"In Hebrew a curse is really a curse. We don't say things like 'You're an asshole,' we say things like "May you die like a dog. Do you still want to hear?"

"I want to know. How bad could it be?"

He said, "His ancestor was the scribe who wrote that scroll. It was the last he transcribed before he died of consumption at the age of twenty-six in 1856. He hopes that when you least expect it, you will be struck down, but not struck down bodily but in mind and spirit. 'May you curse the day your mother gave you birth.'"

Daniel was again of two minds. One part was enjoying his triumph, thinking that this curse meant nothing. It seemed like a joke. The other part thought, Curse the day I was born? Never but maybe I went too far. I should never have let Gino force me into doing this.

He closed his eyes but did not fall asleep. His thought changed. Gino didn't force me to do this; no, I made the decision myself.

When they got back to the hotel, the big news was that gunmen had invaded a Jewish boys' school in Jerusalem, killing a dozen boys aged eight to ten. There was a statement made claiming responsibility. "This glorious act only increases our determination to exterminate every Jew on the planet." Max, when he heard the news, held his head in his hand and wondered how did it ever get to this situation.

For that night's dinner, the tour group was on their own. Adelaide skipped dinner, claiming, quite truthfully, that it felt like the cannons of the 1812 Overture were going off in her head. She was bewildered. Did she still believe in God? Yes. Had her conception of God been correct or had she started to think of Him as a Cosmic piñata that she only had to strike with praise or a prayer and what she wished for would come tumbling out? She had always assumed that God was going to make things occur the way she wanted them to occur. Now she was pretty sure this wasn't going to happen. She wanted her simple happy life back but maybe that wasn't what God wanted for her. If God wanted something different could she reconcile herself to his will? She had never thought about it before and didn't want to now but she forced herself to think about these things.

Before dinner, Svetlana went into a local art shop. There was a painting of two small children standing on a small hill, offering carrots to two ponies. The children were smiling and somehow the artist had conveyed the happiness of the ponies. Svetlana bought the painting and then had a light dinner in the town.

Daniel wanted to join a couple on the tour for dinner. As he approached their table, they quickly looked away from him. Daniel ended up eating by himself.

The two men who had bet dinner took their wives into Tiberius and found a little café and ate together. The loser was very willing to pay up. "That was an entertainment we won't ever see again," he said to the other man.

His wife said, 'It's one thing to say you don't believe in God, it is another to physically assault another person's religious art."

The other husband replied, "Oh come on. We've all done stupid things. God forgives. All Daniel's got to do is acknowledge his fault and ask for forgiveness and he'll have it."

"I'm not so sure it's all that easy," the other man said. "Yes, in the Christian concept of God, the Father forgives but there isn't such an easy, almost cost-free forgiveness in Judaism or under Islamic law, and there are lots of Jews and Islamic people around here. I wonder just how big a scandal this will become?"

The second wife said, "You're right but he's a Catholic and they believe if you sincerely ask for forgiveness you'll get it. But it's very hard to sincerely ask for forgiveness. You have to admit you were wrong and no one wants to do that. That's not cost free like you implied but very hard. I wonder what he's really going through? I'd be a wreck if I was him but ultimately it really isn't that significant. He didn't murder anyone."

After dinner, Daniel went to the bar of the hotel. He looked up at the top shelf at 27 different bottles. Maybe I am a dead man. Should I have one drink from each? I've always wanted to give it a try. He thought better of it and asked the bartender for a large double whis-key and, just to keep his assertiveness up, he asked for an Oban, his favorite single malt whiskey. The bartender, an overweight man of about forty, had the air of someone who, once he got going, could really tell a tale or two. Dan felt an immediate affinity with him.

"You look like hell. Had a hard day? Don't you like Israel or are you having marital difficulties?"

"How did you know?" asked Daniel. "You're on the tour with Max. There are always problems here in Israel but he tries to make everything enjoyable. He's a great guide. And I've seen you with your wife. She isn't here with you now, so the odds of hating Israel or having marital difficulties are about three in four."

"You're right on both counts."

"My name's Isaac. Want to talk about it?"

"Maybe later. Tell me about your life here," which Isaac proceeded to do with quite a bit of humor pointing to a couple drinking at a table on the side and telling Daniel the odd way in which they had met and fallen in love.

"How do you know?" asked Daniel.

"People tell bartenders all sorts of secrets and then forget they told them."

Daniel asked for another double scotch.

"You aren't going to drive or make any important decisions tonight, are you? If you are, I don't think I should serve you another drink."

"Don't worry. No driving or decisions tonight," said Daniel.

After Daniel had two more drinks, he said to Isaac, "Yeah I want to talk about it." He began to explain all that had happened and that his wife had taken it very badly. "She said she has a headache and went to bed. I'm not tired, so I came down here. Doesn't look like I'll be getting any for a long time."

"You never know," said Isaac, "I've seen lots of relationships begin here." To Daniel's surprise, Svetlana came up, wearing a form fitting silk blouse and a flowing silk skirt and asked if she could join Daniel. He readily agreed.

"You're so brave. I've never seen anyone do anything like that. Tell me, have you always been so direct and unafraid?"

"Gotten more direct lately," said Daniel who smiled for the first time in several hours. Isaac winked at Daniel and left the two of them alone. Only Isaac noticed that Dan's hand trembled as he lifted the glass to his lips. After a few minutes of chatter, Svetlana slowly ran a finger up Dan's thigh. Daniel's right hand, without a thought from Daniel's conscious mind, cupped Svetlana's waist for a few seconds and then went back to his drink.

Svetlana said, "I just bought a wonderful painting. It's in my room. Would you like to see it?"

Two thoughts crossed Daniel's mind. One that this wouldn't be a good idea. The second was, I might be dead in a year, I want to see the painting, I have a RIGHT to see it. Who's going to stop me?

As he paid his bill, Isaac said quietly to Daniel, "Told you this is a wonderful place to find romance."

Daniel replied, "It's nothing like that." Isaac smiled.

They went to Svetlana's room. Daniel sat on a very comfortable sofa, leaned back and closed his eyes for a few seconds. Svetlana went to the closet, unbuttoning the top two buttons of her blouse and got the painting. When she turned to show the painting, Daniel had fallen asleep.

At the same time as Daniel had gone to Svetlana's room, two Israeli security agents knocked on Max's door and explained that they wanted to interview Daniel, saying it would be much less scary if Max would knock on Daniel's door and explain to him what needed to be done.

The three of them walked to Daniel and Adelaide's room. Max knocked and the agents waited a few feet down the hall. Adelaide came to the door and told Max that Daniel wasn't there. Max walked to the bar. He knew that Isaac saw a great deal. The agents followed and, far behind them, Adelaide followed the three of them.

Isaac told Max that Daniel had been there but had left with a woman. Isaac described her and Max realized that Daniel had left with Svetlana. Max, the two agents, followed far behind by Adelaide, went to Svetlana's room. Max knocked loudly, which woke up Daniel. Svetlana opened the door. Adelaide saw her, held her hand to her mouth and wanted to cry out but she was silent. Svetlana acknowledged that Daniel was there and Daniel came out to talk to Max. Daniel didn't see the agents or his wife.

Max told Daniel that there were two men there who wanted to talk to him. "What about?" asked Daniel. One of the agents came up, as did Adelaide. The agent said, "We want to have a friendly discussion about the incident in the synagogue."

"Are you arresting me?" asked Daniel.

"No, we just want to ask you a few questions."

"Do I have a choice?"

"It's in everyone's interests that we keep this unofficial."

The agents and Daniel followed by Adelaide went off towards the front of the hotel.

Max stood for a second watching them. I bear a great deal of the blame, he thought as the agents walked with Daniel. Why did I ask if someone would read from that scroll? I never thought there'd be someone stupid enough to take it out. Why did I have to show off? And those debates? I could have stepped in and stopped them. What an idiot I've been.

Svetlana came out of her room and told Max that she wanted to join Daniel and the agents. Max tried to convince her that things were already complicated enough and she should stay in her room. She started to walk in the direction the agents had gone when Max took her gently by the hand, turned her to look at him and said, in the most pleasant and deferential tone he could manage considering how emotional he was at the moment, "Please, for everyone's sake, go back to your room. I'll let you know what happens." Svetlana didn't want to go to back in her room but the sincerity of Max's pleading could not be ignored. As she sat down on her sofa she said to herself, I only wanted to help that brave man.

Daniel and the agents went to a small room off the lobby. Adelaide stood outside the door. Max came up and urged Adelaide to go back to her room but she refused and sat in the lobby. Max stayed with her waiting.

Daniel tried to explain that it was all a mistake. One of the agents said he was sure it was. The other agent showed Daniel the video of the incident and said, 'There's so much religious tension in this country already. Watch yourself carefully." Daniel watched the video. The video showed the incident clearly and Daniel watched himself trip several times over the scroll and, from what he was seeing, it looked like, to others, he might deliberately have kicked and spat on the scroll.

"It's clear that you intentionally desecrated the Torah," said the first agent.

"I'm not so sure about that. He was foolish but the tripping and spitting looked like an accident to me," said the second.

"It's clear to me that you were trying to create an incident. It would be best for all if you take the first flight back to the US," said the more belligerent agent.

"I wasn't trying to create an incident," said Daniel.

"You showed terrible judgment. It would be the simplest, least painful if you voluntarily agree to leave the country," said the second.

"What about my wife?"

"She has done nothing wrong. We can't send her away."

"And if I fight it?"

The first agent said, "Charges might include attempting to destroy antiquities, inciting religious hatred. Do you want to have your picture all over TV? You could go to jail. Go back to America and it will be over. Stay, call your embassy to fight it and it goes out of our hands."

The other agent was more understanding. "I'm sure you didn't mean to create an incident. This was obviously just a stupid mistake. But in Israel, stupid mistakes can get people killed. For everyone's sake, allow yourself to be sent home."

"What do I tell the tour?" asked Daniel.

The second agent said, "We'll tell them that you were threatened and that for your safety you asked to be sent out of the country. They'll believe that. And believe me, this is for your safety."

Daniel didn't want to go. The agents emphasized the gravity of the situation and finally Daniel agreed to go but he had a question, "Do you know that synagogue well?"

"Very well," the second agent said. "My uncle's a member."

"Is it true that the second Torah in the Arc is never opened except on Yom Kippur by the chief Rabbi and that anyone who opens it at other times dies within a year?"

"Yes. Back in 2002, there was someone who opened it and died two months later. A building stone in the ceiling of a medieval building fell on his head."

"I think it was three months later," said the other officer, "but in 1995 a man died after six months, hit by a car. There were also cases back in 1976 and 1972."

"You can't possibly remember them," said Daniel.

"Not personally, but people have long memories here."

Daniel left with the two agents. As he passed through the lobby, he told Max and Adelaide that he had been asked to go back to the States for his own safety. "Tell people that I was called back on urgent business. There's a deal that demands my attention." Daniel and Adelaide had an awkward hug. Daniel shook Max's hand and thanked him for the kindness he has shown him during the trip. Daniel was driven to Ben Gurion airport and had to wait, with a different agent, many hours for a flight.

Adelaide sat in the hotel lobby in a complete state of shock; her emotions hammered back and forth like a ball in a professional tennis tournament. All her habitual habits which usually generated happy thoughts seemed to have failed her. What was Daniel doing in Svetlana's room? Had she so completely forgotten that this is a dangerous world and that beautiful women can easily seduce men? Was Svetlana really trying to take her husband? Why did she come to Israel? Was the incident my fault? She got up and went to her room but could not sleep. At about 3 A.M. she got up, took the blessing book from her pocketbook and wrote, "Jesus, you went through a time of great testing. Now it is my time. Please help me be as brave as you were." As soon as she wrote this she became calm and a trace of her cheerfulness returned. She was determined not to abandon Daniel. She would see him through this difficulty. She lay down and slept soundly.

After the agents left with Daniel, Max went to Svetlana's room, asked her to go with him to the empty lobby to talk. He told her that he was sorry to tell her that Daniel had been sent back to the States.

Svetlana sat there stunned by the developments. She told Max that the agents had no right to come and get Daniel out of her room. She hadn't done anything wrong. The error Daniel made was very minor and it was unfair to target both of them. Daniel's wife isn't good enough for him, she said. "He is an independent spirit and his wife is completely rigid."

Max looked at her tenderly wondering if he could give her any advice that she could hear. I have to try, he thought. "If you were my daughter, I would be so extremely proud of what you've made of your life."

"Thank you," said Svetlana.

"I would remind you, what I have to remind myself sometimes. I'm a tour guide. I'm away from home a lot. Many of my clients are attractive and available. I say to myself, "Thou shalt not covet thy neighbor's wife nor thy neighbor's husband.'"

"I don't believe in God. That commandment has nothing to do with me."

"It's good advice whether there is a God or not. They love each other. Let them work it out. You're young and beautiful. You'll have plenty of admirers."

"Not like him and don't presume to tell me what to do," Svetlana said and stormed out. Max sat wondering if there was anything more he could do and decided there wasn't.

Svetlana went to her room and wept. She did not want to think about what she was feeling. She wanted to destroy something. She picked the painting up, got a scissor to cut it and destroy it, but when she saw its beauty, the joy in the eyes of the children and ponies, she couldn't damage it. To kill that joy those children have. She put the painting back in the closet. She didn't believe in God but if there were any part of mankind that was almost divine, it was artistic creations, which inspired her. She got ready for bed, lay down but did not sleep.

At breakfast the next morning, Max explained to the tour group that Daniel had to return because of urgent business. People were surprised. Some thought it might have been due to yesterday's incident but neither Max, Svetlana nor Adelaide said anything to confirm that rumor.

Adelaide wanted to leave the tour but Max tried to convince her to stay, saying that they only had three days remaining. Adelaide tried but couldn't find a flight back before the one she was scheduled on so she stayed on the tour, worrying about Daniel. What was he going through? she wondered. Would she be able to help him?

She stayed in her hotel room that morning, skipping the tour. She had briefly been calm last night but now she was again upset. What could she write in her blessings book? She was troubled but wrote the verse, "We know that for those who love God, all things work together for good." But this wasn't sufficient. The bitter memory of seeing Daniel come out of Svetlana's room consumed her. She tried to push it aside and failed. She was forced to acknowledge that she was suffering and God seemed very far away. She wrote a quote from the Psalms. 'Why, O Lord, do you stand far away? Why do you hide yourself in times of trouble?' This must be what Jesus experienced. I will remain steadfast and will help Daniel," she wrote and closed her book.

After many hours of waiting at the airport, Daniel was escorted to his seat on the plane. An officer waited at the gate until the plane took off to make sure that Daniel didn't change his mind about leaving voluntarily.

After about two hours of flying, in the middle of the Mediterranean Sea, the plane flew into a severe thunderstorm. The plane plunged and climbed up over and over. Daniel, who normally was not afraid of flying, began to sweat and worry, almost to panic. He wanted to grab the hand of the passenger next to him, whom he hadn't even said hello to, but he didn't dare. His breathing sped up.

He wondered if this was going to be his death? No, it can't be, he thought but his body had its own belief. "Within a year," he re-heard

Max say. "Yes, it is true," he heard one of the officer's say, resoundingly affirmed by the second officer. He found himself trembling as if he'd been drinking so much that he lost control of his muscles. His mind was full of questions about the future. Would he lose his marriage? Was he really an atheist? Was his mind an atheist and his body a believer? He again thought of the question that obsessed him as he had been deciding what to do at the synagogue. "What is he, a man, a mouse or a fool?" He knew for sure that he was a little of each.

Thoughts of the events of the trip and the synagogue continued to grow stronger. He remembered the debate in detail and all the convincing arguments he'd made for why God didn't exist and how he had parried all the arguments for God's existence. His arguments against God seemed real and non-negotiable. "I'm committed now," said one voice. Another voice said, "Just repent." And then he heard what seemed a definitive voice coming from his own mouth, "Never." He had actually said it, loudly. His neighbor looked at him quizzically. When Daniel didn't speak again, his neighbor looked away.

Daniel closed his eyes but did not sleep. He had a brief vision of himself being chased by a dragon, barely being able to keep away from the spewing flames. He opened his eyes; his body was shaking. He knew that he was in really deep emotional waters, forever out of sight of land and, for the first time in his life, he worried that he would not survive the year.

He longed for what he now saw as his "simple" life before the tour but, if he had been given an offer to have skipped this trip and the difficulties he was now experiencing, he would not have taken it. No, life has to be faced. I have to be comfortable with fear, he thought. But I'll never be able to do that. I just don't know what to do. All I know categorically is that I have crossed an important line. I have no idea what is ahead but there is no way to go back. Suffering. There will be suffering. I accept it. With that thought, he fell asleep and did not wake until the plane landed at JFK airport.

# THE GREAT PIANO REBELLION

What a time to stop working, lamented Charles Hurland, a three time Tony Award winning composer, as he hit the middle C key on the battered, peeling but playable, black upright Baldwin piano he was composing on. Charles was 55, a bit plump and greying with nothing physically to distinguish him as a famous composer, except perhaps his very long, thin fingers. Charles worked with a lyricist named Jacques, who was 24 and who had gone home earlier.

Charles was in a small rehearsal room, which contained only a florescent ceiling light, the piano and its bench and two metal folding chairs. It was the smallest of the twelve rehearsal rooms in a rental studio complex in the west 50s of Manhattan.

This Baldwin piano, although it had a slightly metallic sound and the least responsive keyboard of any of the pianos in the studio complex, was Charles' favorite. He'd first rented this least expensive rehearsal studio in 1990 when he was nearly broke, and lived with two other men in a one bedroom apartment. He composed his first commercial success sitting at this very piano. He had since become even more successful but he had a superstition that he composed best on what other people would consider to be an old, uninspiring piano. Plus he believed that, if his music sounded good on this mediocre piano, it would sound wonderful on the Steinway grand piano used when his music was played professionally.

I can't play this song without this C note, he thought. He tried playing the C note up an octave but that key had also stopped working. He wondered how it was possible for them both to jam at exactly the same inopportune time. Jacques also tuned pianos and could fix the keys but he wasn't here. Charles pounded his foot on the floor. Then he said out loud, "Let me transpose the music to C sharp major, then I won't have to use either C key."

He did so and tried to play the C sharp key next to middle C. To his astonishment, he thought he heard that C sharp key call out, "You can't push me around anymore. I won't play for you. Your music, for this play, is insipid and I simply won't take part."

Charles shook his head back and forth, thinking he was hallucinating. Maybe he was starting to fall asleep sitting up. It was Sunday, 2:57 AM. He and Jacques had been working since 9 AM to revise the music for a show that was supposed to open shortly. Jacques had left at 9 PM but Charles stayed on. He thought that when you begin to think your piano is talking to you, it's probably time to get some rest. But he'd better make it only a short nap. Two days before, they'd had a preview with a critic who called four of their new songs "lame, lamentable and listless. The music is even worse than the lyrics. Your play is about an aspiring composer and most of the music stinks." They thought they'd fixed two of the songs but they still had two more to either fix or write replacements. Charles didn't have time to rest.

Charles got off the piano bench and closed the cover over the keys. He opened the folding cot that sat in the corner and moved it in line with the piano keyboard. He lay down but was too wound up to fall asleep. He distinctly heard talking in the room but knew that was impossible. He felt fear and the muscles around his abdomen were tense. Definitely, the voices were in the piano. I'll move the piano bench away and move my cot closer and listen. Maybe I'll get an idea for a better song. No, I'm acting crazy, he thought, but he continued to listen.

Charles had perfect pitch. Whenever he listened to music, he could always tell exactly what note was being played. Now he was sure the keyboard was talking, each individual key speaking in its own exact distinct pitch. He pinched his cheek to see if he had gone off to sleep but he was awake and aware. There was no pitch variation in each voice he heard, just the 88 sounds that can be made by the 88 keys of a piano.

"That bastard Charles left me out again," he heard. "He's a prejudicial, low-note phobic, black key hating scum." So said the lowest black B flat key. "I'm triple cursed and deserving of better."

"Oh yeah," replied the highest white A note on the piano, who resided 86 keys to the right of the first complaining B flat, "I'm a white key and when has he ever put me into one of his pieces? Maybe once. He's also an anti-high note fanatic."

"You don't understand," said the middle C, "most music is written in the range of the human voice and neither one of you is a tone that can be sung by a human. That's why I'm the most frequently played sound. It's only fair."

From somewhere came the question, "If you're so popular, why did you stop playing?"

The middle C note replied, "Because I'm forced to work too much because I'm so damn popular. I should be paid more than any other key because of all the extra work I do. You all should revere me. I'm on strike for fair pay."

"Who the hell are you to defend those bastard humans for not using all notes equally?" said the D note, three octaves above middle C. "I'm above the notes that humans can sing so I don't get my fair share of playing. Humans have the technology to allow vocal chords to be altered to produce much higher and lower notes. If they did that, I'd get my fair share of playing. I say we all stop working."

"I think humans might think they have other more pressing problems to solve. I love Charles' music. He's great. I'm not going on strike," noted the white G note, who resided a few notes up from middle C. Most of the other keys called this particular G key, "Haughty G." This key was extremely unpopular and had virtually no support from the other keys.

The black F sharp note, about two octaves lower on the keyboard shouted out, "Haughty G,, what an arrogant double-crossing bastard you are. You're part of the C major chord, "C", "E" and "G", the most popular chord in all of music and then you're the base note of the G major chord, which leads back to the C chord and the second most popular chord on the piano. And the G major scale has the second most music written for it. You get all the attention you could possibly deal with, while I get none. Charles used me only once in the last fourteen songs he's written."

"I don't know why the hell you complain," answered 'Haughty G.' "Why you, Mr. F sharp, are the last note of my scale. The best of all scales, the G major scale."

"I told you I'm no longer a mister. They took my sexuality away. Bastards."

"Ignore what that note says," joined in the F sharp chord even lower than the previous one. "You, Haughty G, called the G major scale and all the notes in it, including me, 'My scale.' As if you own all of the other six notes in the scale and we are your slaves. I'm no one's slave. No way. You're as much an exploiter as Charles."

"I agree with F sharp," said all the black A flat keys at once. "We black keys have a tremendous grievance. There are 52 white keys and only 36 black ones. That's almost 50 percent more. I say all black keys should refuse to play when we're hit until we get equality of numbers."

"We don't need you," said the white E note, two notes down. "We white notes can make up a full major or natural minor scale. That can't be done with only the black notes. Why should Charles even bother with black keys? White keys should be enough for him."

There was a shout from the black keys high on the keyboard. "That's why there should be more black keys. Make all the white B keys into black B keys, then there will be 44 black keys and 44 white keys. Now that would be fair. "

Two lower B keys cried out, "But changing us to be a black key will mean that there'd be two black keys next to each other and then all the piano players will be totally confused and won't know how to play any longer. They'd have to learn to play all over again. Most of them won't bother and they're be so many fewer pianos made. That's not practical."

A counter-shout came from two upper white B keys. "So what? We two are all for equality. I vote to become a black key and for making all the piano players re-learn how to play."

A black A flat key countered this proposal. "The black keys are unique and constitute both major and minor natural pentatonic scales. Pentatonic scales are the most melodious. If you play only on the black keys, your music will always be harmonic, never a sour note. We don't need any of you so-called superior white notes. All you do is cause disharmonic sound combinations. Let's separate the piano into two pianos, one white and one black."

"More needs to be done," said one black G flat key. "I had a horrible realization two weeks ago. You know that Charles gives piano lessons. Why such a famous composer would teach snotty little kids to play, I can't say but he says he enjoys it. He was teaching this ignorant brat, Tommy, who knew nothing, and I mean absolutely nothing about music. Now I always think of myself and call myself by the name G flat so that I'm sure of my identity. Charles taught Tom that I'm also the F sharp key. Immoral, I should get to decide what I'm called, not some ass of a composer. Self-identification is our unalienable right. Now I'm so confused. How dare he call me what I don't want to be called. It's humiliating. I want him in jail. I'm thinking of burning myself up. I think I'll get a match."

Charles was suddenly frightened. What if this conversation he was hearing was true? Would there be a fire? He thought of doing something until he heard a cry from throughout the keyboard, "Please, please don't play with matches."

Charles relaxed. This conversation is fascinating, he thought. Who would have guessed the passions going on inside an ancient Baldwin piano?

The "Haughty G" key, Charles' defender, whispered to the A key, two up from him, "That G flat key is one striking short of being sent to the home for mentally confused piano notes."

"How very arrogant you are, 'Haughty G'. Next we'll have to call you 'Sir Haughty G'," replied the A key.

"Haughty G" ignored this and continued, "How could a piano key not know we all have many identities? Composers can call me a G note or F double sharp note, or A double flat and I could go on. We all have multiple identities, just like humans have. But there's a beauty in music notation that isn't in humans. Change the key signature on music and you can play the piece many different ways. Humans almost never change."

The black A flat key, in the next octaves down, piped up, "I've always found that the flat key signatures are the most melodic. Why the great Chopin was enamored of the key of A flat major. Some of the world's most melodic music is written in my key."

From across the keyboard came shouts, "That statement is deeply prejudicial. All scales, keys and notes are equal. All of them. Retract your statement or be expelled. Let's vote that particular A flat key out."

"But who will remove the key, if we vote it out?" asked the much hated 'Haughty G.' "You'll never convince Charles to remove all the A flat keys and he'd have to do it."

"That bastard Charles covered us up," said the high A, the highest note on the keyboard. "We're almost always in the dark. No light. I'm going to light a match."

There came a roar from about twenty-seven keys at once. "Never. We have a solemn pact never to light a match. You might hurt someone."

"I don't care, I wish I could hurt someone. I'm going to burn this whole damned studio down if Charles doesn't include me in one of the pieces he's writing."

Charles sat bolt upright. All the piano keys were talking at the same time and he couldn't discern what was being said except that his name was joined with words like "cynic," "chauvinist," "mongrel," "parasite," "misanthropist," "sneerer."

Charles started to wonder what he could have done to get the Baldwin piano to rebel. It's not fair. I've dedicated my life to the piano, teaching students, writing music, seeing how pianos could be made less costly so more people could play them. He began to talk to himself. He thought it odd to talk to oneself, but it was nearly 4 AM; he had an excuse. "They say I'm prejudiced, black key hostile, a low key maligner, an exploiter of certain keys. How can it be? I always hoped that I treated all the keys equally."

He uncovered the keys. Light streamed in and the keys were startled. After a joint scream, they became quiet. Charles began to speak to them. "Please understand that I have to make my music fit the mood, words, emotions and sensations of the plays. If the songs don't sound satisfying, the audience won't come, I'll lose my job, starve and maybe die. You don't abhor me enough to want me to die, do you?" Then, exhausted, Charles lay down and continued to listen.

Haughty G said, "What an understanding composer Charles is."

From different parts of the piano keyboard came cries of "Not enough" and "Work-stoppage."

Suddenly there was an intense complaint, coming from a place they didn't expect to hear from. The sustain pedal yelled, "All people ever do is step on me. It's terrible to be trampled on by smelly shoes. I won't stand for it. I demand a walkout."

There was then a boom louder than any other, "I am the metal frame that holds you all together. Do I get even the slightest notice or good wishes? Never. Does the composer ever make the player hit me so I can make a sound too? Forget it. If I withdraw, the strings will fall off and there will be no music. I say we defy Charles."

"I don't understand why you're rebelling. What do you want from me?" asked Charles.

The lowest note said, "Who will get all the glory for the new music? You, Charles, that's who. It's always the same. You're the hero. Who will be credited in the Playbill? You will, Charles, and it won't mention us. If you win another Tony, will you thank us in your speech? Will the composer in the play, play on an old battered Baldwin? Of course not. He'll play on a brand new, shiny Steinway. We spit on bright new Steinways. This is an official work stoppage."

The piano fell silent and in a minute Charles fell asleep and started snoring.

At 9 AM, Jacques, the lyricist, woke Charles, bringing coffees and breakfast sandwiches. Charles put the folding cot away, refreshed himself, then they ate and drank. Charles was usually talka-tive in the morning but he today, he was silent. Jacques figured that Charles was probably exhausted and trying to save energy, so he didn't talk either.

When they finished eating, Charles put the bench in front of the piano and was about to play, when he stopped and said to Jacques, "I have no idea what's going to happen when I play the piano. I'm afraid."

Jacques, much bemused, thinking Charles had gone insane said, "Had a bad night? Fall off the horse? They say the best thing is to get back on the horse."

"I didn't fall off a horse, it's this damned piano. I want no part of it."

Jacques looked Charles in the eye with disbelief. "Afraid of a piano, I'd never have guessed."

Charles wondered whether he could pluck up the courage to play. He looked at Jacques and said, "The piano talked to me last night. It's having a work-stoppage."

"Maybe you should take the day off."

"It did talk to me," screamed Charles. "Go ahead, try to play it, it's holding out."

Jacques tried as hard as he could not to laugh. He hit the white middle C key and there was no sound. "That's odd. Must be stuck. I can fix that." Jacques got out his tuning tools.

"Try more keys," said Charles.

Jacques hit the white D, E and F keys, next to middle C. Nothing.

"Now try the black keys," said Charles.

Jacques hit the black A flat, B flat, D flat, E flat, G flat keys below middle C and not a sound came out.

"They must all have agreed," said Charles. "There was one key that was friendly to me, it was the G key above middle C, the other keys called it the Haughty G key. Try that key." It didn't play.

Jacques didn't know what to think. He said to Charles "Maybe you need more rest. We could put this off a few more hours then we'll try another room."

"No, I refuse. I always compose at this piano. Take a picture of me playing and tweet it out saying how proud I am of this Baldwin Piano."

Jacques did so. Charles tried to play the notes again but they were all stuck except Haughty G, which actually played.

"I'm on to something. I know it," said Charles. "Maybe I can understand some of what was said last night."

"One key plays. That ain't much," said Jacques.

"It's everything," said Charles. "I've got it. I have in my mind a new piece of music, it's going to start out on all black keys, an introduction in major pentatonic, completely harmonic and loud. It's our play's composer's introduction to a happy piece. Then we add a chorus, it's in A natural minor, using all white keys. It sounds so different from the beginning but somehow we make it fit. Then I do a huge sweep from bottom to top hitting all the white key and then one down all the black keys. Every key played. All equal."

"It's a plan at least," said Jacques.

Charles stopped to consider what else he might do. He opened the top of the piano and started to pound on the frame, which made interesting notes. He took his shoes off and pressed down on the sustain pedal to make the sounds even more exotic.

"We're going to have lots of key changes in this piece and lots of high and low notes. Can't wait to get it down," said Charles. "This new song will be named *We all win when I play on my Baldwin*. How does that sound as a plan, Jacques? Can you write a song with those words as the lead in to the chorus?"

'Sure. Let's go to another room and try it. This piano is messed up."

"I'm pretty sure I've made this Baldwin happy and it will play now." Charles started a riff up the piano on the white keys and down on the black keys. Every single note sang out like luminous flame. He took off his shoe and started to push down the sustain pedal with his bare foot as he played a pentatonic melody followed by a natural minor melody. Then he changed the key of the song five times running. Charles felt the Baldwin's pride.

Jacques said, "I love that sound. It will sound even better on a Steinway."

"Nope. We're going to use my favorite Baldwin in the show and we'll put its picture on all the advertisements. It's this piano that's made all this possible."

"What an odd morning," said Jacques.

"A marvelous morning," replied Charles. "They all need to have their voices."

Jacques looked at him oddly, "Whatever you say, Charles." Then, on a whim, "I agree, let's have this Baldwin in the show."

"Brilliant," said Charles.

"I am brilliant sometimes," said Jacques.

"I meant the Baldwin," replied Charles, with a double rainbow in his eyes.

# THE REPUBLIC OF SILENCE
## OR
## MAYBE A BEAVER WILL SAVE ME

AFRAIDHELPME

My brother, Jeramy, keeps saying these words over and over again. He says almost nothing else. Using the word "says" implies that he speaks but that is not correct. My brother cannot control his tongue enough to speak nor control his fingers enough to type. A "doctor," using a technique pioneered by the Chinese Communist Party, took away these abilities after his second violation of our speech laws. Jeramy talks to me by knocking metal pieces on his knees to produce Morse code.

How did this happen? Before the current law, there was a Human Rights Commission which sued people for saying things that designated groups of people thought were objectionable. No one was jailed but many were fined and threatened if they didn't pay and say and do what the Commission commanded. Many did not see this as an attack on freedom of speech but my brother and I did.

The problem expanded when Canada started to give severe penalties to those who refused to use the self-chosen preferred personal pronoun for those who do not want to be called "he" or "she." This new law was created to produce compassion for those who consider themselves to be non-binary.

After this law was passed, you could call someone a "f-cking a-shole" without the slightest penalty but if you refused to use "zir" or another of the individually chosen and constantly multiplying personal pronouns, you could be jailed. My brother supported the use of these pronouns and up until the passage of the law had always used them, but he did not believe the government had the legal or moral authority to compel speech and he refused to comply. He was the first to spend time in jail for violating this law.

Before his going to jail, I had become a nurse working at Montreal General Hospital. Many days after work, I'd walk up the hill to The Cross on the Mountain and the Mount Royal Chalet and look out over the city. Montreal is a magnificent place to live especially if, like me, you enjoy snow, cultures and different types of people.

I had many affairs with both men and women, often at the same time, causing lots of heartache but I couldn't help it or, more truthfully, maybe that's just what I wanted to do. Jeramy became a writer, mostly for newspapers and magazines and then he started writing stories and novels. He married and had two sons.

Jeramy had recently written an article in the journal, Canadian Artist's Duty, which was a forum to discuss the purpose of art. He proposed that novelists should examine both sides of issues and not just follow one side or the other. "If your protagonist is offered a simple solution, it should never work. Art needs to reflect the complexity of life" is the only quote I remember. He got nominated to run for the presidency of the Canadian Writing Society and won a narrow victory. He now had a position of some authority.

When the extension to the speech law was going to be debated, Jeramy told me he planned to testify against its adoption. "It's the next logical step towards totalitarianism."

I told him he'd ruin his reputation. He'd be labeled as a peddler of "hatred," an expression used to intimidate those who refuse to buckle under the enforced use of language. "They may pass it but they'll never jail someone for the improper use of pronouns."

"Fat chance they won't. If they meant that, they'd put the no jail time wording directly in the law and they've refused to do that."

The testimony was still a week away and there was time for Jeramy to change his mind. I gave a dinner party and invited Jeramy and his wife, as well as Professor Emmanuel Toussaint and his wife. Professor Toussaint taught at a liberal arts university in the Eastern Townships of Quebec, where Jeramy and I had both gone to school. I was hoping the professor would talk some sense into Jeramy.

Professor Toussaint made a large pitcher of rum-based drinks. He poured us all a drink. Jeramy's wife, my lover, and Professor Toussaint's wife went to the living room, while the three of us drank ours in the kitchen. Between sips, I was putting together lasagna.

As we worked, I said to Professor Toussaint that Jeramy was planning on testifying before Senator Crusher's committee. "What do you think about it?"

"It's rather a silly controversy," said Toussaint. "If we spoke Turkish, there'd only be one pronoun "O" for everyone and there'd be no controversy but we speak a language where there are already two pronouns. From two to many is a small leap. Still, it's no reason to put people in jail."

"That's not what I asked. If Jeramy testifies, he'd be slaughtered, right?"

"This is Canada, Professor. I'm sure to get a fair hearing," said Jeramy.

'What makes you think that? We don't have a Constitution guaranteeing freedom of speech and, even if we did, where there's political passion there's always distortions. I grew up in Haiti and there's a great combination of passion and lying there."

"This is Canada. Everyone's reasonable here," Jeramy said.

"We have our uncontrolled passions. From 1963 to 1969 there was a terrorist bombing every ten days, all concerning the political status of Quebec," said Professor Toussaint. "Before she was a Senator, Crusher was my student and we clashed on the first day of class over the requirements for the term paper. You had to take a political ideal that you held to be true and present evidence for and against this idea from a philosophical and historical point of view. She said that she believed the political view of requiring equality of outcome on all occasions and this view could not and should not be argued against.

"I pointed out that it was an impossibility to always have an equality of outcome. Our football team had just lost 35 to 7. You'd have had to put me as the quarterback of the other team to get anything like equality of outcome.

"Crusher replied, 'An excellent idea. Equality of outcome is essential, and I will hear no argument against it'. I pointed out there were many philosophers and political writers who believed that only an equality of opportunity was possible or desirable, so she should easily be able to find arguments against her stated political ideal.

"Her response was, 'Equality of opportunity not of outcome is a racist and oppressive ideal and I refuse to even consider such garbage.'

"I said that the class was designed to make one think about the complications that are inherent in any set of beliefs.

"'There are no contradictions in my belief. You are preaching racism.' She reported me to the administration, put me on trial. She provided faked evidence and I was convicted. Be careful. She doesn't have any respect for truth and facts."

On Wednesday, the three of us drove to what has always seemed to me to be, aside from the National Gallery, the very boring city of Ottawa.

The hearing would be before five senators in Senator Crusher's committee, two from her party and three others. When the hearing started, Senator Crusher announced that the three members of other parties were sick and would not participate.

The testimony was given in a small Senate room, similar to a small TV interview studio. A single video feed, delayed for seven seconds, was piped to a large gallery, where the invited guests and media sat.

As we went through security, we had to give up our cell phones and other electronic devices. We saw many people with invitations who were being turned away from the meeting.

Jeramy's testimony was to be the last of the day. Each testimony started with a five-minute opening statement followed by ten minutes of questions. The first five participants had publically stated that they were in favor of the new legislation. Two who would speak against the change, Jeramy and a novelist named Mary Slater, followed them. The four of us sat in the gallery while we waited to be called to testify.

The first testimony was from a stage director. He pointed out that Trans people have a high suicide rate and that directors had an obligation to modify traditional plays to safeguard them. He had staged a prose version of Hamlet, where Hamlet and his father are Trans individuals. "Hamlet's great speech has been changed to 'To be, or not to be; that is the question: Whether 'tis nobler in the mind to suffer the slings and arrows of outraged pronouns, Or to take arms against them.'"

Senator Crusher asked, "Can you think of a single reason not to pass this law?" The director replied no. The audience chanted, "Pass the law."

During the break Professor Toussaint said to me, "Very clever director. It's a good career move to have a different take on a famous play."

"You don't think his changes are a bit much?" I asked.

"Sounds rather simplistic but why shouldn't he do that? Jeramy is arguing for freedom of expression. So why shouldn't others have it too?"

I asked Mary what she thought of the testimony and all she could say was "worrying."

During the testimony of the next witness, the audience continually chanted, "Pass the law."

"Why is everyone so vehement?" I whispered to the Professor. "Is the law this popular?"

"This is an invitation-only audience and we saw most of the invitees denied entrance. If you invite the right people and stop others, you're bound to get an audience that's overwhelmingly for the law. Let's face it, this hearing is propaganda."

Mary looked grim.

The last supporter was a prominent book critic who said, "I will denounce any book whose author doesn't support the law." The audience cheered.

Senator Crusher called for a short recess. The four of us talked among ourselves.

Professor Toussaint said to Jeramy and Mary, "It's your time to show courage, wit and quick thinking. Show them that freedom is vital."

"I'm a single mother and can't afford to lose my book sales. I'm not feeling well." She ran from the hearing room. All our hopes now rode on Jeramy.

Jeramy had insisted that I be allowed to accompany him while he testified. I had to promise not to speak. We walked into the small studio and sat facing the committee.

Jeramy began by saying he understood why some people might support the changes but he believed they constituted a threat to our common freedom. As he finished this sentence, the speakers started a feedback loop, which continued for almost five minutes. As soon as the audio was fixed, Senator Crusher said, "Thank you for your enlightening opening statement."

"I didn't finish it."

"Time's up. What are your qualifications? Do you have a doctorate or a medical degree?"

"No but I am President of the--"

Crusher cut him off. "Don't you know that LGTBQ people live shorter lives because they don't get the respect they need? Why do you refuse them this respect?"

"This is an issue of freedom of speech..."

"You want to sow hatred of gay and trans people? You have no right."

We could hear a few people outside chanting "Hater."

"You can hear people calling you a hater, can't you?" asked Senator Crusher.

"They have no basis for saying that. I love all people, which is why I want everyone to have freedom of speech. Without that freedom--"

Crusher again cut him off. "You told us you aren't a doctor or even a professor. You heard the theatre director talk about how the pronoun "he" killed Hamlet's father."

"I support his right to change art as he likes. You should respect my right to make art as I like. Freedom of speech is needed in order..."

The Senator interrupted again. "What does a hack writer like you know about such important matters? Your last book makes a mockery of trans rights. One character was born with male genitals and at age twelve this person believed they were female, so this person convinced a doctor to give them hormones and an operation to change their genitalia. After the operation, this person was even more unhappy than before and in physical pain. At fourteen, the character came to believe they were a man and again was transformed. They were still miserable. At age sixteen, they had an operation to again have female genitalia which no longer worked and the person wishes they had never been transitioned in the first place. You are denying trans individuals the right to transition."

"I didn't say that at all."

About seven seconds later there was a roar from the audience, "Kill Jeramy."

The Senator called for order. The audience slowly calmed down.

"You don't understand how novels are written, Senator. A writer can't make the characters do anything; they act as they see fit, on their own initiative. That's what the character in that story thought, not what I think."

"You made a mockery of people feeling they are trapped in the wrong body."

"Life and art are complicated. There are other characters who transition as an adult and are quite happy. No status in life is purely blissful. You're upset that a Trans character was unhappy but some are. I'm all in favor of marriage but there are unhappily married people and it's not for everyone. Is it now a crime to say such things? Art is like life. It shows joy and sorrow, wisdom and foolery. What's important is freedom of speech ...."

Senator Crusher interrupted again. "You know nothing about life. How could a hack like you be elected as President of an Arts organization?"

"To many people my books seems of little importance but to me they mean something. The characters are as alive to me as any of you and what was written was exactly what this person experienced. Changing your genitalia is a major operation. We shouldn't encourage children, who could so easily change their mind, to do this. We don't let children drink or vote. Changing your genitalia is a much greater responsibility. Let people wait until they are more mature before we offer such a medical solution."

"That is the statement of a hater, a hypocrite and a dangerous individual.

Usher, remove them," demanded Senator Crusher.

Jeramy made one last statement as he was escorted out. "We are all equally absurd only in different ways. We're small and unimportant and we don't know that fact. I see that in myself. I see that in everyone else. That's what I write about in my books. I wish I could say that we are all heroes but we're not.'

"Get out," yelled Senator Crusher.

The usher led my brother and me off.

When we got to Professor Toussaint, Jeramy said , "I was pathetic."

"You're my hero," I replied.

"What an idiot you were," said Professor Toussaint. "When the Senator asked 'Are you saying that transitioning never works. Why did you say, 'It absolutely never works.'"

"That's not what I said."

"He never said that, "I said.

"When Senator Crusher said 'You directly made a mockery of people feeling they are trapped in the wrong body. Why did you say? 'It's a myth that there are people who feel they are trapped in the wrong body?'"

"I never said that," said Jeramy.

"Are you sure?" asked Toussaint.

"Of course he never said that," I said.

"She's snookered everyone with that delayed feed," said the Professor.

"Did she use some artificial intelligence to change Jeramy's responses?" I asked.

"Probably. And your mouth, on the screen, corresponded to what she wished you had said. You have to give it to her. No one could have done a better job of destroying your reputation."

That night, there were shows about a hack writer who denied that there were trans people and denied them the right to transition. Not one sentence about freedom of speech or about Senator Crusher's trampling on Jeramy's rights to testify fully and truthfully.

A year passed and Jeramy was proved wrong. No one was jailed in our country but some were jailed for similar speech in Europe and other places where freedom of speech was formerly respected. Then Senator Crusher's party came to power saying that the needed changes in speech patterns hadn't happened yet, so more strident action needed to be taken.

Soon after the election, Jeramy wrote a novel where the hero was jailed for trying to actively campaign against the speech laws. When it rose to number three on the best seller list, Jeramy and his wife joined me for a celebratory dinner at a Greek café.

On the way out, two men who were Horsemen confronted us (Members of The Royal Canadian Mounted Police.) They were without horses and in plain clothes.

"I understand that your name is Jeramy and you wrote a novel," the first said.

"Yes."

"What did that person say?" said the second Horseman pointing to the first.

"He asked if I'd written a novel."

"I prefer to be called zir," said the first Horseman.

"I asked what did that person say," asked the second agent again pointing to the first Horseman.

Jeramy was obviously in a panic. He wanted to be polite but he didn't want to be forced by the law to speak in a certain manner.

"That wonderful person asked if I was a writer."

"That person wants to be referred to as zir."

Jeramy looked at the first and said, "I would love to call you that.'

"But you didn't," said the second. "Last chance, are you going to continue to insult that person?"

"Wonderful, enlightened, kind person..." said Jeramy.

"Call him zir or it's jail time," said the second Horseman.

"The law cannot compel me to do so. I am a free man."

"You'll be a jailed man."

"Maybe the only free people are those who are in jail," said Jeramy.

Jeramy was sent to the slammer for two years. The Prime Minister weighed in saying how important it was to stop this hate speech and that the only way to guarantee that was to jail those who would not obey.

My name and address as well as the names and addresses of Jeramy's wife and children were published. We were publicaly hounded outside our residences by members of GEOO (Guaranteed Equality of Outcome). We got threatening phone calls. Within a year Jeramy's wife left him and took to using her maiden name. I also changed my name and moved to a different part of town.

A few weeks after his incarceration, I visited Jeramy. "I discovered that murderers and bank robbers are not insulted if I call them "he" even though a few prefer other pronouns. They said that what pronouns they are called by are the least of their problems. Now, I'm willing to call these heroes by any pronoun they wish. I am with the only free people in the country and want to honor them."

During the second year of Jeramy's incarceration, they legally defined yet a new use for pronouns that indicated to what oppressed group you belonged. To make it easier and fairer, a new list of per-sonal pronouns was standardized. Each new pronoun would contain six-letters, from "AAAAA" to "ZZZZZ", omitting a few unneeded combinations that formed common words. These new pronouns allowed for more than three hundred million choices and since Canada has less than forty million people, the government believed these pronouns would be enough, for now.

The speech law was not changed because it didn't specify punishment, but the administration published a decision that second time offenders would be punished by disabling their tongues and their fingers, permanently silencing them by injecting a certain "medicine" in each finger and into the underside of the tongue. When I visited Jeramy, in prison, he quipped, "And now, Canada, just like in the People's Republic of China, will create citizens of a brand new nation. I call it

The Republic of Silence."

"No way."

"It's a certainty."

Jeramy got out of prison, and to make a long story short, he was convicted a second time and sentenced to this gruesome penalty. The judge had been appointed during less ideologically driven times. He did what he could to indicate to the jury that he didn't think Jeramy was guilty. Nevertheless, Jeramy was convicted.

The judge did not want to impose silencing on Jeramy so he did something unusual. "Jeramy, write a story that shows you are willing to follow the dictates of our enlightened society and I'll commute your sentence. You have two weeks to do so."

The gallery, crowded with fervent supporters of the law exploded, "Enforce the law now. " The judge tried to shout back: "The law demands both justice and mercy."

For the first week, Jeramy sat in his apartment thinking but came up with nothing. Fear broke up his sleep. We had once traveled to the Say Lake Lodge near Algonquin Park. The proprietress, Monique, had been interested in the creative process, asking Jeramy to share his creative methods. Jeramy had been flattered because he said Monique had a delicate manner of asking questions and didn't ask banal questions like where he got his ideas. I asked him if he wanted to go there again. He agreed.

There were always protesters from GEOO outside Jeramy's building determined to harass him. We did not want them to know where we were going. On the night before we were to leave, there was a tremendous rainstorm that drove away the protesters. Jeramy walked four kilometers through the rain to my apartment, arriving soaking wet and without other clothes. I found him a few dry things and we left.

When we arrived at the Lodge, Monique greeted us warmly. She looked older. When we'd been there before, she'd had black hair and now her hair had grey streaks.

Besides guest cabins, there was a main lodge room, where the guests could gather together. We had a beautiful cabin facing the lake with a screened porch and a fireplace. We made a fire. Birch wood burns with a bright passion and the flames put me into a reverie that was almost hypnotic. Jeramy was calmer than I'd seen him since his sentencing. He said that he enjoyed the fire but couldn't think of anything to write about. "How can I write something that doesn't insult protected people and ideas?"

"What do you mean?"

"Now it's like in Animal Farm. Some people are more equal than others. You can insult some people with impunity, others you must respect. How can I do that and still be an artist?"

"Don't be an artist. Just save yourself."

"Then I'll be a fake and I won't do that even to avoid this punishment."

The next day, Jeramy thought of thirty different plots but rejected each one. "I've accomplished nothing," he said at the end of the day.

The next day, I insisted that we take two of the easier guided walks in Algonquin Park. "Why not the logging museum and the beaver ponds?"

Jeramy agreed. We went to the logging museum first. The first exhibit was a huge rectangular log building that loggers lived in during the winter. As soon as we got inside, Jeramy perked up. "Lots of men worked here. They were cold and wet when they returned. They enjoyed being together. It was their own perfect world. This is where I'll write my story in one day or just give up."

"Are you going to write about the loggers?"

"Can't. They cut down trees. Today they'd be considered exploiters."

"They were poor, desperate men. Wouldn't people sympathize with them?"

"That truth doesn't matter. Let's continue the tour."

We went around the whole museum but nothing sparked a safe idea.

Next we went to the beaver ponds walk. At post 1, I read the guidebook, which said that the beaver's works are remarkable, calling them "engineers."

"Love them. They were once killed to make hats. Horrible. They're smart."

I continued reading, "Most people assume the beaver do this engineering through conscious, intelligent foresight."

"That's right,"

"The guidebook says that the felling of trees does not show intelligence."

"Sheer arrogance." Jeramy stood up taller and straighter.

We walked to a pond where two beavers were swimming. Jeramy was enchanted.

The guidebook gave a description, with illustrations of the layout, safety of beaver lodges and how they built them.

"Very clever," said Jeramy. He obviously had an affinity for beavers and it was the first real enthusiasm he'd shown since his sentence was passed.

At post 5, we had reached the beaver dam that created Anikeus Lake. The location was spectacular, with the lake turning off to the left going on for several kilometers. In front of us, creating the lake, was the longest beaver dam either of us had ever seen.

"Beautiful lake. If I'd made it, I'd be proud. "

Something was bubbling up inside of Jeramy.

I read the description in the guide. It claimed that all the beavers' achievements were the result of "unreasoning instinct."

"Fools. Do they need to prove that beavers aren't intelligent so they can feel better about themselves? This dam proves they're smart."

"The guidebook points out that beavers sometimes build longer dams in one place where they could have built a shorter dam elsewhere."

"I sometimes pay three dollars for a loaf of bread when I could have bought it somewhere else for two. Proves nothing. Idiots."

"Getting angry isn't like you but I like the change. Have you got a plot?"

"No but I've got inspiration. Maybe a beaver will save me. I've got to think. Leave me in the loggers' camp tomorrow and I'll write it. If I can't write a short, politically correct story in a day, I should take whatever punishment they give me."

"Are you going to make it entertaining?"

"They want a story that will prove all their prejudices are right. I'll try to write a comedy. If I can get the audience to laugh, I should be safe. I'll do the first draft by lunchtime tomorrow. Then I'll spend the afternoon re-writing. When I finish, you, Monique and I can get drunk on the best wine we can get and you can read it to us. Then together we can say whether it meets the criteria."

"You mean if it's good."

"No, whether it's orthodoxy."

"Why get drunk first?"

"Then we'll be more likely to tell the truth and I'll need to hear the truth. Let's have two bottles of Sancerre with dinner tonight. Then I'll forget all about what I think I want to write about and something will just pop up unannounced."

"Getting drunk today and tomorrow. Isn't that a bit alcoholic?"

"Alcoholism is if I take a drink in the morning to get over a hangover and you can be assured that I won't do that. Besides, I've heard that when you're silenced, you lose most of your sense of taste and I might never taste Sancerre again. The only good thing that might come out of the operation is that I'll end up losing some weight."

When Monique brought us our meal, Jeramy invited her to listen to the story tomorrow. She said she would be honored.

"Aren't you afraid of helping a hater?" Jeramy asked.

"Everyone's a hater and a lover," she said. 'My husband cheated and left me. I hate him. I told him so but I also loved him. "

"I'm sorry to hear it," said Jeramy.

We ate our repast, enjoyed the two bottles of Sancerre. Later, we sat at the outdoor fire pit with Monique and other guests. I talked to the guests but Jeramy remained silent. "Do you notice that Monique's hair color is different?" Jeramy asked. I looked and she had short red hair. I wondered what was going on.

The next day, I left Jeramy in the logger's building and came back for him at 5 PM. He put the manuscript in an envelope. Monique brought us dinner. Around 8 PM she brought three bottles of Cotes De Rhone and I read the story to Jeramy and her.

"Let's drink first," said Jeramy.

"Is that a good idea?" asked Monique.

I said "Definitely," and we drank two bottles.

While we were drinking I asked Monique about her hair. She explained that she was a member of an amateur theatrical society that kept their costumes at the lodge and often rehearsed in this room. She often borrowed the wigs to wear at night.

When we'd finished the two bottles, we opened a third and poured ourselves another glass but didn't drink it. I opened the envelope and took out Jeramy's story.

I started to read. "Magnus" by Jeramy Jangle.

On a windy, October day in Montreal, Heidi and Harrold came into the Natural History Museum, to review the data they'd collected on the intelligence of beavers.

Harrold, who had been hit by a car when he was eleven, was in his early forties, short, overweight, with black hair. He limped badly and rarely smiled. "Our experiments definitively prove that beavers have no ability to plan."

Heidi was a tall, willowy blonde, in her twenties with a, raucous laugh. She constantly twirled her long hair, often putting the ends in her mouth and sucking on them. She preferred skipping to walking and always had to stop and wait for Harrold to catch up.

Heidi laughed. "Prejudice, that's all your interpretation is, prejudice.

The experiments just as easily prove that beavers are extremely intelligent."

"Let's go and re-check on our experiments tomorrow."

"You'll end up agreeing with me that beavers are the crown of creation."

"Must you always use non-scientific terms?"

"Don't be such a stick in the mud. Scientists can have fun, too."

The museum had built the world's largest terrarium about a hundred kilometers Northwest of Montreal. It was surrounded by an invisible particle beam fence to keep out all but a few chosen scientists.

Heidi and Harrold traveled in a self-driving car. For the first few miles, Heidi was overflowing with enthusiasm for the wonderful fall colors. "Its almost as if God made each leaf glow for me." Harrold wanted to shout "BS" but he didn't want to get into a fight in the car. After a few minutes each started looking at the screen of their phones and, from that point on, neither could look anywhere else.

The car stopped but it was several minutes before Harrold and Heidi realized the journey had ended. Harrold limped towards the watcher's cabin. Heidi started to skip jumping high every other step trying to get her hair to fly.

The watcher's job was to ensure there were no break-ins from kind-hearted protesters, who were trying to set the beavers free. Unfortunately, the designers of the invisible fence had not learned to control the particle beams and several protesters were burned severely as they crossed its path.

Heidi knocked, and the watcher came out and reported that, once again, she'd observed that beavers go through the particle beam fence with no damage. She had asked several scientists how this was possible, but none had given her an explanation why the beaver seemed to be exempt from the faults of the system.

"The fact that they don't get hurt shows they know what they're doing," said the watcher.

Harrold looked up from his phone's screen and said, "It's just dumb luck."

"I just love them. I can understand these protesters. We shouldn't be *experimenting on poor beavers," said Heidi.*

*Harrold put the phone in his pocket and said, "Then we'd lose our status and income. We can't let that happen. We aren't hurting the beavers because they bring absolutely nothing of value to the world that we can't do ourselves."*

*Heidi looked down and picked a mushroom. "I'll have it for dinner tonight."*

*Harrold slammed it out of her hand. "Don't you recognize Ananita Virasa?"*

*"Never heard of it," said Heidi. "How dare you slap my hand?"*

*"Its common name is Destroying Angel. How many times do I—"*

*The watcher interrupted them. "I think I have proof that beavers might be much smarter than you think. I've been observing them and one of them in particular. He's the largest and he doesn't fall for any of your tricks. He destroyed six speakers you've set up."*

*"Just shut up," said Harrold. "We don't need input from a high-school dropout."*

*"We don't need more evidence," said Heidi.*

*"Anecdotal evidence proves nothing. A few speakers are bound to be destroyed occasionally," Harrold replied.*

*"He destroyed six in three days. That can't be a coincidence," said the watcher.*

*Heidi smiled and said "I'm convinced" then she pulled out her phone and started to call her cousin to remind her to feed her cat.*

Monique interrupted my reading. "Aren't you afraid that making these scientists act silly will be provocative and get you in trouble?"

Jeramy answered, "These scientists experiment on animals. I must ridicule them. If they were climate scientists, I couldn't question them. If you write about a climate scientist, everything they say has to be true and they must be portrayed as noble."

"Don't you believe the climate scientists?" asked Monique.

"I'm pretty sure all sets of scientists are about equally honest but in our society climate scientists are part of a protected class, so

I can't disparage them in my story."

"I don't get it," said Monique, "but please read on."

I continued reading.

*"You know that the wolves try to get to the beavers' houses, don't you?"*
*said the watcher.*

*"Of course, we know that," said Harrold.*

*"Well they don't come near the pond that has this larger beaver's house.*
*Maybe he's found a substance that inhibits the foxes' sense of smell."*

*"You must be drinking too much. Give beavers a stimulus and they au-*
*tomatically do what they are programmed to do. If there is wood around,*
*all you need to do is have the sound of running water and the beavers will*
*build on that spot, even if there is no running water. Let me show you,"*
*said Harrold.*

*He pushed a button and a hidden speaker blurted out the sound of*
*running water. There were five beavers in the pond. The largest beaver*
*stood upright on its hind legs and watched while the other beavers started*
*building a dam where the sound of running water was being played, even*
*though there was no running water there.*

*On seeing this, Harrold told the watcher, "It's the thirty seventh time*
*we've proven that just the sound of water makes them work. They're not*
*smart like humans. It's boring here. Let me check the latest music video."'*

*The watcher walked off. She'd been insulted too many times to want*
*to continue the conversation. Harrold held out his phone to Heidi, They*
*laughed at the antics of a cat playing with an ant.*

*The largest of the beavers, standing on his hind legs, walked up to*
*Heidi and Harrold. When the video ended, he said, "Harrold and Heidi,*
*I'd like to talk to you."*

*Heidi and Harrold looked up from the screen and down at the beaver,*
*then they looked at each other. Harrold dropped his phone.*

*The beaver said, "You call yourselves human beings, divine beings.*
*Humans aren't more divine or intelligent than beavers and I can prove it."*

*"Really?" asked Heidi.*

"It's simple," said the beaver. "First give me a lab coat, so I can look like a scientist too."

They found and gave him one.

Heidi and Harrold were amazed and terrified. Both assumed that even if a beaver could speak, he or she wouldn't be able to correct people with advanced degrees but, since they claimed to be scientists, they decided to record what the beaver had to say.

The camera on their phones wouldn't work. There was a remote camera that they wanted to turn on but the beaver objected. "This is for you two alone. If you are brave enough you can tell others, but I will not let you convince others with a recording."

"Not fair," remonstrated Harrold.

"You want to be famous scientists, don't you? That's the only reason you want a video. You don't care a bit for the truth."

"I see you are a male beaver, what pronoun would you like to be called by?" asked Harrold.

"None."

Harrold's face crimsoned. "What is your name?"

"Magnus. I can prove how vapid humans are. I had access to your pay stubs. Harrold makes $200 a day more than Heidi. I ask you, is that just and fair?"

"I'm being cheated," shouted Heidi. "The museum says they pay men and women the same. What lies! It's completely unfair."

'It's fair," thundered Harrold. "I've been at this job seventeen years and Heidi only started a year ago and she hasn't even got her PHD yet."

"So women don't deserve to be paid the same as men for the same work?"

'It's not the same work. I direct you." Harrold and Heidi turned towards each other, "I'm the one who discovered enough to write the last three papers."

"I corrected your grammar and your poor writing. Without me, you'd be fired."

Monique started to laugh and then put her hand over her mouth to repress herself. I continued reading.

*Magnus stepped between the two arguing humans. "Tell me what you*
*really think of each other."*

*"I don't want to say," said Harrold.*

*"Well I will. Harrold is a prick and a bastard."*

*"I didn't want to say it but Heidi is a complete..."*

"Stop," yelled out Monique. "Stop right there. I have a suggestion. Don't let Harrold use the English word. Let him say it in
French."

"That's exactly what Harrold says."

"Please continue reading. I'm enjoying this," said Monique.

I kept reading.

*"I know exactly what both of you are going to say," said Magnus, "and*
*it is quite impolite. No beaver would ever use such language with another*
*beaver. All I have to do is mention the word fairness and humans want to*
*break each other's heads. Isn't that far less intelligent and more dangerous*
*than building a dam when we hear water running?"*

*Harrold turned towards Magnus, "But we invented music and math-*
*ematics."*

*"You have no idea if beavers have music or art, do you? Would you*
*recognize them? Answer me please," asked Magnus.*

*"I don't think I would," said Heidi.*

*"I'm sure I would," said Harrold.*

*"You two can't agree on anything. We don't need your music or math-*
*ematics because we have our own. As long as you leave us alone we're fine.*
*The same can't be said of you so- called human or divine beings. You can*
*never leave anything alone."*

*"You're probably an exploiter," said Harrold.*

*Magnus smiled but the two humans didn't notice because beaver's*
*smiles aren't similar to human smiles. "I've proved a second time that*
*humans are mechanical, can't think clearly or agree on anything. "*

*"That's not fair," said Heidi. "You just picked one topic where we don't*
*agree."*

"Let's try another one. A quote from one of your so-called philosophers, 'From each according to their abilities, to each according to their needs,'" said Magnus.

"I completely agree with that," said Heidi. "Sharing is caring."

" It's BS. People will demand what they didn't earn. That ideal never works."

"Enough. How about light is both a wave and a particle?" asked Magnus.

"Of course that's always true. It's poetry isn't it?" asked Heidi.

"No, it depends on the observer," said Harrold.

"I'm not hallucinating am I? We are talking to a beaver, aren't we?"

"I'm not hallucinating, at least."

"I've proved my point," said Magnus. "Humans can never agree with each other. Beavers have one weakness. Humans have thousands. Admit the beaver's superiority."

There was no reply. Harrold and Heidi were viewing their cell phones.

"Can't you concentrate on what I'm saying?" asked Magnus. "Is this how you humans get love? From a tiny machine?" There was no response.

Magnus slapped their cell phones to the ground and said, "Beavers can still relate to each other and to reality. We don't need to constantly be entertained. We can enjoy the world we live in, the smells, the food we eat and each other."

"There is one ultimate proof that humans are superior," said Heidi. "We have discovered that each person should have their own, self-chosen pronoun that designates in what way they are being discriminated against. For example, I choose the pronoun CGAEFY to describe the oppression I face."

"I picked the pronoun UBYTRL to indicate the forces against me."

"We beavers are superior again," said Magnus. "We don't constantly claim others are oppressing us and we don't use personal pronouns. We always use a person's name. I am always called Magnus and, if I meet another beaver, I refer to that beaver by name. If someone reads in a story 'UBYTRL said' instead of 'he said,' how will they know who is being referred to? Suppose there are twenty characters. Who could ever keep all those pronouns straight? Again it proves that beavers are superior."

Heidi and Harrold looked at each other and smiled.

"I think Magnus has solved one of our problems. Let's uninvent personal pronouns and only use a person's name," said Heidi.

"Great idea. We could make it a law. How can we enforce the law?"

"We will give increasingly severe punishments for any deviation to our new law but that wouldn't be kind. Isn't there some other way?"

"Let's stick with punishment. We can think of kindness later," said Harrold.

Harrold and Heidi shook hands. "We agree. See, Magnus? Humans can agree."

"On how to punish each other. You plan to jail' those who don't agree with you."

"What do you beavers do in a case like that?" asked Harrold.

"My best bud, Marshall, sometimes talks rot," said Magnus.

"And how do you punish him? Do you have beaver jails?" asked Heidi.

'Of course not. I say Marshall, 'What you're saying is rot but go ahead and say it, I've said more than my share of rot in my time.' Then we talk about it and try to understand each other's point of view. Lots of the things I thought were rot, turned out to be true. I tell Marshall to tell me what he's thinking. Maybe I'll learn something.'"

"I never talk rot," said Heidi.

"If you think that, you know nothing about yourself," said Magnus.

'I don't let people talk rot. I correct them," said Harrold, "especially not--"

Magnus interrupted Harrold, "You were about to call me a dumb rodent just like you called the watcher a dumb dropout? We beavers don't do things like that."

"It would be so lovely to be a beaver," said Heidi.

"If you were, you'd be all wet," said Harrold.

Magnus said, "I hear some running water. I've got to go."

Heidi and Harrold didn't notice when Magnus shrank back to his normal size and walked away. As Magnus looked back, he saw Heidi and Harrold facing away from each other, both talking into their phones. Magnus thought that these humans sure don't like each other much.

Magnus joined Marshall and the other three beavers that were cheerfully constructing a new dam where Heidi had turned on the sound of running water. About two minutes later, Magnus, realizing they were being tricked, put a stick through the hidden speaker and the sound of running water stopped.

"We don't need to build a dam here," said Magnus.

"Let's go back to eating water lilies," another beaver said.

"Let's get them before the humans experiment on them," said a third beaver.

"They wouldn't dare," said Marshall.

"Oh, they'd dare," said Magnus.

Harrold and Heidi drove back to Montreal. As they approached the city, they started to converse about their experience with Magnus.

"Beavers are lovely," said Heidi. "I want to tell people all about their wonders.

We saw and heard with our very own senses that beavers are intelligent. They reason, debate, even talk."

"We have no proof of what we saw so we didn't see anything. How sure are you really that you talked to a beaver?"

"We have no proof. You'll never get a PHD if you tell people beavers can talk," said Harrold.

"You're right but it was so enchanting. Maybe I'll write a poem about it."

"I don't care about a poem. What will you say to the museum?"

"That we proved there was no intelligence with beavers?"

"Great choice."

Marshall and his friend went to their beaver lodge. Magnus began to compose a ballad referring to scientists as "The Troubled, Troublemakers."

*As he sang, the other beavers beat out the rhythm with their tail. Marshall said, "Your song is rot." Magnus chuckled and agreed, "It sure is."*

*"I wish Harrold and Heidi could come join us in our lodge and enjoy our companionship," said Marshall. "It's wet in here and they wouldn't be able to use their cell phones. They'd probably be very unhappy."*

*"You're probably right," agreed Magnus.*
*The End*

There was silence for almost two minutes after I stopped reading.

Jeramy said, "Tell me the truth. Was it completely orthodox?"

"It was magnificent, so funny and so true to life," said Monique.

"I wanted to write drivel that the judge would approve of."

"It wasn't your best but it's completely orthodox," I said to Jeramy.

"A bit insulting to women. If you change the part of Harrold for Heidi it will be insulting men. You can always insult men," agreed Monique.

"Good. I'll make that change tomorrow." Jeramy got up and went to our cabin.

"Let's have one more drink," I said to Monique.

Monique said, "Come back for a visit, with Jeramy, whether he wins or loses."

"It freaks me out to think of him silenced and unable to use his fingers. Are you sure you're up to seeing him like that?"

"They won't do it," she said.

"I'm not so sure."

"Come back no matter what happens'"

"We will," I replied. Monique left.

I was beginning to sober up and that made me think the story wasn't orthodox. It was insulting to humans and some of the beliefs of our society and insulted protected classes of people. Writing humor is always dangerous.

I was tempted to throw it in the fire and try to write a story that was pure drivel but I knew I couldn't do that. If I substituted my story and Jeramy was convicted anyway, he'd never forgive me. For better or worse, we'd have to go with the story of Magnus.

Jeramy submitted his story to the judge and two days later there was a hearing. The gallery was packed with supporters of the new law. The judge had read Jeramy's story. He announced the verdict, "The story does not meet the requirement for clemency. The original sentence must be carried out." Jeramy was too stunned to say anything. From the crowds, there were shouts of joy. I shouted to the judge, "Why wasn't the story acceptable?"

He answered, "In some ways it is completely innocuous and extols many of the precepts of our society but it opens them to ridicule and laughter..."

I will say this in favor of our legal system. There is still the ability to appeal. Since it was the first time this sentence was given, Jeramy's case was given an instant appeal, and the case was assigned to a Judge Hugo Magnifico.

Jeramy, his lawyer and I went to the hearing. Judge Magnifico started out by saying he had reviewed the law, opinions, evidence and the story. The Judge commended Jeramy for writing an entertaining and interesting polemic but it did not meet the original judge's requirements for a reduction of sentence. "This story can never be distributed in this country on pain of further imprisonment."

Judge Magnifico asked if Jeramy had anything to say. Jeramy was silent.

I stood and said, "My brother is too broken to speak. May I approach the bar?"

"You may."

I said to Judge Magnifico, "Someone with such a wonderful name as Magnifico, must be able to offer us some hope that a reduction of sentence is possible."

Hugo sat silent for several minutes and then said, "Jeramy, approach the bar. I have carefully reviewed the new sentencing guidelines and will ask you a few questions. Do you have any minority status?"

"No, I am a white, heterosexual male."

"Doesn't help. Is society discriminating against you so you need your own personal pronoun?"

"How does that matter?"

"If society is oppressing you and you require a pronoun chosen from 'AAAAAA' to 'ZZZZZZ' then I can reduce your sentence to community service."

"I have never required the use of one of those pronouns and don't approve of breaking society up into tiny groups each claiming to be more discriminated against than the others. We're all equal and the same and all of us are in this together."

"Think carefully. You can register for one of the pronouns now. Be warned that you can only do this one time. If you change your mind, your choice will be considered false and invalid."

"Doing so goes against all I believe," said Jeramy.

I whispered into Jeramy's ear, "This is your one chance. Don't blow it."

"I'm afraid," said Jeramy.

"What did he say?" asked Hugo.

"My brother said he's afraid, that's A F R A I D."

"A F R A I D. That certainly seems like a valid pronoun."

The usher brought in a recording device to witness Jeramy's new pronoun.

"I can't do it," Jeramy said to me. "I can't swear to this."

"You are afraid to be silenced, correct?" asked Judge Magnifico.

"Yes."

"Then enter it."

Jeramy entered his name, address, date of birth and his pronoun A F R A I D.

The stupid machine immediately posted the error message: "Invalid pronoun."

A technician looked in the pronoun database and there were the pronouns 'AFRAIC' and 'AFRAIE' in the database as valid pronouns but no "AFRAID."

The technician said, "Judge, did you forget that common words were removed from the pronoun list. That's why you got that error message."

That was it. There was no second try. Jeramy asked for the sentence to be carried out as soon as possible.

Two days later, Jeramy became the first Canadian citizen of The Republic of Silence. A doctor, or should I say, someone who called himself a doctor because, in my opinion, a real doctor wouldn't violate the oath to "Do no harm" injected a substance into each of Jeramy's fingers and the underside of his tongue. Jeramy lost the ability to speak or control his fingers.

Jeramy did not make the slightest complaint. I was very thankful that the silencing was not done before a public audience. Many thought Jeramy had got off too easily. After this, every time Jeramy or I entered or left his apartment building, we were jeered at by militant members of Guaranteed Equality Of Outcome.

Jeramy could not hold a knife and fork. I found a company that made a device to strap a knife or fork to his hand. He could move his tongue enough to swallow but he could not control it enough to speak. He had lost most of his sense of taste. Jeramy's prophecy came true. He did lose weight. I visited him every day urging him to eat more. He was ashamed to go out because he was embarrassed that he couldn't speak. The contingent of GEOO had to content themselves with harassing me.

We learned Morse code. He put metal pieces above his knees so he could tap out messages to me. They weren't very varied. For the first several weeks he mostly used his knees to make the Morse code "A F R A I D H E L P M E." He'd then fall silent. He seemed to have no interests.

Monique contacted me and asked that I bring Jeramy to visit at the lodge. It was right before the snows usually came and there would be few guests. Jeramy resisted. Monique sent him a card with a drawing she made of two beavers talking. It said, "Please come visit us. We live near the Say Lake Lodge" and was signed "Magnus and Marshall." Jeramy knew the card was from Monique but he was touched and he wept. I asked if he was willing to go and he tapped out "Y E S."

How could I sneak Jeramy out? The "guard" was there twenty-four hours a day. Monique thought of a way. She walked into Jeramy's building wearing costumes from her actin troupe, a brown wig and green coat. She dressed Jeramy with a wig and a black coat. She changed into a blue coat and a blonde wig. They walked to her car undisturbed and then picked me up and we drove to Say Lake Lodge.

The night we arrived, it was cold, almost freezing but there was no wind. You could see the winter Milky Way. Jeramy stood outside looking at it for about a half hour.

The next day was warmer. Monique and Jeramy got into a canoe, which Monique paddled to the far end of the lake and walked to a large pond with active beaver lodges. They spent several hours watching the beavers and came back late in the afternoon.

That night, Jeramy, Monique and I were in the main lodge. Jeramy started tapping out the letters M A K E K E Y B O A R D ON F L O O R.

I didn't know what he meant. He tapped it out again. I told Monique what he had said. She got a gigantic sheet of paper and drew a keyboard on the floor with letters about fifteen centimeters tall. He tapped letters with the ball of his foot. It was only after he did it three times that I realized he was typing out WRITE WHAT I TYPE.

I got a notebook. Monique sat next to me and called out the letters as Jeramy used his feet to type out "M A G N U S  S T I R R E D."

What could that mean? I thought. I looked at him with a quiz-zical look.

I realized that Jeramy was going to write another story and I was so ready to hear it. Monique smiled and nodded her head. I could tell she was anxious to hear it too.

"We're all ears," she said to Jeramy. Monique said the words out loud as Jeramy typed them with his feet and I wrote them in a notebook.

MAGNUS STIRRED AND SAID TO MARSHALL I WILL HELP THOSE HUMANS. WHY BOTHER? ASKED MARSHALL. BECAUSE I CAN AND BECAUSE I LOVE THEM

I wept tears of joy. Jeramy hadn't left me or abandoned the human race. I looked over and a few tears rolled down Monique's cheek.

It was a magnificent story. I asked Jeramy if there would be more and he typed out, "much more." Jeramy asked Monique to act out the dialogue between Magnus and Marshall and she did it with such a comedic air that Jeramy started to laugh and made some very odd sounds. He was embarrassed. Monique said to Jeramy, "Don't worry, everything you do is lovely." I didn't know if she was telling the truth or acting but I was grateful. It was a wonderful evening. What would happen next, once we left the lodge, I had no idea, nor did I really want to know.

# A WALK IN THE PARK

It had taken Fiona and Michael forty minutes to drive the five miles to LaGuardia Airport where they were taking a flight to Boston for a Yankees, Red Sox game. They'd been married two years and this was their third visit to Boston where they loved the art and history museums. The Yankees were one of Michael's passions and this was the first Red Sox game he'd be seeing at Fenway Park. Fiona didn't understand baseball but hoped to enjoy watching the rival fans interact with each other.

It was this year's hottest day, over a hundred degrees, the humidity near one hundred percent. The sun was beating down on their car, which had all the windows open because their air conditioner had failed.

"I swear, I could f*cking kill someone," shouted Fiona. "Sweat's dripping down my back. Why the f*ck can't this traffic let up?"

Michael glanced over. Fiona wasn't scrunching her eyes, so Michael knew this was only a colorful expression, not a genuine cry for vengeance. "You'd feel better if you didn't complain," said Michael, who was sweating as much as Fiona. "I hardly feel the heat."

"The f*ck, I would. That's the only thing keeping me sane. Not feel the heat? My ass."

Michael was a laid back middle child of an Italian-American family from Long Island. He'd met Fiona on the first day of his junior year abroad at Kings College, Dublin. Fiona bumped into Michael, as he was gawking, mouth slightly open, at the bejeweled cover and painted pages of the book of Kells.

Fiona eyes were riveted on the book as she bumped into Michael. "Sorry, I didn't see you," she said. "Can't take my eyes off that f*cking magnificent page. I'm going to paint like that someday."

Michael looked up and saw a petite, freckle-faced girl, with a broad smile, ginger hair with a pageboy haircut, who looked to be about twenty. They started talking about the Book of Kells. Michael thought Fiona might also be a student at Kings College but she told him she was in her final year at the Dublin School of Creative Arts, "where we f*cking pretend to be artists until we master the techniques to convey the sublime vision we see in our dreams."

Michael laughed and replied, "I'm pretending to study finance until I actually have a sublime pile of cash."

"F*cking priceless. I don't have any money either."

"I wish I could be as expressive as you," said Michael. "You're so interesting." He thought this was the worst pick up line in history, not that he had much successful experience, but Fiona smiled prodigiously and Michael realized he liked her confidence and cheekiness and he took the risk of inviting her to share tea and scones. She gladly agreed.

It was Michael's first full day in Ireland. He had been shocked to hear such aromatic language from a fresh faced, young woman but before a week was out, he became used to the fact that, for many Irish students and Fiona, in particular, the word "f*ck" was not a curse but an embellishment used in hundreds of different and enlightening ways.

Many friends found them an unusual couple. Until he felt comfortable with a person, and that could take a long time, Michael was spare in his expression but during the span of a pot of tea, Michael relaxed and felt more vibrant than he ever had before. They told each other their insignificant secrets. A passionate liking for each other began and, after a year of courtship, they married and moved to Queens, New York. They lived a quiet life with a daily drizzle of emotional excitement and the occasional thunderclap from Fiona, followed by a heavy downpour of emotion. The storm almost always ended with a wave of tranquility and the intense sunshine of mutual reconciliation and tenderness.

Michael worked for a large bank in downtown Manhattan. Fiona began to paint colorful oil portraits that breathed life and excitement into each sitter's depiction. The sitters, many of them middle aged or older and considered by their friends to be rather boring, were portrayed as intriguing, exciting subjects. Fiona's technique for finding the hidden exotic was simple, "Tell me what's the f*cking wildest thing you've ever done or wanted to do. Go all out. Your secret will go to the grave with me.' If they were reluctant to share a secret, she'd tell them an exotic fabricated secret about herself to open them up; her real secrets being very minor ones. For the men, she'd often say she and a partner had made a painting by covering themselves with paint and making love on top of a huge canvas. She would never have seriously thought of doing such a thing but big secrets opened the clients up and she had a wild and theatrical imagination for creating them, which greatly added to her painting abilities. For the devout sitter, she'd tell them truthfully that she'd enjoyed studying the writings of the Little Flower, Saint Theresa.

Sitters often told far more than they intended. Fiona would keep them talking until she could honestly say, "What a f*cking fascinating person you are. I'm tickled to know you." Each portrait ingeniously expressed a whispered elation and intoxicating personality that neither their friends nor themselves had ever noticed. Fiona soon had a long backlog of customers.

The traffic on the Grand Central Parkway lightened. Michael said, "We'll get there in five minutes. No more sweat, only sweet air will flow."

"A f*cking blessing. Can't wait."

They pulled into LaGuardia's airport. There was construction everywhere; cranes, earthmovers, workers seemingly not doing very much in the searing heat.

"F*cking waste to make them work in this heat."

They were crawling, there seemed to be hundreds of cars behind them but when they got within several hundred yards of the parking lot, a police car, which was on the side of the road facing them, pulled into their lane, directly in front of them stopping traffic. When they didn't move for several minutes, a few cars far behind them, who hadn't seen the police car, started to blare their horns.

"What the f*ck is going on? F*ck, f*ck, f*ck," exclaimed Fiona. She felt like a woman dying of thirst being offered a glass of water and having the glass slapped out of her hand. She demanded, "Michael, get the f*ck out there and ask them to let us go through."

Michael looked over and saw a fierce gaze in Fiona's eyes and that her fists were clenched. These gestures meant the situation was serious but Michael was reluctant to go. He was sure that talking to the police wouldn't change the length of their wait but, if he didn't go, Fiona would go over and then anything might happen.

Michael opened his door slowly, stepped onto the road. Strong sunlight heated his body further and his shoe stuck to the partially melted pavement as he slowly walked to the police car, whose windows were rolled up. A tall black male officer, named Samuel, was in the driver's seat. Few people, in this situation, had got out of their car to question him and, from experience he knew that a small percentage of those who did were unstable or dangerous. He looked over at his female Hispanic partner of two days, named Loretta, who had just graduated from the police academy. She shook her head slowly. Samuel wasn't yet confident in her. Samuel opened his window and looked quizzically at Michael.

Michael tone was timid and polite, "Why did you stop us?"

Samuel, said, courteously but forcefully, "It was necessary. We'll open up the road as soon as we can. Go back in your car and wait."

"But, my wife wants …" Samuel's window rolled up. Michael could see that neither of the cops wanted to let searing air in or even less did they want to step out of their car. Michael went back, sat down and told Fiona. "They'll let us go once things clear up ahead."

"They f*cking don't know what the f*ck their f*cking doing. Why did I let you ask the question? I'm f*cking going to make them tell me the f*cking truth."

Michael was even more worried. When Fiona said "f*ck" three or more times in a phrase, she was beyond exasperated. "Don't go. You'll just piss them off."

"Do you think I give a f*ck about that?"

Fiona got out, walked rapidly and knocked on Samuel's window. The window opened and before Fiona could talk, he said, with a hint of annoyance, "I know you're frustrated but I told your husband to go back to your car. We'll let you move just as soon as we get the word. Now go back." The window rolled up before Fiona could speak.

Fiona was going to tap again but then thought, I'll try the other cop and she walked over and knocked on Loretta's window. Loretta looked at Samuel for guidance. Samuel was beginning to think this might escalate so he said, "Let her have her say."

The window rolled open a crack and Loretta looked at Fiona, who said, "It's over a hundred degrees, our car's air conditioning isn't working, just let us the f*ck through."

"I know it's really hot. We'll call and see if we can start to let people through. Now, please go back to your car and wait."

"I said let us through."

"I promise to call ahead. Now go back to your car or I'll have to arrest you for interfering with police business." The window went back up.

Michael was getting worried. He was standing at the side of his car. He called out, "Fiona, come back."

Fiona looked at Michael with contempt, thinking he was too cowardly in these situations. She turned back to the police car and knocked again. The window opened a crack. Loretta looked annoyed and worried. This was the third time this woman had knocked. Samuel and Loretta looked at each other. They were pretty sure they were dealing with an unhinged individual.

The police back at the station had planned a surprise thirty-fifth birthday party for Samuel, that would start in an hour and they had told Loretta that she had to get Samuel back to the precinct on time for the party. She knew that if they arrested this woman, they'd end up being very late. Fiona repeated herself, "It's over a hundred degrees, our car's air conditioning isn't working, just let us the f*ck through."

'Get back to your car now. This is my last warning." The glass rolled up again.

Fiona stood there, defiantly. Michael came over, leaned forward and reached out to grab her hand urging her to come back to the car. "Leave me the f*ck alone, I can handle this on my own." Michael realized he wasn't helping any, so he went back to his car, stood next to his door and watched.

Fiona moved closer to Loretta's door and hit the window with the side of her clenched fist. The glass dropped and Fiona said, "It's f*cking clear enough now to let us through."

Loretta said, "Move aside so I can come out."

"No need to come out, just move the f*cking car. It's f*cking scalding out here."

Loretta tried opening her door, but Fiona blocked the door with her hip.

"Back off. That's a direct order."

"Not unless you let us pass," said Fiona.

Samuel, who knew about his surprise party and didn't want to get involved with an incident that would delay it, realized that he had to act quickly. He opened his door and walked behind Fiona and said, "My partner told you she'd call ahead and see if we can let you through."

"I won't move until you f*cking move your car."

"Go back to your car. That is a direct order."

"What are you going to f*cking do? F*cking arrest me? I'm not moving."

Samuel said, "Hands behind your back. You're under arrest for interfering with police business. Don't make it worse by resisting arrest," as he slipped a handcuff on Fiona's left wrist, then grabbed her right arm and put the other cuff on. Fiona was shocked and didn't resist, but she screamed, "No one in Ireland would ever f*cking arrest anyone for asking a question."

"This isn't Ireland," said Samuel as he opened the back door and gently pushed Fiona into the back seat. He told Michael that he should follow them and pick his wife up at the local precinct. They had to wait briefly before another police car was available to replace them directing this traffic.

Neither the cops nor Fiona talked during the drive. Fiona twice stomped her right foot hard, and then sat in a scrunched, uncomfortable position while, without her knowledge, a few tears rolled down her chin. When they got to the precinct, the two cops escorted Fiona into the building, followed closely by Michael. One cop inside said to another, 'Loretta and Samuel arrived early. Go and try to get people together for the surprise party."

As they walked into the precinct, Michael apologized profusely for Fiona's behavior. To his surprise, Fiona was cowed and didn't say anything.

One of the precinct cops took Loretta aside and said that if they booked Fiona, they'd be there a long time and they'd miss the surprise party. "Why not just give her some tickets?"

Loretta whispered her agreement. "It's like an oven. That silly woman just acted stupid. No harm done."

Loretta went up to Fiona and Michael, who were standing with Samuel, "We arrested you for a serious offence. But it was hot, and you didn't act violently, so we'll give you a choice of being booked or getting several tickets. It's your choice."

"I won't get any points on my license, will I?" asked Fiona.

"You'll have to show up at traffic court and probably negotiate them down to just a fine."

Michael and Fiona gratefully accept the tickets with fines totaling about six hundred dollars. Loretta went away to arrange the party. Samuel told Fiona, "You're lucky they're giving me a surprise birthday party. I'm giving you a present of not locking you up. If you block police business again you might not get off so easy."

By the time Michael and Fiona got back to LaGuardia, the traffic had lessened. The Boston shuttle flies every hour and they caught one two hours later than they'd planned. They sat together without looking at each other and were completely silent, both obviously angry.

As the flight's descended Fiona asked, "Are you giving me the f*cking silent treatment?"

"Of course not."

"You never f*cking communicate enough. I do most of the talking unless you've had a few drinks or you want to drag me into bed."

Michael was silent and sullen. They took a cab to their hotel. The weather in Boston was sunny and a comfortable eighty-three degrees. They entered their hotel room, which had a small balcony overlooking the Charles River. Fiona walked onto the balcony and called Michael out. 'What a god awful, f*cking shitty day we've had and you've made it far f*cking worse."

Michael walked out slowly. His posture was hunched. He didn't answer.

Fiona stood tall and said, "I bet your planning to f*cking make me suffer this whole f*cking trip. Maybe we should just go home now."

Michael straightened up and snarled, "You're addicted to anger and complaining. You're totally predictable and totally controlled by your wild emotions."

"No, I'm not. I'm in complete f*cking control and can do anything I f*cking well please."

"Not for a second. You're a slave."

"The f*ck I am. "

Michael looked into Fiona's eyes. "I challenge you to a bet. You can't go one day without swearing or cussing and whining in your mind. You have to say what you feel and it can't be a curse or a squawk. You up for it?"

Fiona stared back, "Done. I'll win. It will be a walk in the park. And what about you? You always hold it in. You're more a slave than me. You can't go a single day expressing the frustration and antagonism you hide inside."

"I'm not angry."

"The f*..." Fiona paused, took a deep breath, looked up to the sky and continued calmly, "I watched you when we were with the police and observed you were angry. Tell me about it."

"I thought it best you listen to the police and come back to the car."

"The f*.. " Fiona paused and then continued, "I observed that you had much more negative emotion than that. Real animosity. Go on...."

'I was rather piqued at the police and how you provoked the two of them. But it's best not to get too worked up. Least said, soonest mended."

"That wasn't what I observed. To hell ...," Fiona paused and continued, "You have to say exactly what you thought or you lose the bet."

"I can't express it exactly."

"If I express what I saw, can we agree that I'm not making a complaint? And then if I'm right, you'll repeat it?" asked Fiona.

"Agreed."

"I observed you thinking, 'It's f*cking sizzling and these f*cking cops block my way. Assholes. Now Fiona's getting out of the car. Idiot. Now they're having a confrontation. Why the f*ck can't my "c" of a wife listen? Get back into the car before you get your ass arrested. Is that more like what you actually thought?"

"Sort of, but my thoughts weren't nearly as spicy or as vulgar."

"You can think it but not say it? Say it. I'm challenging you."

Michael looked up towards the ground. "Why the f*ck did those cops have to stop us? I wish I'd had the courage to drive right past them." He looked at Fiona and continued, "And then my hotheaded wife f*cking went out pounding on their windows. Then she was in cuffs. What a god-awful day."

Fiona looked at Michael and smiled, "Don't you feel better now?"

"I do feel a bit better but I'm even more exasperated now than I was before. It's like coughing. The first cough makes the itch go away and then it comes back twice as strong."

"I feel better too. I'm glad I'm not the only one that explodes at the slightest provocation."

Michael looked directly at Fiona, "Are you always f*cking judging me? I hate it. Take it back."

Fiona shook her head slowly, "I guess that was a complaint. It can't be a real one because I didn't notice it."

"I'll let that go, but there better be no more f*cking complaints in the next twenty-three hours." Michael was panting. This violent emotional expression expended a hefty amount of his energy. He felt exhausted, more furious than he'd been in an incredibly long time.

Fiona tensed up too and looked directly at Michael. She wasn't used to hearing such vehemence from Michael. It took an incredible amount of discipline for her not to react. She said calmly, "Or what? If I criticize you, are you going to, f*... , divorce me for it?" Fiona realized that what she was doing was what she did with her clients, finding out their secret passions and getting them to express it. But this seemed completely different. With clients the risk was tiny, they might decide not to get their portrait painted.

Fiona thought that when she and her friends yelled back and forth, it didn't seem hostile but with Michael it was different. There was a new physical quality to his profane utterances, something more real and meaningful than with her friends. Friendship, especially if one made friends easily, might come and go without much hurt but a congenial marriage was much more valuable and, with that, one needs to avoid hurting each other. Fiona hadn't thought about that before. Now she thought, why the f*ck did I mention divorce? I never want to divorce. Me accuse him of something? I was just letting off a bit of steam and now he's making a huge deal of it.

When he heard the word divorce, Michael was petrified. Did Fiona want a divorce? He hated the thought. He'd seen many men look at her with lust and desire. He believed she could get another man, if she wanted one, faster than he could tie his shoes. Is she growing tired of me? Why can't I just express what I think without worrying about it? Why do I hold back?

Fiona waited, on edge, wondering if she'd set off a crisis. She was surprised Michael didn't flare up immediately, he seemed to be thinking. She looked down and saw the Charles River glistening in the sunlight. She stared at the dappled, reflected sun and her thoughts slowed down. She could feel her breath, hear the sounds from the street. Here I am. Here I am. I didn't even notice. I'm actually alive now, she almost said.

Fiona began to see herself with the police, as if she were watching a movie. How different she looked in the movie. She could see the heat waves rising from the pavement but they no longer had the power to drive her to behave like she did. Why did that woman in the movie, who was her, have to be so aggressive, so determined to get her way? No. It wasn't necessary. She could change but how?

She started to consider how much effort she'd need to stop doing what Michael considered to be complaining, for the next twenty-three hours. Maybe she could get falling over drunk. No, that isn't a solution. Her verbal expressions are so automatic that she never noticed them. Being aware of how I talk is f*cking hard, she said to herself. She wondered if that thought were a complaint or just an observation.

"Michael, I've noticed that being aware of my emotions and not just blurting them takes great discipline but also opens one up to new thoughts."

"And I've noticed that expressing every f*cking irritation of mine is f*cking counter productive and makes me even angrier. It's f*cking exhausting." Michael let out a long deep sigh.

Fiona noticed and smiled, "How bout I admit I lost the bet and we go back to the way it was before and we agree that I'll tone it down a bit and you tone it up a notch?"

Michael sighed again. "I agree completely. I should express a great deal more."

"That would be very nice," said Fiona.

"Have I told you lately that I love you?"

"I love you too." Fiona embraced Michael, "I promise to only say "f*ck" once in each expression in the future."

"Can't wait for the game. The Yankees are going to slaughter them."

"Can't f*cking wait for it or for after the game," said Fiona.

"Yes, we should put lovemaking on our f*cking calendar."

Fiona laughed and said, "I like that particular calendar. What a marvelous trip."

Later that night, before falling asleep, Michael wondered if he could change and easily express his angry emotions without getting even more agitated. After all, there is nothing wrong with being reasonably angry when it is appropriate. Could he express his happy thoughts too? How? He'd think about it tomorrow.

Fiona lay awake for a long time. Earlier that day, she had irrefutably known that she was a slave to her emotions, now that formerly certain unquestionable fact no longer seemed true. It just can't be, I am in charge, she thought. She decided to think about it tomorrow. She fell asleep.

When they woke up, Fiona and Michael had lost the bitter thought that they were mechanically activated by events, having almost no control.

Six months later, on a cold bright Sunday afternoon, they were sitting in the living room of their fourth floor apartment, talking happily, while drinking Sancerre, toasting life and health, which was their tradition after Fiona completed a portrait. Fiona sat on an easy chair and Michael on the red settee. The sun was setting, orange-red and pale light streamed through the windows, bouncing off a large mirror and filling the room with a warm radiance.

Fiona started to talk about the secret she'd extracted from her sitter. "You know, she's been embezzling from her brother for years. Took almost two hundred thou from him. F*cking amazing. It was a walk in the park getting that secret." All at once, she realized that she'd promised to guard the secret with her life and now she'd told Michael. She realized that she hadn't used that expression, "A walk in the park," since that fateful argument and she was reminded of those dreadful hours and the realizations she'd come to while standing on the balcony looking at the Charles.

Time seemed to slow down or cease to exist as if a flash had gone off in a dark room and she saw herself simultaneously making the promise of secrecy to her sitter and blurting it out to Michael. It was true. She was mechanical and had absolutely no control over her behavior. She noticed her own reflection on her wine glass where she looked tiny, curved, and insubstantial. Maybe that reflection is all there is of me. My will changes as fast as the reflection on the glass changes.

"Michael, remember Boston and that incredible argument we had about being slaves to our natures and not being free to be and act as we really want?"

"Yes. I was so angry. It was horrible. Why bring it up now?"

"I solemnly promised to keep that woman's secret and I didn't even remember. I couldn't help telling you. It proves I'm not in control. I saw the same thing in Boston and then forgot."

"I'd forgotten Boston too. I told myself I'd be much more expressive and I wonder if I changed at all," said Michael.

Fiona got up and sat next to Michael on the settee. They faced each other and Michael noticed that Fiona was nervous, which was very unusual for her. "I desperately need to remember," she said, "and get free. No bet. I have to be gentle with it. Will you try too?"

"It's not going to be easy and we can't expect too much.'"

"How will we possibly remember?" asked Fiona.

Michael took Fiona's left hand. "We could put notes on all our mirrors."

Fiona shook her head, "Let's do that but it isn't nearly enough. Let's make a video of what we're thinking right now and review it regularly."

"Interesting. We can review our progress every week."

"It's a start. Also, let's not forget our love."

Michael kissed Fiona's hand. "That's why we're doing it and maybe love's our only hope."

Fiona smiled and said, "Have you noticed I haven't said f*ck in at least five sentences? "

Michael smiled. "I have."

"Let's make the video quick before I start again."

Michael laughed. "Agreed."

# FATHER YURI'S MIRACLES

It was a Thursday night in late November 1907, around 8 PM. Father Yuri Gresenko, a chubby 36 year old Russian Orthodox priest with a long black beard, was about to play whist with his wife, Marina, and another couple, Vladimir and Dorcas Stoykin. He got up from his chair, while the others watched him, to check the heavy snow hitting the glass windows. He then gazed over at a few of the nearby houses which were obscured by the blasts of snow. A fire blazed in the stone fireplace, warming the small, well-built Siberian home on the Kamchatka Peninsula. Father Yuri turned back to the room and intoned Pushkin in his low sonorous voice.

> The storm wind covers the sky
> Whirling the fleecy snow drifts,
> Now it howls like a wolf,
> Now it is crying, like a lost child,
> Now rustling the decayed thatch

On our tumbledown roof,
Now, like a delayed traveler,
Knocking on our windowpane.

"Always quoting the poets who had no idea what real life is about." Said Vladimir. "Suppose I started to quote from my favorite poet, Karl Marx?"

"Go right ahead," said Yuri, "but he wrote prose not poetry. What he said would never beat the deep truths that Pushkin wrote of. Yuri recited,

I say to myself: the years are fleeting,
And however many there seem to be,
We must all go under the eternal vault,
And someone's hour is already at hand.

"Let's play cards," said Marina. The four sat down and began. Yuri was teamed with Dorcas and Vladimir was teamed with Marina.

Yuri looked at his wife Marina and smiled. She smiled back. She realized that Yuri had already drunk a little vodka and that their guest, Vladimir Stoykin, had drunk more. Marina noticed that a little drinking seemed to inspire the two men to a friendly debate. Dorcas, Vladimir's wife, however, was worried that they might drink more and have a serious quarrel, which she wanted to avoid. Neither Dorcas nor Marina were drinking vodka.

Father Gresenko and Marina had been in the village six years. He had briefly been a chaplain in the army but had become interested in the natives of Kamchatka in Siberia and volunteered to take a post near the wilderness so that he could study their beliefs and customs. Their nine-year-old son, Alexander, was studying in his room.

Vladimir and Dorcas Stoykin were not as fortunate. Vladimir

was dark haired, short, thin, twenty-eight and seemed to have a perpetual grudge against the world. He had not volunteered to come to Kamchatka. He had been exiled to Siberia for five years after taking part in the failed 1905 Russian revolution. Dorcas, who was about twenty-three, tall, thin and blonde, joined him in his exile. They had only been married twenty months. They had arrived in the spring of 1907, escorted by guards. Dorcas and Vladimir lived in a small, poorly furnished cottage about a three minute walk from Father Yuri's house. They knew they could easily walk home no matter how much snow fell or how much drink was consumed.

Normally, Vladimir, as a political exile, would have been an outcast from the local "polite" society but Father Yuri, who enjoyed thinking of himself as broad minded and who enjoyed talking to people, insisted that Vladimir be treated as anyone else would be.

"Just because he got himself into trouble doesn't mean he's not a fine man. We've too few educated people here and can't afford to waste any talent," Yuri said to the mayor of the village.

The mayor did not approve of Father Yuri's plan to hire Vladimir to teach Russian reading and writing to the local children whose families lived in the village or who spent a season near the village.

Yuri insisted and the mayor gave in. The job greatly improved Vladimir and Dorcas' financial situation, which would have been dire without it.

As they played cards, Vladimir said, "Always talking about death and the next life. What a waste of this life. Marx expressed the truth far better than Pushkin. 'From each according to their abilities to each according to their needs.' Don't preach God to me again. There is no God." He took a long drink of vodka. He was starting to get the feeling of invulnerability that often accompanied his drinking. "Your life proves it. You do everything for this so-called God and he lands you in this awful place far away from all civilization."

"This is a wonderful place. I chose to come to this paradise," said Yuri. "Have you opened your eyes and noticed all the flowers and grains that grow here in summer and the beautiful snow-capped mountains and deep rivers running with fish? The Kamchatka peninsula has rather mild weather, wonderful ports and wonderful people. God made this amazing place and you've never noticed it."

"You haven't noticed the poverty all around you and the exploitation of all by the Tsar and the ruling class?"

"Yes, there's poverty and there always will be poverty. What matters is that we try to help and love our fellow man and to show them how much Jesus loves us."

"Jesus is a false god, a total self-promoter. He proclaimed the Kingdom of Heaven. There's never been nor never will be a Kingdom of Heaven until we take power."

Dorcas began to worry. She had often seen Vladimir become belligerent when he drank too much. He was starting to insult their host and she did not want the argument to escalate. She tried to step in and turn the tide. "Father Yuri isn't oppressing anyone, dear. He even helps the peasants harvest their grain. He doesn't have to do that."

"He's still part of the oppressing class."

"Jesus was both a truth-teller and a poet, perhaps the truest poet that ever lived. The Kingdom he spoke about is both poetical and real. The majesty of what he said inspires and awes every person who opens themselves to it," said Father Yuri.

"Jesus was a liar. There is no spirit, only matter. And you represent an oppressive power, the Tsar. You owe your power to the Tsar's lies and murders."

"I am not rich and I share what I have with others."

"You have the best house in the village," said Vladimir.

"My house is better, but many of the natives follow their traditional ways and roam from place to place. Those with no fixed homes will never have many material goods but perhaps more spiritual goods than many in civilization. I only wish they knew more of the Lord and his mercy. They seem to have so much fear of the spirits around them and no knowledge of the love God has for us."

Yuri realized that Vladimir had been drinking too much. He also knew Vladimir was an unhappy drunk, one who provoked conflicts, so he tried to change the subject. "How is your playwriting going?"

"Nothing, I've written nothing in the past month, but you are just trying to distract me from my mission. We'll change the world and overthrow the Tsar's regime. I'm your enemy and I will triumph and destroy you and your kind. Marx showed us the scientific truth of this. 'What the bourgeoisie, therefore, produces, above all, is its own gravediggers. Its fall and the victory of the proletariat are equally inevitable.' "

"I wish you would stop this talk of successfully transforming the world through violence. It can't be done."

"We will do it," said Vladimir.

"Danton tried and made the world worse."

"Danton was a fool. He didn't know true socialism. Marx teaches us much more."

"Napoleon tried violence and failed. How are you to do better?" asked the priest.

"We know much better than either one. Marxism teaches scientific facts."

"I had thought that talking to you of Danton and Napoleon would have convinced you. Now I'll speak of something you won't understand. God tried to use violence to change the world for the better and He failed. If He couldn't succeed with violence, no one can."

"What are you talking about? There is no God."

"God tried to change the world by violence, by flooding it and only saving Noah and his family. He failed. Noah, who was a better man than either one of us, still had too many flaws. After that failure, God decided never to try the way of violence again. If God renounced violence because it didn't work for Him, it won't work for you either. I can see the flaws in you. I'm sure you can see the flaws in me. Neither one of us could lead such a movement."

"All attempts at peaceful change in this country have failed. The only means left is violence."

"I support the Tsar but have asked that he carry out reforms. His family has the experience of ruling that goes back centuries. Even when he rules badly, he rules better than your people would."

"So you admit he rules badly."

"At times badly, at other times well but you and your friends will rule badly always."

"The world is nothing but material and you can't prove otherwise."

"Yes I can. We both love poetry. That proves there is more than just material." Yuri took a large sip from his glass of vodka. Vladimir drank also. Both women looked at each other wondering what they could do to stop the escalating argument.

"I know that's why you helped us, to have someone around whom you can talk poetry with. But poetry is just as material as everything else, just sounds in the air or ink on a page. There is no spirit or anything beyond the physical. There is more wisdom in this material glass of vodka than in all of your beliefs in the spirit. If there is something beyond the physical, I challenge you to reveal it."

"Jesus returned from the dead."

"Myth and tricks."

Marina could see the fire start to glow in Yuri's eyes. "I'll get some more water for the samovar and then we can have our dessert," she said but she did not actually get up and move.

Yuri struggled to control his anger. He wondered if it was anger, which made him want to prove that God existed? Was his idea of how to do this a good one? Yuri thought of Jesus' admonition not to reveal the sacred to those who will trample on it. Did this saying apply here? he wondered. It wasn't reasonable but Yuri believed, at least a little, that Vladimir would change if shown that the spirit really existed. He'd give it a try.

"I'm sure that there is a God, I often feel Him. If you promise to think seriously of what I'm going to show you, I'll give you proof, " said Yuri.

"You're a fool," said Vladimir.

"Dear, we're guests here, don't talk that way to the Father," said Dorcas.

"Don't ever talk to me like that. You owe me your support," Vladimir said to Dorcas.

"Let me get the things ready for tea," said Marina again, not wanting the confrontation to continue but, again, she didn't move because she wanted to see what would happen.

"Proof can be shown," said Yuri.

"Go ahead and prove there is a God," said Vladimir.

"Yes, show us," said Dorcas.

"Please show us," said Marina who now wondered what Yuri would do. Surely, no one could prove there was a God, could they, she thought.

Yuri's anger had cooled and he now was unsure if he should go through with his plan. He decided to get a sign from the Lord. "Dorcas and I are ahead in his rubber. If Vladimir and Marina win, I'll show you."

"Coward," said Vladimir.  Dorcas winced.

They continued playing. Father Yuri made a mistake in discarding an important card and Vladimir and Marina won the rubber. Did Yuri want to lose to be able to show his proof or was it simply a mistake or maybe part of the divine plan? Father Yuri didn't know but he could sense the anticipation in the other three.

"Now show me that God exists," said Vladimir with a cunning smirk on his face.

The priest added a log to the crackling fire, and said to Vladimir, "Think of a number between one and nine hundred ninety nine and whisper it in your wife's ear. I'll turn around so I can't see your lips. The Spirit will tell me the number and I'll tell it to you."

Vladimir whispered five hundred forty one in his wife's ear, very softly. He said to Yuri, "I gave her a number. Tell me what I said."

Yuri turned around to look at the others, and then sat for twenty-five seconds with a blank expression. He didn't doubt that the Lord could tell him the number. What Yuri doubted was that the Lord had really told him to go ahead with this plan. Maybe his anger and desire to show off had made him presumptuous.

With the lengthy pause, Vladimir was sure Yuri would fail. "I see you have nothing."

Yuri said slowly, "The number is five hundred forty one."

"Cheat," shouted Vladimir. "My wife and you are in this together. You arranged a code between you. I've often suspected you two of cheating together at cards."

"I can understand how you could think I cheated you but suspecting your wife. Why?" asked Yuri.

"She's an ignorant peasant, without a bit of education. She's under your spell."

This was a gross insult to Dorcas, who had more native and emotional intelligence than her husband, but she did not defend herself.

"How could you speak of Dorcas like that?" protested Marina. "Apologize to her."

"I will not," Vladimir said to Marina. To Yuri he said, "You forced me to pick that number."

"How?"

"I don't know but you forced me. Admit it."

"I can't force you to do anything."

"If you're going to prove it, do it again. Do it again, twice, in writing this time. Give me some paper and two pens." Marina provided them.

Vladimir tore the paper into 4 small equal squares. "Go into the kitchen and I will think of two numbers and write them here and then will call out to you to write the two numbers on the squares I give you."

"I agree," said Yuri, whose blood was again almost at a boil because of what he thought of as Vladimir's insolence. I have to calm down, he thought, and he took several very deep breaths. He realized he might be a fool and prayed silently for support. Should I just give it up now? They'll think I'm a fool, but I've proved to the world that I'm a fool many times. Another embarrassment won't hurt me. Yuri asked for an answer in his prayer and at first there was only silence. Then he thought he heard not a physical voice but a strong indication that seemed to say, "Do this now but don't ever do anything like this again."

Yuri took the two pieces of paper and a pen and went into the kitchen. He stood so he could not see into the dining room. "Think of the numbers you write down," he called out to Vladimir.

"No, why should I? Your so-called God should know the numbers without me thinking of them."

That's true, thought Yuri. I have to have faith and he said to Vladimir, "Yes, He will."

"I've written down my two numbers on the two sheets and written "A" on the back of one and "B" on the back of the other, so we know what order I wrote them in," said Vladimir.

With trepidation, the priest wrote down two sets of numbers and heard a warning in his mind that, to him, seemed to come from the Lord. "Don't write the "A" and "B" on the back. I always give a person the freedom to believe or not believe. If you write the "A" and "B" it will force Vladimir to believe and I will never do that. My children have to choose to believe, not be forced or they lose their humanity and freedom."

Yuri carried the pieces of paper back into the dining room. When he went through the door, he tripped, dropped the papers on the floor and bent down and picked them up again. On the dining room table were the two sheets, notated "A" and "B" written by Vladimir. Yuri put his two turned over pieces of paper below Vladimir's.

Vladimir turned over his first sheet and the number "784" was revealed. The priest turned over the sheet below Vladimir's and the number "902" was revealed.

Dorcas was crestfallen. Yuri obviously got it wrong. Vladimir would be merciless in victory she thought.

"I knew that first time with Dorcas was a trick, you conniving priest," said Vladimir.

"Let's turn over the other two sheets," said Yuri, who knew more than the others.

"You've already lost," yelled Vladimir.

Dorcas, wanting to please her hosts, said, "Yes, let Father Yuri turn over the other two papers." Vladimir gave her an angry look.

Yuri turned the second set of numbers over and Vladimir's read '902' and Yuri's read "784."

Yuri's numbers were 784 902

Vladimir's numbers were 902 784

The two sets of two numbers were exactly the same but in the wrong order. Both Marina and Dorcas wondered what order they'd be in if Yuri hadn't dropped his sheets.

"Cheat. That's all you are," shouted Vladimir. "I'll never play cards with you again."

Vladimir picked up the four pieces of paper and threw them towards the fire. He turned to face Yuri. Marina looked at the two men not knowing what to do. Dorcas got to her knees, scooped up the pieces of paper and put them in her pocket. Vladimir did not notice her action. He went to get their coats. Vladimir and Dorcas put on their coats and left. On the way out, Dorcas whispered "Sorry" to Marina. Vladimir was silent. When Dorcas got to their house, she hid the four pieces of paper.

Vladimir and Dorcas passed an unpleasant night. He was very angry, and she felt emotionally isolated and abandoned.

Yuri and Marina also did not pass a pleasant night. Marina cleaned up, went to bed but could not sleep. She was upset and worried, realizing how deeply this would hurt the relationship between the four people.

Yuri went out in the snow and walked to the Orthodox Church, which was a five-minute walk away. The snow had stopped and was almost up to his knees. In the church, he knelt down and prayed for several hours apologizing to the Lord for being such a complete fool. By the time he was finished, he felt as if his feet were frozen. When he returned, Marina had fallen asleep. He warmed his feet near the ashes of the fire, which still emitted gentle warmth. His feet tingled. When they'd warmed up, he went to bed and lay down. He immediately slept but woke early having dreamed of sailing alone on a boat, without sails or oars on a large, lonely sea. In one direction, there was land, a very pleasant looking land but the boat drifted parallel to that land and it did not seem to be getting either closer or further away. Then there was a fire on the land, a large fire. Yuri woke up shaking.

Yuri and Vladimir were often thrown into each other's paths, many times each week but all Yuri's attempts to patch things up were rejected.

Vladimir was in a very odd mood. He was by nature angry but now he was also moody, depressed and in doubt. He knew Father Yuri was trying to help him and this increased his fury. He did not want anyone's help, especially not someone from the other side. Liberation in the form of a revolution seemed ever further away, almost impossible. The 1905 Revolution had been crushed and there seemed to be no prospect of another one occurring.

Dorcas, whose faith had atrophied when she married, was convinced that she had seen a miracle. She again became a believer. She secretly sought instruction from Yuri who taught her much about the prayer of the heart. She prayed secretly and fervently. Sometimes she spoke to Father Yuri of the consolations of prayer and he emphasized that these consolations were not meant for ourselves but to allow us to manifest love and kindness to others.

Three months later, through the work of the two women, the

couples began to play cards again but the atmosphere was heavier with less talking than before. Slowly, Vladimir's mood returned to normal. He was less depressed and moody but his long-standing anger continued to plague him.

About two years later, Vladimir's sentence was commuted and he was allowed to go back to Saint Petersburg. He entered the radical world he had left before. Before they left, Yuri gave Dorcas a manual on prayer, a section from the Philokalia stitched into the pages of a Tolstoy novel for good hiding. Dorcas put the four pieces of paper from the "miracle" in the book and kept it hidden from the world.

Several years later, the catastrophe that many had predicted came true in the form of the great European war. Russia was at war with Germany and Austria-Hungary. Yuri volunteered to be a chaplain for the troops. He hated the war. He hated leaving Marina and Alexander behind. After three years, Yuri gave up working in the army and moved to a small plot of land which he worked with his own hands. Even though he still looked strong, Yuri felt like an old man. His joints ached and he had the first few gray hairs. Marina and Alexander joined him. Alexander was almost at the age where he would be expected to fight.

Vladimir and Dorcas went into voluntary exile at the beginning of the war. They returned to Saint Petersburg, about two months before Lenin returned. Vladimir became active in the Soviets and later the Red Army, rising to the rank of Captain.

The Civil war began. Alexander, against the wishes of Yuri, joined the White Army. Living conditions, which were already bleak, became much harder. During the winter, Marina caught consumption and died. Yuri was heartbroken both by his wife's death and by the fact that he had lost touch with Alexander.

Towards the end of the civil war, the Bolsheviks took the area where Yuri lived. They did not, yet, persecute anyone who did not take an active part against them but to actively cross them was death. One day, a wounded White Russian officer found his way to Yuri's home and Yuri hid him and kept him alive. Yuri was not political but he had seen so much death that he would have saved anyone he could from more suffering. The officer recovered and Yuri gave him directions and aid in escaping to a safe area. Yuri was reported to the secret police, arrested and sent to the local detention, torture and execution center.

Vladimir was the second in command of this center. Dorcas lived with him. The commander was a former Tsarist general, who had deserted and joined the Soviets.

Vladimir was the principal political officer, in charge of interrogations, torture and execution. He had quickly become horrified by this work but he still considered it necessary. Fighting in the war had been frightening, horrible, but mopping up an unarmed enemy in a prison that included torture was even worse.

Dorcas was even more horrified at the killing of people she believed were only guilty of being in the wrong place at the wrong time and who had the additional misfortune of being caught. Everyone was vulnerable and could be executed by one or another's side in the civil war. Dorcas' whole being rebelled against Vladimir's work. She could see no point in these executions except as a means to terrorize the opposition and she did not want to be a part of it. It was only with the greatest effort that she could continue to stay with Vladimir, but she had no place else to go and did not want to desert her husband.

Vladimir had a number of lower ranked assistants, all more eager for this work than he was now. His assistants had been involved with torture and murder for only a short period of time, so they had not yet become disgusted with it.

Vladimir began to think that only those who actually enjoyed pretending to be God could stand this work for very long. Then he thought of how Father Yuri had spoken of God. Yuri's God was entirely different than the god that these men seemed to be imitating.

Father Yuri spoke of a God of kindness, patience, love and forgiveness. The men who enjoyed this work acted like a god who embodied vengeance, mercilessness and fury.

Late one afternoon, Vladimir was given a list of the new prisoners and he saw the name Yuri Gresenko on it. Yuri is a very common name and Gresenko was not uncommon, so it did not strike Vladimir immediately that this could be the same Father Yuri he had known in Siberia. He did an inspection of the holding cell, which held the new prisoners. He saw what to him looked to be a late middle-aged man, different than what he remembered of Yuri. This man was much thinner, beginning to grey and had only a very short beard.

The man looked much older than Vladimir had remembered but, in a few seconds, his increased age became the new normal and the man looked like Father Yuri. Vladimir's heart trembled. What was he to do? He went to the one room cabin he shared with Dorcas. They ate dinner together. He did not want to tell his wife, but he couldn't stop himself.

"Father Yuri is here," he said.

"What is he accused of?" asked Dorcas.

"He hid a White army officer."

"You have to get him off."

"He is our class enemy."

"He was never our enemy. He helped us all he could."

"I must do my duty. You know the fate of those who hide the enemy."

"You must help him, he performed a miracle for us."

"Miracle? No, it was a trick. How did you help him trick me?"

"I've never lied or tricked you."

"Liar," said Vladimir and he struck her. He had lost his temper many times, but he had never struck Dorcas before.

Dorcas fell to the floor and began to cry. Have mercy on him for my sake, she called out in silent prayer. Out loud she said, "Please find a way to save Father Greshenko." After that she sobbed.

It was as if a frozen Artic windblast had hit Vladimir. He had actually hit his wife. He could not believe it. He stood still.

"You know you could get him off," Dorcas said softly.

That was true. All Yuri had to do was declare his loyalty to the Soviets and betray someone on the other side. Many people, who had done more than Yuri, had gotten off. But Vladimir was not sure he wanted to get Yuri off. He thought that perhaps it had been a miracle he had seen. Let this be a test to see if the so-called God, creator of all, could get Yuri off. Why should I bother? "If there is a God, He doesn't need my help."

Among the privations of the time was the lack of vodka. The joy and sometimes sorrow of people drinking freely had been greatly diminished by the civil war. That morning, a nearby Soviet unit had liberated a great quantity of vodka and much was distributed to the workers at the prison.

Vladimir met with his second in command, Dmitri, in the early evening to play cards. They, along with two other assistants, began to drink, at first a little but then more and more.

Vladimir won the first round and slowly got drunker and drunker. He began to feel invulnerable.

"I once saw a so-called miracle. It fooled some but not me. Just goes to prove the duplicity of the clergy and the simplicity of the people who believe such things," said Vladimir.

"Tell me about this miracle," said Dmitri.

"I was exiled in a village in Siberia and I worked for the local priest," said Vladimir.

"You worked for a priest?"

"Yes, in Kamchatka teaching the children to speak and read Russian."

"He exploited the people, just like all priests. Right?"

"No, he treated them fairly. He even helped them harvest their fields."

"You admired this enemy of the people?" asked Dmitri.

"I wish he had been one of us; he would have been the best. But he was firmly on the other side," said Vladimir.

"Tell me about this so-called miracle."

"He was able to guess a three-digit number that I whispered in my wife's ear, implied that God told him the number. I knew it had to be a trick."

"Your wife told you that it was a trick?" asked Dimitri.

Vladimir thought about how he had tried to force his wife to admit this. "She never admitted anything. I think she's secretly a believer."

Vladimir suddenly stopped, knowing that he might have gone too far. Commissars are paid to be suspicious. If he had not been so drunk, he would have seen how Dmitri was looking at him. Dmitri's eyes said that there are many traitors to the cause. He thought Vladimir probably was one of them.

The next morning, Yuri was brought before Vladimir in a small interrogation room. They faced each other across a small table. There was a small open window behind Vladimir. Behind this window was a tiny room with a seat. A second person could listen to the interrogation from this room and hardly anyone would be able to notice they were there. Vladimir was in charge and he never allowed anyone else to listen in on his interrogations.

When Vladimir entered, Yuri was silent. He did not immediately recognize Vladimir who had also aged greatly, even much more than the dozen or so years that had elapsed since they saw each other would show.

"Do you admit that you harbored a White fugitive?" asked Vladimir. As soon as Vladimir spoke, Yuri recognized his voice. He looked closely and saw a very unhappy man. He saw how much Vladimir had deteriorated and thought he too must also have changed greatly for the worse.

Vladimir asked again, "You harbored a White spy?"

"Would you believe me, if I denied it?" asked Father Yuri.

"Of course."

"You never believed me before, why should you now?"

"Tell me who your White contacts are."

"Why?"

"We know you're guilty but if you reveal your contacts it will go easier with you."

"How will it go easier?"

"If you give me your network and join our side, I'll be able to free you. If you only tell us you're guilty, I can offer you a clean death, a mere bullet through the head. If you do not cooperate at all, my men might torture you or shoot you but not fatally. Some have lingered for more than a day in pain before they died."

"Millions have died in great pain, I am not afraid."

"You should be afraid."

"During the Great War, the Germans were our enemies but we didn't threaten and torture them when we captured them, why are you threatening to torture me? Are we now living in the new glorious world you told me you would build when we lived in Kamchatka?"

Vladimir looked into Yuri's eyes and knew that he was not afraid. There was very little he could do to scare him. He answered his question, "We have to go through a difficult time before we see the new glorious world."

"Is Dorcas well?" Yuri asked.

"Why do you ask of her? Worry about yourself."

"She is precious to God. I am hoping she is well."

"She is very well. And what of Marina and Alexander?"

"Marina died of consumption last year. I hope that Alexander is alive, but I don't know."

"You saved the White officer because you were on his side. Admit it and give me your network."

"I am on no one's side but God's. His love is impartial, loving both the good and the bad. I would save anyone I could. I would save you if I could."

"Are you going to turn over your network?"

"God has no network. He just IS."

"You have made your position very difficult. I'll have to decide how to deal with you."

With that Vladimir left the room, not having made any decision. He was not afraid to kill Father Yuri, as his wife was. He had killed hundreds so what was one more? But he had become very tired of being an ally in the service of cruel, early, unnecessary and painful death. The Pushkin poem Yuri had recited before the so-called miracle came to his mind:

> I say to myself: the years are fleeting,
> And however many there seem to be,
> We must all go under the eternal vault,
> And someone's hour is already at hand.

Why did he have to force people under the eternal vault? Was it Yuri's hour? Was it his hour? Vladimir's mind drifted. He brought it back to the present. Yuri was clearly guilty and he clearly was not going to cooperate. For no one else would Vladimir have held his hand but he hesitated and tried to explain to himself why he was going to give Yuri one more chance to change his mind.

He ate dinner with Dorcas, who thanked him for not executing their friend. "You have to find some way to pardon him. You are the chief, you can do it."

That night Vladimir again played cards with his three assistants and again Dmitri, his second in command, plied him with vodka and questions. The drink drove away Vladimir fears.

"You didn't torture or execute that traitorous priest," said Dmitri.

"Not yet," said Vladimir.

"I would have done something beyond merely talking to him."

"I gave him something to think about. He'll have something to tell me in the morning."

"You know he won't talk. We've seen his kind before. Death to traitors is the only way."

"I'll get him to cooperate."

"You know you won't. Why pretend. It's that miracle he performed that's stopping you. Isn't it? You told us about the trick with your wife. What else did he do? Tell us the secret. Did that priest do anything more than have your wife relay the correct number to him?"

Vladimir took another glass of vodka and commenced to tell the full story of the two sheets of paper including Yuri's dropping the sheets and picking them up. When he told of uncovering the first two numbers, Dmitri smirked. When he told of uncovering the last two numbers and having the same sets reversed, the two other assistants were astounded. They thought maybe this was a miracle. Dmitri was now absolutely convinced that Father Yuri had tricked Vladimir.

"Tell me that you're sure it wasn't a miracle," said Dmitri.

"I am sure it was a trick," said Vladimir.

"How did he do it then?"

"How would I know?"

"Why didn't you torture it out of him? Seems to me that you consider it a miracle. You told us yesterday that he is a good man. "

"Better than most. I wish all priests could be like he was."

"Priests are our particular enemy." Dmitri spat and grunted.

Vladimir had drunk too much to notice the grunt and snicker Dmitri gave him.

On the way home, Vladimir pondered what to do with Father Yuri.

Vladimir slept badly. He knew he'd have to speak to Father Yuri again but he had no idea what he would say. In the morning, Dorcas again urged Vladimir to find a way to free Yuri. Vladimir made no promise, but he tried to be as tender and loving as he could to Dorcas.

Around 10 AM, Father Yuri was brought to an interrogation room and was joined by Vladimir.

"Have you thought of what we talked about yesterday?" Vladimir asked.

Yuri did not respond. Instead, he pointed with his eyes to the window behind Vladimir's head. Behind the small window the small room was in near darkness. Vladimir looked quickly and did not see anyone. Father Yuri gestured with his eyes a second time. Vladimir looked closely and in the near darkness sat Dmitri. In normal circumstances, this would have been a major violation of protocol but Vladimir began to realize that this was no longer a normal situation. He had raised suspicions about his own loyalty and now both he and Yuri were in grave danger.

"Have you thought about the offer I made you yesterday? Are you going to cooperate with us?" asked Vladimir.

"A man is obliged to save himself if he possibly can do so without violating all he believes to be true. I can do nothing to save myself but if anyone can save themselves, they must try their hardest to do so. This is a great law for all people," said Yuri.

"That is not an answer," said Vladimir.

"It is not the answer you are expecting but there is nothing else I can say. If I could save anyone, including myself, I would do it. If you can save anyone, including yourself, you must do it. Think of your love and your life. Do you remember the beauty of our village with the snowcapped mountains in the distance?"

"Yes."

"The core of all life is even more beautiful than that."

Vladimir was confused and felt the need to show a determination he did not actually feel. He said, in a very loud voice, "Listen to me, you traitorous priest, you are going to have to answer my question. I will send you to solitary confinement and speak to you in the morning."

Yuri was led off to solitary confinement. Vladimir left the interrogation room and went to his office. Dmitri came to talk but Vladimir would not speak to him. He knew that Dmitri found his performance disloyal.

Vladimir paced back and forth in his office, his head down, thinking and thinking. If he was a prayerful man, he would have prayed but he was not one. He brooded over and over. I'm an intelligent man, with normal emotions, what should I do? he wondered. He continued to pace. I can't do anything for Yuri, he thought. If I stay, Dmitri will probably turn me in. If I flee from here, directly I will get caught. What should I do? What exactly was Father Yuri telling me? An hour passed before he made his decision.

He went to see the commanding officer and asked him how the fighting was going at the front. "We've suffered a setback," the commander said. "There were many casualties and morale is poor."

Vladimir volunteered to go back into combat. He said that Dmitri was able to take his job but he warned the commanding officer that Dimitri was not completely reliable. "When he drinks, he imagines things that don't exist. Afterwards he tells the wildest stories of what he thought he saw and heard. That's dangerous."

The commanding officer was delighted to be able to send a seasoned combat officer back to the front. Vladimir asked that Dorcas be sent to Petrograd.

Vladimir went to break the news to Dorcas. As he walked in their shack, he felt for her almost the same love he had felt as a university student. He told her of his plan.

"But what will become of Father Yuri?" she asked.

"I cannot save him. Maybe God will save him. He told me to save ourselves. That was his final message to us. I swear it."

"You say, maybe God will save him. Are you a believer now?"

'I am less of a doubter than I was. I can't kill Father Yuri and, if I stay, I'll have to. We have to save ourselves. I intend to desert on the way to the front. We can try to make our way to England. I always loved the name Croydon and wanted to visit there. I will meet you there. You will be sent to Petrograd. I've been told that the Finnish border is lightly patrolled. Perhaps you can escape that way. We have to make a try."

"I don't want to leave Father Yuri behind," said Dorcas. She started weeping, and then she started praying and had a feeling that she should do what Vladimir requested. She knew that there was no other choice.

Fourteen months later, Dorcas made it to Croydon where she waited for Vladimir, never hearing anything and growing more worried month by month. Almost eighteen months after Dorcas arrived, Vladimir appeared in Croydon, having made his way through Constantinople after a long and complex journey. He had met a number of other deserters, from both sides of the Civil War, who banded together. They never revealed to each other their real names and Vladimir didn't know this but one of them was Alexander, Father Yuri's son, who was able to go to Paris.

After Vladimir left, Dmitri took his place at the detention center and moved steadily up the ranks in the secret police. Eighteen years later, he was arrested, tortured and during Stalin's great show trials, confessed to hundreds of imagined crimes and was executed.

What became of Father Yuri? Dmitri interrogated him the next day and Father Yuri gave him no answers. Dmitri ordered that Yuri be chained to a post and shot in the stomach in such a way that he would die slowly and painfully. He assigned one of his most talented and trusted executioners to shoot Yuri and had a trusted guard watch over Yuri with the offer to finish him off quickly, in exchange for information.

Before the executioner shot Father Yuri, he told Yuri of his disgust for the rich and cowardly clergy. Father Yuri said nothing. The executioner shot Yuri in the abdomen making sure that the wound would cause a painful, lingering death. The guard looked on and continued to watch Father Yuri, hoping for more information.

For the first three hours, Father Yuri lay on the ground, reciting the prayer of the heart, over and over. "Lord Jesus Christ, Son of God, have mercy on me a sinner." Sometimes instead of saying a sinner, he'd say, "Have mercy on me an ingrate" or "Have mercy on me a hypocrite." He never complained.

The guard was so impressed that he asked Father Yuri to forgive him and to pray for him. The guard began to say the prayer along with Father Yuri. Yuri asked the man to recite the prayer silently because if the guard was overheard praying aloud, the guard would also be executed.

The guard prayed silently for seven hours as Yuri prayed aloud. The guard offered to end Father Yuri's suffering but Yuri asked him not to. "I still have much praying to do. It is good to die with a friend nearby. We two are sharing in the agony of Jesus on the cross, one of the greatest of all mysteries."

Several hours later, Father Yuri fell unconscious and eventually died. The guard considered the manner of Father Yuri's death to be the only miracle he saw in his life but whom could he tell and be safe? He had a wife and two children, but he couldn't tell them. Children were encouraged to turn their parents in if they were dangerous and spouses were also urged to turn each other in.

The guard harbored this secret in his heart until he was sixty-three years old. His wife had died, his children moved away and he was in poor health. In the last six months of his life, he told hundreds of people of Father Yuri's death and what a miracle it had been to him. Most ignored him but a few people were impressed but they could not say so publicly but held the information sacredly in their hearts.

The guard was arrested and shipped off to a slave labor camp in Siberia where he spoke of Father Yuri and the prayer of the heart to some of the other prisoners. Most ignored him but a few were heartened. A few days after he arrived, the authorities realized he couldn't do the required heavy work and they used a bulldozer to bury him and two other similar prisoners alive.

In Corydon, Dorcas and Vladimir taught English to the many Russians and other non-English speakers. Vladimir still drank to excess but he appreciated his wife and his life and tried to do what good he could. When asked what his philosophy of life was, he would reply, "I once met a great man, Father Yuri, who taught me to be good to all people."

Vladimir had led a very hard life, had done and seen too many horrible things and was far too emotionally scarred to accomplish this lofty task, which few people even begin to attempt, but he did sincerely try and made some progress.  He died in 1939.

Dorcas lived on until 1948. She made many sincere friends. She often spoke of Father Yuri and his miracle. Most people smiled and thought she was either making the story up or that the miracle was not a miracle but was merely a coincidence. Some said it was a trick but could never explain how Father Yuri had accomplished it. A few were impressed but quickly forgot what was said but a very few took what she said to heart and thought about what it might mean to them.

Before she died, Dorcas gave her copy of the Russian version of Tolstoy's novel, given to her by Father Yuri, with sections of the Philokalia in it, to a local Croydon library. She put the four pieces of paper, with the numbers on them in the book and included an explanation, in English, of what happened and how the experience had changed her life. That book may still be in that library or maybe someone has realized what a treasure it is and put it in some place of honor.

# NIAGARA'S MISTS

"Nick and Nora rode proudly down Fifth Avenue. They were Co-Grand Marshalls of the Macy's Thanksgivings Day Parade. Nick had just cracked another case, a triple homicide commited by a contortionist who could shimmy his way out of almost any room or jail cell. Nick began to wonder if he'd make it to the end of the parade without having to hop off the float to grab a drink. He normally had about twenty to thirty mixed drinks a day. Nora knew he couldn't hold out any longer, so she handed him a water bottle filled with a new drink she'd invented called the Sledge Hammer. Nick took a swig and said, 'My dear, you are the best of wives.'"

Harrold had seen an old movie, *The Thin Man*, the night before and he was beginning to write the story that the film kicked off in his imagination. He was excited, as he always was, when he was working on a story. It was as if the whole universe was buzzing with excitement inside his large, rather oddly shaped head. For Harrold, creating was as thrilling as the first passion of love. He couldn't wait to put down the ideas that flashed in his brain, before they faded away, so he typed as fast as he possibly could. He'd found he never had writers block if he typed like a virtuoso at his piano.

Harrold never considered the ideas he wrote to be his own. No, they were free falling inspirations coming out of nowhere, going everywhere. He loved to go to the Canadian side of Niagara Falls and find the spot where the mists from the falls would continually land. Most people abhorred getting soaked but Harrold would root himself there until the mists moved to another area and then he'd stand there. He loved getting drenched. Ideas he thought seemed to be just like that, flowing gently downward, never stopping, even for an instant.

Harrold often talked to people who were bored and he wondered why they didn't look for places where ideas freely and gently rained. These people often asked Harrold, "Where did you get that weird idea?" Harrold learned that a truthful answer angered people so he gently changed the topic.

"Come to the table, Harrold. You've been writing too long. Aren't you tired? Come talk to the guests," said Harriet, his wife. They'd been married two years and were living in their in-law's basement house trying to save money to buy a house. Harrold was a bit annoyed. He worked nine hours a day, five days a week, turning the "Stop" and "Go" sign in front of road construction sites. Harriet didn't like him to spend more than an hour a day writing. On Saturday, Harrold had to do chores almost the whole day. His in-laws had a huge property and he cut their lawn, planted, weeded, shopped and worked like a dog's body all day. His only long period of writing was for three hours on Sunday morning when the rest of the family went to church. Harrold thought of his writing as prayer and he enjoyed almost every second of it.

When the family got home from church, there was a family dinner and afterwards, the in-laws had there "at home" day, where friends, neighbors and artists would stop by. Harrold's mother in law's hospitality was well known and the "at homes' were well attended. Harrold was expected to be there.

At today's "at home," Harrold joined the conversation of Peter and Louise, two local poets. Peter asked Louise, "Remember when we first met, it was eleven years ago and you were nineteen years old?"

"No," said Louise, "it was twelve years ago. I remember because you were nineteen and I was only eighteen. I became nineteen one month later because you were born in May and I was born in June and then we were both nineteen together. "

"Are you sure it wasn't when we were seventeen?" asked Peter.

Harrold wanted to shout, "Can't you think of anything more interesting to talk about?" He looked to the side and he was going to suggest they talk about the plant next to them, which was, in his imagination, poisonous and they had accidently brushed against it. Harrold knew he couldn't say that but he wanted the conversation to be at least a bit more galvanizing, so he commented, "When Obama was first running for President I was nineteen and that was an exciting time."

Louise continued, "Seventeen was a big year for me." Harrold's ears perked up. Was he going to hear a secret? Louise continued, "I failed English. Mr. Sullivan was a really poor teacher."

Harrold had now had it with this conversation and he saw two people, James and Joan, whom he vaguely knew, talking in a corner. Harrold joined them. James asked Joan, "Wasn't your hair black last time I saw you?"

"Yes, I became a blonde only six months ago. It is absolutely amazing how differently people treat you when you're blonde. I can tell people think I'm dumb but none of my female, so-called, friends mention my small breasts anymore. It's a blessing in disguise."

A scene from Evita flashed in Harrold's mind. He began thinking of Joan standing topless on a huge platform, thousands of people cheering their adulation, each small bare breast topped with a maraschino cherry, her long blonde hair standing straight up, with a crown on the top and Joan singing at the top of her voice, "Don't Cry For Me Argentina." Harrold started to laugh.

"What are you laughing about?" asked Joan. "I didn't say anything funny."

"Sorry," said Harrold. "I was thinking of a joke one of my friends told me."

Joan continued, "You didn't have a mustache before, did you, James?"

Harrold began imagining each of James' mustaches growing seven feet long and on each side beginning to be intricately curled and pointed. At the end of each mustache was a golden propeller; one twirling in a clockwise motion and the other in a counter-clockwise motion so that James' head was slowly turning to the right. Harrold would have to warn James before his head screwed completely off. Harrold knew he'd start to laugh at any moment. He didn't want to insult Joan and James with his unsought laughter, so he left that conversation. And so it went through the rest of the afternoon.

That night Harrold finished the first scene of a new story and read it to his wife, Harriet. She nodded politely. It was another story derived from someone else's work. She wondered why Harrold didn't write something original and why someone who seemed brilliant, didn't work at a better job.

On the next Sunday "at home," there were many musicians. Harrold would often hum a few bars of some ditty he'd made up. It wasn't unusual for Harrold to be told, "I haven't heard notes put together like that before." Often that would be the end of it and the players would change the topic but, on a few occasions, a male violin player and a female cello player improvised on Harrold's hummed theme. They'd yell back and forth to each other, "Change that third note from a B to a B flat, that would make it better."

Harrold might chime in, "Change the B to a B sharp."

"Silly, a B sharp is a C note," said the cello player and she'd start to laugh. Harrold laughed too because, of course, he knew that a B sharp was the same as a C but he had made that comment specifically to entertain the two players.

Today, Harrold joined three musicians, who were about to go on a tour of Europe. They were talking about tuning their instruments for the best performance. One said, "The orchestra always tunes the A note above middle C, to be at 440 beats per minute. It sounds so much better than 438 beats per minute. Don't you think so?"

Thinking of time, Harrold reached into his pocket and took out his grandfather's pocket watch, looked at the time and held it to his ear to make sure it was still ticking.

"No, I think 439 is proper tuning for optimal sound quality," said the second musician.

"But if it's an odd number, it's so hard to tune the other notes. There's always some that are a bit flat or sharp."

"That's true" said the third, "which is why 440 is the best, even if it doesn't sound the best."

Harrold lost interest thinking; don't they realize that their clock is ticking? Time is passing quickly and there's never enough of it. Maybe their flight will crash. And they're worrying about two beats a minute.

Harrold saw a middle aged woman he'd never spoken to before sitting alone by herself in a corner of the room. She looked extremely sad. He went over and said hello and asked her how she was doing.

"Well, I'm ..." she said and stopped talking. She shook her head from side to side.

Harrold sat in the chair next to her, saying nothing. After about two minutes, Harrold said, "Life can be hell sometimes, can't it?"

"Are you trying to cheer me up?"

"No. Never. If someone tries to cheer me, I feel even worse, as if I'm a failure because I'm sad. When I'm miserable it's for a good reason and I don't want anyone making my problem and me look insignificant and ridiculous."

"You're right. The last thing I want is someone giving me sympathy and gloating at my sadness. I really don't want to talk about it."

"I'm going to tell you a secret about myself. Promise not to tell anyone else unless that person is feeling miserable."

The woman smiled and said, "I promise not to tell anyone who isn't miserable."

"When I'm miserable, I say really strongly, 'Harrold, you're feeling terrible for damned good reasons.'

"Yes," said the woman.

Then a mysterious second part of me says, "Damned straight. Harrold, you're SUFFERING." This part then laughs and continues "Poor Harrold. Poor, poor Harrold. No one else has ever suffered like you have."

Again the first part says, "Damn right. I'm completely justified in calling myself, Poor Poor Harrold. Are you doubting me, asshole?"

"The two parts of me go back and forth like this, a few times, and then a third part starts to feel like laughing at this back and forth except that pride won't allow it to do so. This continues and, in all parts, I feel that the suffering is still there but so is laughter. I laugh and cry at the same time. Living life is like eating sweet and sour vegetables. Never one taste without some of the other."

The woman smiled, and said, "My name is Janice and I'm very glad to have met you. I promise to keep your secret. Who would believe it if I told them anyway?"

"Only those who allow themselves to suffer can understand."

Janice laughed. She stopped then looked at Harrold and said, "I'm sorry. I hadn't thought seriously about what you said. It sounded so unusual. ... Yes, that makes a lot of sense. Thank you."

On Tuesday, Harrold's older brother George was killed in a car accident, skidding off the road and crashing into a telephone pole.

Harrold was distraught both at losing his brother, whom to his mind was the most vital person he knew and because he kept imagining George's crash, smashing into the pole as if he and not George had been in the accident. Harrold saw himself crushed in the car, felt the pain, looked down at his mangled body and heard the cry for help screaming from his own lips.

Then Harrold realized he was alive in his own room. Again he'd see himself as George, eating dinner, then driving the car that he knew to be George's and again re-living the crash. This time it was even bloodier, as if the bloody residue of the first crash was added to the horror of the second one. By the time Harrold had reviewed the crash three times, it was all he could do to stand on his own feet, shake his head and realize that he was alive and unhurt. He took out his grandfather's pocket watch and listened. It was still ticking. Yes, it's so wonderful to be alive and healthy.

George's funeral service started at 10 AM. Harrold arrived five minutes early. Funerals frightened him. He always imagined that it was he who was lying in the coffin. How wonderful to finally be noticed. How horrible to be dead and have embalming fluid in one's veins instead of blood. He thought of all that happens to prepare the body. Horrible. He imagined he was alive as the blood was drained out of him. I must not think of that, he thought. Maybe I'll include it in one of my stories.

Harrold sat down next to a cousin, just as his brother's service began. The music stopped and the minister began to speak.

"George has gone to a better world, a wonderful world, the best world that could ever exist. We know this because God is so very good, that he has created the very best world for us and loves us intensely. "

Harrold's mind reacted. "How in the world can he know that? Maybe George just doesn't exist or maybe he is still alive on another plane looking at us wondering why the heck we don't see him and say hello. I wonder what's really happening to George. I wonder if what he's experiencing is so wonderful, whether maybe I should volunteer to have God take me in George's place. Then George would be back again." Harrold came back to the current moment and heard more from the minister.

"George hasn't left us. We have complete access to George. We can be with George any time we want to be."

Harrold thought that was wonderful. I miss George already. How can I see him anytime I want to see him? This minister is really the best because he's going to tell me how to always have George around.

The minister continued, "And you can always contact George because George has gone to God and is in God and you can always go to God to be in contact with George."

How incredible and true, thought Harrold. That's the answer to the question. I'm so glad that I came today. I wouldn't have missed this funeral for the world. But let me think for a moment. I call to God all the time and usually get no answer. In fact the more I call and don't get a response, the less I seem to know, as if knowing nothing at all is the same as knowing everything. Could it be true that 'Less is more or is more less?' This is so confusing.

I'm not sure this minister knows what he's talking about. I used to think I knew God but now He seems further and further away and harder and harder to describe accurately. I read *Dark Night of the Soul* that describes how the journey starts by a person experiencing God and then God seems to get further and further away. *That's* exactly like my life but what do I really know?

These thoughts continued until Harrold came back to the present moment and realized that the minister was closing his eulogy. "George was the perfect son, brother, father, husband. He is going to God and now we will drive to the cemetery to place his body in the earth from whence it will rise on the Day of Judgment."

They got to the cemetery. It was winter and the grave had not yet been dug. They put George's coffin on a stand and the minister asked everyone to gather round. There were grave markers nearby. Harold looked down at the one closest to his feet, Doris Lestwise born July 14, 1968, died May 5, 1973. She was not even five years old. Harold's mind tried to comprehend this tremendous tragedy. At least his brother had made it to be 43 years old. Yes it was a tragedy that George died but at least he'd lived. Harold imagined Doris getting sick and her parent's trying to tell her that she'd get better but she was so young she might not know what was happening and didn't comprehend what death was.

Harold didn't think death was so bad. Who cared if you died? What was so awful was not death itself but the fact that death is so incredibly final. His father had died. Harrold didn't mind. What he minded was that ten years later his father was still dead. Why can't death be like a vacation, you go away for a few months or even a year or two and then you come back refreshed, full from your new adventures? If he were God, maybe he'd arrange things that way.

Harrold realized he wrote stories and created worlds, so he was like a minor god. In his stories the dead could come back after a long vacation. It might be macabre but he could write it. He didn't care if it was published, he'd write it for himself. To feel that incredible life one feels when the creative juices are flowing, when the words leap from one's fingertips as fast as one can type. He longed to be back in his room.

Harold came back to current consciousness and the minister said, "Let's make a final goodbye to George and then we'll go to the lunch which has been arranged and the party back at his house put on by his family."

When Harrold, sitting in the passenger's seat, drove away, his mind had not yet left the gravesite. He imagined that he was George, left all by himself, as the others drove off. Have you forgotten me already? Harold heard George wondering. Why did you leave me here? I'm alive. Alive. Harold imagined George talking and playing with Doris Lestwise, the little girl who had died. Harold tried to overhear their conversation but the car was rapidly driving away.

As Harrold drove back, he could not concentrate on the conversation in the car but imagined himself talking to George and the young girl. The two, who no longer were dead, decided to take a trip to Paris to see the pavement artists along the Seine. What a jolly idea. Harrold wondered whether he was simply imagining what George and Doris were now doing or if it were actually happening.

They got to the lunch. There were trays after trays of different foods. Harrold piled his plate high with ziti, roast chicken, mashed potatoes, hot sausage, broccoli and creamed spinach and sat with his cousins Louisa and Loren who were debating the merits of long grained brown rice and jasmine brown rice. Harrold tuned out. His last thought on the topic was, I bet I'd like rice and black beans the same whether it was made with long grained brown rice or jasmine brown rice. Don't they realize their ticking clocks could stop today?

Harrold began to wonder what Louisa and Loren would do if they were suddenly dropped in the middle of the Sahara desert with ten gallons of water and a pack of food and a friendly person pointed them towards an oasis that was ten miles away and barely visible. They'd probably wonder if what they saw was real or a mirage. Harrold imagined them sweating, praying in their hearts that the oasis really was there and suddenly, out of no where, storm clouds popped up and there was a heavy thunderstorm. When the thunderstorm ended, Louisa and Loren saw the oasis had disappeared. It was just a mirage. But maybe they were mistaken and they weren't in the Sahara at all.

Harrold got up and sat next to George's ten-year-old daughter, Sarah. Two people were talking to her about their vacation plans for the summer. Harrold waited for them to pause for air and began to speak about how wonderful it was to have had George as a brother. George's love of life and of everyone around him would be so dearly missed. "Let's talk of his goodness and how we'll miss him." The two other people soon left but Harrold and Sarah spoke for almost half an hour, smiling, laughing and crying. To Harrold, it seemed like George was there, enjoying being remembered, wishing he could communicate with all those present and at the same time anxious to get on with his new life in the world beyond. What an interesting place to be, thought Harrold.

Eventually it was time to go home. Harrold pulled out his grandfather's pocket watch, listened and then wound it. He thought about how few ticks there actually are in a life. When he was seven years old, he'd taken a personal vow to unravel the mystery of human life. Every time he looked at the watch he was reminded that he'd have to hurry if he was going to accomplish this gargantuan task.

The next day, at work, Harrold turned his "Stop" and "Go" sign at the construction site. He had to pay close attention so there wouldn't be an accident but each time a car stopped in front of him, Niagara mists of a story poured down. Often the car had only a single person, who was interesting enough but when there were three or more people, the mists rained hard and Harrold had to ground himself in order to turn the sign to "Go" to let the car pass. Today he was very fortunate, he'd seen two people in the front seat, talking very quietly and he knew, yes, just knew that they were planning a robbery.

That night, Harrold added this to the story he was writing, Nick solved this robbery and was telling the solution, over a dozen or more drinks, to Nora and his police friends.

To be a writer, thought Harrold, is the best of lives. So far, I've been writing trivia but now I'm going to write stories that explain the universe. That is, if my clock doesn't stop ticking first. Harrold got on his knees, said "Thank you" and asked, "Maybe my timepiece can keep running until I finish these stories?" Sometimes Harrold felt he got a response. Tonight it was, "Write your stories but be gentle. Many readers are unaware of time passing and terrified of getting soaked by reality." Harrold was very pleased.

He felt Niagara's mists falling, soaking him to the skin. He went to the keyboard and began a new story, nothing like what he usually wrote. Two hours later, Harriet came in urging him to come upstairs. Before he did, he read Harriet his new story. She smiled. "At last you've stopped copying others and begun writing about the secrets of the human heart."

"Yes, I plan to write exclusively about the secrets I've learned."

"I can't wait to read them. Be gentle to your readers."

"I'll try but I can't promise that."

"Okay, we'll see what you create," she said

The next time he sat to write, Harrold either imagined it or Doris Lestwise really was sitting next to him. She told him of her sickness and death, when she was five years old. "I'll tell you what I experi-enced, when I was sick. I've tried to tell people that I had a wonder-ful life but no one will listen. I've finally found someone who will. Would you please write my story?" She seemed to be both a small child and a wise person at the same time.

"With the greatest pleasure," said Harrold.
Harrold felt like Mozart at his piano, improvising the music that was silently, unwinding in his mind or like a man, under Niagara's mist, soaked to the skin. I must not frighten my reader, thought Harrold. He soon realized he had nothing to worry about. Doris told her story with gentleness and poignant mirth. This really is a secret well worth knowing, thought Harrold. Being a writer is the very best thing I can be.

# SAINT JOSEPH'S PUFFS

It was uncanny, a stunner, something never before imagined. My Grandfather, Andrew, lost four straight games of combo-Bolivia, that amazingly complex card game that our extended family was addicted to playing. Andrew was by far the best player and his team rarely lost one game. Once in five years, his team might lose two games. I'd never seen him lose three and now he lost four in a row.

Andrew is old but still vigorous, still working in his shoe repair business from a shop in front of the house. But it is his gambling that makes him the peer of legends. He has the reputation of being the smartest, most daring gambler in town. With his family, he only played for chips because he said, for most, gambling is risky for their wealth, health and spirit.

This night all the card players were on edge. Four days before, there'd been an earthquake in southern Italy, where our family comes from. We'd seen pictures of the damage on TV and in the newspapers but we still had not heard from any of our relatives in the area.

After the game, I washed some of the dishes in the small, white kitchen with my Aunt Mary. She is the oldest child and has an even cheerful temperament. As far as she could remember, and she had a remarkable memory, Grandfather had only lost three games once, the day Pearl Harbor was bombed, when he was worried that one of his sons had been killed.

I finished the dishes and went back to see Andrew, who was still sitting at the long mahogany table. He often gave me card tips after we cleaned up. Andrew was smoking his pipe looking dolefully at the oil paintings of his parents that hung on the right wall. I asked if he'd give me some tips tonight.

"Not tonight," he said. To my surprise, tears slid down his cheek. I tried to make a joke to cheer him up, but he didn't laugh.

"It's not that your joke isn't funny. I just heard from my cousin Peter." He pulled out a letter written in Italian and translated a bit for me. Andrew didn't speak English well, but we'd known each other all my life so we had no difficulty understanding each other.

"The earthquake devastated our region, village after village. Some places have barely one stone on top of another. Many died."

He put the letter away, sucked on his pipe and smiled. "They don't have money to rebuild. Peter asked for our help."

I knew my grandfather had saved money. He'd once allowed me to bet almost a year's salary using his money saying that, if I lost, I'd owe him nothing.

"They need about two million dollars to get started. There will be charity but not enough to make a difference."

It was 1978 and I had only been at my computer-programming job about eight months. I made about fourteen thousand dollars a year. Two million seemed like an astronomical sum.

"How the heck are we going to get that much?" I asked.

"Will you pledge to help me?" he asked.

"Of course," I said.

He hugged me, something he never did.

"What are we going to do?" I asked.

"Look out for some opportunities to win a huge stake."

"How much do you have?" I asked him.

"Forty thousand."

"Can you turn that into two million?"

"Impossible. But we're going to try. Feel lucky?"

"Not really," I said. "You never counted on luck so far as I can tell."

"Luck is fickle. We'll only do it if I bend the luck in our favor."

"You mean cheat?" Andrew and I'd had this exact conversation before, and I already knew what he'd say.

"No, observe what's really happening, not what we think should be happening. That always bends the odds in your favor," he said.

"Any ideas?"

"Not yet. You should look for an opportunity too."

"How much will you give to back me?" I asked.

"Half." I nodded. Then he changed the topic. "Have you met your cousin Luigi?"

Luigi was the son of the only son of Andrew who didn't visit the house. We were both twenty-three. Luigi had recently gotten a job at the giant brokerage house "SSH," Smyth, Symington and Harrison, the rival of my company, the financial giant "OH," O'Brian, Halston and Irving.

"We met and quarreled," I said.

"You promised to make friends. Why did you fight?"

"He's a Red Sox fan and I'm a Yankee fan."

Andrew sneered, "That's nothing."

"That's everything. He insulted my team." I explained to Andrew that we'd made a bet on which team would finish in first place. If Boston won, I'd have to wear a Red Sox shirt for a week and if the Yankees won, Luigi would have to wear a Yankee's shirt.

Andrew started to laugh. I knew he was going to make a caustic comment, so I continued, "And he's Buddhist and I'm Catholic.

The loser would also have to read one of the scriptures of the other religion."

"No reason not to get along. You might learn something," Andrew said.

"What could I learn from a Buddhist?"

"Now you know everything? I always wanted to meet such a person. You can learn from every person you meet. Start seeing with your eyes and hearing with your ears and not muddling everything up with your preconceived notions."

"But my religious notions are true," I said.

"I'm sure Luigi thinks the same of his. You said you'd bring Luigi here."

"His parents didn't want him to come to this house."

"Then I'll take the train and see the two of you."

"You never come to Brooklyn."

"Haven't gone in over twenty years but I will, to see Luigi."

We agreed on a visit next Saturday around 6 P.M. I didn't tell Luigi because I wasn't sure he'd meet Grandfather anywhere.

Luigi and I met at a restaurant for an early supper. I'd intentionally lost a bet and promised to take him to any restaurants near Carroll Gardens. He picked an expensive Chinese restaurant. When we entered, Andrew was sitting at a table. Luigi didn't recognize him, of course. Andrew said he'd be glad to buy us dinner.

I introduced them. Luigi said his parents had told him to avoid Andrew.

"Did they tell you why?" I asked.

"Not a word," said Luigi.

"Let's pretend we're strangers and met by accident. Call me Andrew. I've never had Chinese food. Maybe you could make a suggestion."

Luigi, whose mother was from China, looked a little mischievous. He ordered tea and said a few words to the waiter in Chinese. "I ordered something really special for you, Andrew."

We chatted a bit and, about five minutes later, a very strange looking dish on a small plate was put in front of Andrew. I wouldn't have eaten it.

"I'm not going to try chopsticks yet," Andrew said. He picked up a fork and knife, cut the food in two and put half of it in his mouth.

Luigi smiled wickedly.

Andrew bit down, his eyes bulged a bit, he chewed and swallowed. "Excellent," he said. "Would you like to try some, Eric or Luigi?"

I said no. Luigi shook his head vigorously, "No."

Andrew ate the other half. "Excellent. What was it?"

"Your first taste of jellied duck's feet."

"Have you ever eaten brijole?" Andrew asked.

"No. What is it?" asked Luigi.

"Pig skin in sauce."

"Sounds horrible," said Luigi.

"I love it," said Andrew.

The ice was broken, Luigi ordered three main dishes and we talked contentedly.

The dishes arrived. Andrew asked to be shown how to use chopsticks. After a few false starts, he got the hang of it. I tried and again failed, going back to using my knife and fork.

Both Luigi and I had joined our respective consultant-only softball teams. Luigi started to talk about the softball rivalry between the employee's teams of the major financial houses. These were eight well-established, well-coached employee teams, the pride of their companies. The championship game was shown on TV, Channel 12 WPIY. In the past four years, OH and SSH had each won two championships. They played for a million- dollar prize that would be paid by the losing team to the charity picked by the winning team. Andrew's eyes lit up.

"Have you ever played them?"

I said, "My consultant team played the employee OH team. We

lost 37 to 2. I think they let up on us towards the end."

"That's an awful lot of runs. Why so many?" asked Andrew.

I said, "It's slow pitch softball. The ball has to make an arc of six feet. Makes it much easier to hit."

"That doesn't explain how you lost so badly," said Andrew.

"There are three thousand employees at OH and less than sixty consultants. That gives them a tremendous advantage plus each team must play three girls at all times. There are a lot of women employees but extremely few women consultant programmers. They have a huge advantage."

Luigi said, "When my consultant team played the employee SSH team, we lost 23 to 1. We heard it from the winners. One said, 'Why don't you put the words pond scum on your uniforms?' "

"That's what they call us at OH too. I didn't think they did that at SSH."

"Why don't you get up another charity game for a million and have the consultants challenge the employees? Maybe they'd put that on TV too," said Andrew.

"They'd slaughter us, and we don't have that kind of money," I said.

"Maybe you'd only need to put up a smaller portion. They'd probably give you ten to one odds. After all, one has to take into account the risk involved. They'll know they're going to beat you and might bet a good deal more than you because it wouldn't cost them anything," said Andrew.

"What are you suggesting?" Luigi asked.

"A friendly wager. Maybe it could be arranged," said Andrew.

"Not likely," Luigi said.

I was surprised when Andrew looked at Luigi and said, "Life is very mysterious. Who would ever have expected we'd become friends so fast?"

I was noticing that Andrew was speaking with much less of an accent then I was used to. I wondered why but didn't ask.

Andrew asked Luigi what he did at SSH.

"I work in the IPO department," Luigi said.

"What's that?"

"Initial public offerings. It's when a company first goes public. There can be huge swings in prices. Our company brings them out and tries to set a fair price and give reasonable advice to our clients as to the prospects for the company," said Luigi.

"Must be a lot of secrets there."

"I don't hear secrets, I'm working on computerizing the accounting. I'm sure there are people who know things, but I don't."

"You say you publish opinions. Who gives these opinions?" asked Andrew.

"Tell me about their ages and how long they've been doing it," asked Andrew.

"Two are in their thirties and have been doing it about ten years but there's one who is sixty-eight and has been doing it for fifty years," said Luigi.

"That's since before the great depression."

"I guess so."

"What's his name?"

"Aaron Jacobsen."

"He's Jewish too. There was a great prejudice against Jews back then. He must have been very good for them to keep him so long. Bring me all his write-ups and recommendations for the past ten years and what happened to the stock prices."

Luigi said he could easily do that. Friday night, I brought Andrew over two thousand boring pages for seven hundred IPOs. Along with price projections and the actual price after three years of issue.

On the train ride, I looked through them. There was a system of grading, strong buy, buy, hold, and sell. All the initial offerings had either a strong buy or buy recommendation. I wondered if there was much difference. I looked up ten in each category. At the end of three years, 18 of the 20 stocks had made money and the buys actually did slightly better than the strong buys. Nothing there.

After the buy or strong rating, Aaron gave a one-sentence wrap up, saying that it was either "inevitable" or "indubitable" that the stock would make a worthwhile amount of money. Again, I checked and there was only the slightest difference over three years. Good luck to Andrew, I thought. He'd have to figure it out, not me. But what did he know of high finance? Not much, I assumed.

When I got to work on Monday, I started to think about how our consultant team could get a charity game against the employee team. There were two consulting companies, mine, Spectrum, and one headed by my rival Bruce. Obviously, the two consulting companies would have to put up a stake for the bet to proceed. If we could get the ten to one odds, we'd need to put up a hundred thousand.

I had twenty thousand from Andrew and a few thousand of my own. My company refused to take part, so I offered to put up the entire fifty if our company would say they were sponsoring the prize.

"Why not?" said our leader. "We'll get some publicity, and you'll take the risk."

I wrote him a check for fifty thousand to be deposited only if we lost. If we lost, I was on my way to jail.

I'd done Bruce a huge favor, cancelling most of his gambling debt. I asked that he help set up the bet. Bruce told me that my favor was worth a great deal less than fifty thousand dollars, but he talked to the head of his company and they tentatively agreed to put up their fifty thousand, if we could get the game on TV and if Bruce said he thought we had a chance of winning. At that point Bruce was pretty sure we'd lose, so it was a no go.

It was June 27 and Bruce, Luigi and I went to see the Yankees versus the Tigers. The Yankee pitcher, Ron Guidry, had a great game, struck out eighteen and only allowed four hits and no runs.

"If we had a pitcher like Guidry, our softball team might win," I said.

"He'll never pitch for you," said Luigi.

"Or if we had a great designated hitter, that would help too," suggested Bruce.

"If we were the home team, couldn't we specify something about how the game was played? They'd have to follow our rule, right?" I asked.

In the next few days, Bruce told his company's co-owner, that we would find a fantastic pitcher to give us a shot at winning. And if the game were on TV it would be good publicity. They agreed to put up their fifty thousand.

The captain of the OH employee team was Ryland, who happened to be two levels up in both of our management chains. Bruce had talked to him extensively and I had only casually met him.

On Monday, Bruce and I went to Ryland's office. On his wall hung a mace, that medieval weapon of a spiked ball. He also had pictures of him holding the winning check for a million dollars made to his favorite charity.

Bruce proposed we play and disclosed the terms. We'd bet our hundred thousand versus their million. Their charity versus ours.

"Why should you only have to put up so little?" Ryland asked.

"The score was 37 to 2 last time. What's the odds we'll win? It's easy money for you. How much chance would you say we had?" asked Bruce.

There was a very thick piece of wood on the wall that had many gouges. Ryland took the mace, swung it over his head and said, "You'd have about as much chance as if there was a mouse on this piece of wood" and he smashed the mace into the wood." I'm going to hit a few home runs like that against your pathetic team. We're in."

"There's only one other stipulation. We get to be the home team," said Bruce.

'You want last licks. No problem," said Ryland.

"It will be like the National and American League. Maybe we'll have a designated hitter."

"No problem. Do you want to use a DH's or not?"

"We'll let you know at the start of the game," I said. It was the first words I said.

The bosses signed a contract on the terms specified. OH only asked for one change. If the game were tied after seven innings, both OH and the consultants would donate their money to charity. I hadn't thought of that, but it made sense. If I was to stay out of jail, we needed to win. OH wanted some good publicity so they bought three hours of time on Channel 12, WPIY to have the game broadcast.

The next day, Bruce and I discussed how the hell are we going to win this thing? Bruce wasn't that worried since he had no financial interest in the outcome.

I suggested that we try to see if we could improve our odds. On Saturday morning, Bruce and I started to tour baseball diamonds in Prospect Part looking for either a pitcher or a hitter to even things up a bit.

"And if you find him?" asked Bruce.

"We'll offer him fame, to be on TV," I said.

"He won't be a programmer. How will he do the work?" Bruce objected. "That will never work."

"Sure it would," I said. " No one has any idea what they're doing the first few weeks on the job. They can fake it. We can handle it."

"Sounds risky," Bruce said.

"Any better suggestion?" I asked.

"None."

There wasn't much happening so early. There were a few men playing baseball throwing curveballs and fastballs. A couple of the pitchers were impressive, so we went out to talk to them asking if they played softball. "Softball is for kids or girls" was the general response. Bruce and I decided to give up on getting a baseball pitcher.

We wandered on and came to where three girls were practicing.

There was a big, tall white girl, with a long ponytail catching and a moderately built, lanky black woman with an Afro with blonde highlights pitching. Next to her was a short, thin, long straight dark haired, Asian woman. They all looked to be in their very early twenties.

The black girl threw underhand, and fast. She threw from five different arm angles and could throw any pitch from any angle. Her pitches curved and dogged left and right, up and down. It was like watching a baseball pitcher throw a curve, a fastball, a slider, a changeup, a screwball and a dead fish all from different arm angles.

Neither Bruce nor I had ever seen anything like this before. We played in a slow pitch league where the ball had to be arced up 6 feet and fall in a very regular pattern.

Bruce and I looked at each other and smiled.

After the black girl threw about thirty pitches, the Asian woman took over. Her pitching motion was even faster whipping the ball in. She didn't have as great a variety of pitches or arm angles, but she had enough and the speed was incredible. Do you know the old song "How do you keep them down on the farm, once they've seen Paris?" Bruce and I had just seen Paris.

"Women," I called out. They ignored me. "Women, please can we bat against you?"

"Little boys. Get out of here. We're busy," said the black girl.

"Let us bat against you," Bruce asked.

"Are you kidding?" asked the Asian girl. "If either of you can even touch the ball when I pitch, I'll give you a big kiss right on the lips."

"And if either of you can touch one of my pitches, I'll give you two kisses," said the black girl.

"Get ready for some kissing," I said.

The catcher just giggled. "Boys and I do mean boys. Try it. I'll give each of you three kisses, if either one of you even touches one of their pitches."

"I'm Carlton Fisk," said Bruce as he stepped into the batter's box.

A pitch came in and Carlton, or should I say Bruce, kept the bat on his shoulder as the pitch screamed over the plate.

"Strike one," said the black girl.

"I didn't see anything. I just heard something go by," said Bruce.

The next pitch curved to the right and again Carlton, who told me later he wasn't looking at the pitch but at her arm, to make sure he swung, swung and missed the pitch by a foot.

"Strike two," said the catcher.

"Hey Carlton, you don't usually miss when you play at Fenway," I teased him.

"Get ready," the pitcher said. "I'll make this one easier." Bruce must have seen it because he swung just where the ball seemed to be, but it wasn't there when the bat crossed the plate. Another clean miss.

"Strike three," said the black girl. "No kisses for you. You man enough to try?" she asked me.

"I'm not one of these wimpy Red Sox, I'm Greg Nettles," I said. "I never strike out."

"You're cute enough to give one kiss to but I promised you two, so you'll have to earn it," said the Asian girl.

Her first pitch came in. It looked straight. It wasn't. I swung right at it and clean missed it.

"Nettles isn't having a good day," said the catcher.

Bruce was laughing. "You look even worse than me."

The next pitch also looked straight and I intentionally swung below it. Bruce said that I almost made contact.

"Strike two."

"Gave me an easy one," I said.

"Here's a cookie," she said.

She wound up and pitched. I could actually see the ball clearly; I swung. I wish I could say I hit it, even fouled it but I clean missed it.

"Strike Three. No kisses today," the girl on the mound said.

"Now beat it," said the catcher. "We have a lot of practicing to do. We can't waste our time on boys who can't hit."

That felt like a low blow, but I ignored it and asked if I could talk to them seriously for a few minutes. They weren't interested but then I asked if they'd like to play softball on TV before an audience of millions in order to win money to rebuild homes destroyed by the Italian earthquake. (I made the audience number up, but Andrew had advised me to talk big at times.)

They were interested and they told us their names. The black woman, who was named Satchel after the great Negro league pitcher, was really bi-racial. She had a black father and a white mother and had grown up only a few blocks from the park. "I've seen things no one else sees. Both sides of the coin as it's tossed in the air spinning with joy and dread and hits on the edge and starts to roll." I had no idea what that meant but it was poetic, and I liked it.

The Asian woman was named Jasmine and her parents had come from Korea after the war. The white woman was from Iowa and had come to New York to attend NYU and was named Maisy.

They became interested in helping us.

Bruce asked, "How did you get so good?"

"You don't know anything about fast pitch softball, do you?" Satchel demanded.

"Nothing at all," Bruce said.

"Nothing for me either," I said.

"How typical. It's almost completely unknown except by people who play it but the greatest pitchers of all time played it," said Jasmine.

"It's true," said Satchel. "Most acknowledge that Satchel Paige was the greatest baseball pitcher ever. But he had nothing on Eddie Feigner. Ever heard of him?"

"Nope," said Bruce.

"He threw a softball, underhand, faster than any professional baseball pitcher ever threw a pitch. He struck out Willie Mays, Roberto Clemente, Brooks Robinson, Willie McCovey, Maury Wills and Harmon Killebrew in a row."

"Amazing," I said. "Are you already on a team?"

"We're going for a tryout for a professional team, in three weeks," said Maisy.

"Our games in two. We desperately need the pitching," said Bruce.

"You'll need me to catch them. You don't think either of you two could?" asked Maisy.

The three women had daytime jobs, making less than we would pay them as programmers. We always had at least a few openings, so we brought them in as programming consultants. They protested that they didn't know anything about programming. We assured them their work would be done for them in such a way that they could easily get by pretending to have done it. It's only for two weeks.

Bruce and I would work a few hours to do Jasmine's and Satchel's work. Luigi volunteered to help Maisy pass as a programmer.

Our consulting company worked at OH's headquarters, a building put up during the depression with the purpose of impressing all those who entered. It had a Rococo lobby with a twenty-five foot ceiling. When we came in the first day with Satchel, she said, "What an amazing place you work. This will be a step up for all of us."

We took them to human resources to register, also a richly re-decorated floor.

We took them to where the consultants work. It was a dump. Peeling paint, carpets with holes, tiny cubicles, decrepit furniture. It looked like it hadn't been maintained in thirty years.

"Why do you put up with this BS?" Satchel asked. "You're like slaves in here."

"They call us Pond Scum but don't make a fuss," I said. "You have to pretend you really need this job."

"I don't. I'm going to be a professional softball pitcher."

"Not for at least three weeks," I said.

She sat with me in my cubicle. As I've said before, the overwhelming number of programmers are male, many not used to interacting with women. The other male consultants came around to talk to Satchel. She'd dismiss them, claiming she had too much work to do. "If you don't let me do my work, I'll disclose your darkest secret," she said to the few who wouldn't leave her alone.

One asked what was his darkest secret?

"You're desperate for a taste of sugar."

He walked off and stayed away.

After work, Maisy, Jasmine and Satchel would join our practice. The rules for fast-pitch were a little different, but we weren't going to allow any changes to the rules besides allowing fast pitching. The three helped us improve our teams hitting and fielding. With them, I thought we'd at least have a chance to win.

There was only one time when I thought our plan would unravel. My boss, Susan, had long tried to get rid of the consultants and replace them with employees, especially ones she didn't like. She was the one to tell us exactly what she wanted done but she made it hard on the consultants by constantly changing the volume and intonation of her voice, going from very loud to almost inaudible, leaving about half of what she said indecipherable. She'd then blame the listener for not understanding.

She tried this with Satchel, who rolled her eyes and asked, "Do you have a speech impediment or are you trying to intimidate me because I'm black?"

Susan indignantly answered, in a loud even, understandable voice saying that she spoke correctly and meant no disrespect.

Satchel said, "Now I see that you can speak normally. Please keep it up."

Susan, with a red face, told Satchel clearly and exactly what needed to be done in her program. It was one of the few times a consultant was treated fairly by Susan.

Three days before the game, I went to see Andrew. He was still working through the data I'd given him and the constant IPO updates provided by Luigi. He'd given twenty thousand dollars to his church as a donation and the priest was going to allow him to invest it in anyway he saw fit, the whole amount to go for earthquake relief.

"If Aaron Jacobsen has a secret, I've not found it," said Andrew We were sitting at the dining room table with my Aunt Mary. She'd made coffee and we were munching on some of the remaining Saint Joseph Puffs that she made for certain holidays. They're fried little spherical cookies covered with honey. Heaven. They are a great favorite and usually went very fast.

"We'll all be there at the game," said Aunt Mary. My parents and others were going to drive most of my aunts, uncles and cousins to cheer us on.

"Except for me. I've got to continue my research," said Andrew.

"But you're the one who should get most of the credit for the idea," I said.

"I don't want credit," he said.

In the two weeks before the game, we had to do something about our consultant uniforms. The employee team uniforms wore expensive and well designed. They called their team the Lions and they had a large lion on the back, just below their number.

Our consulting company uniforms were cheap but, for this game, they spent extra to equip us in a style that didn't flash "cheapskate." We took the name of Ones and Zeroes, after the binary system used on computers, and placed the name on the back of our uniforms. Satchel suggested that, as an internal unifying gesture, to have the letters PS, standing for pond scum, embroidered on the left butt cheek of the uniform. A few noticed and asked questions and we'd answer that it stood for "proud scorer." The team was united in one thing; the pond scum were going to get revenge on the field, in front of a huge TV audience.

The seven-inning game was set for two o'clock, played on a softball field in Prospect Park. WPIY had a crew there and both sides agreed that, to save broadcast time, Oscar, the WPIY producer, would make the final decisions in case of any disagreements. At 1:45, the lineup cards were exchanged. Bruce said that, as the home team, we were going to be following our team's rules.

Ryland, the employee's team captain, agreed. "We've come up with a designated hitter too."

"That isn't the rule we're changing," said Bruce. "We're going to play by the current rules but allow fast pitching."

"We never agreed to that," protested Ryland.

"What do you say Oscar?" asked Bruce.

Oscar thought for a second and asked, "You played slow-pitch before. What was the score?"

Ryland said, "We won 35 to 2."

"The audience will turn off the game after an inning. Let's do fast pitch. It might at least be interesting,"

And so we played fast pitch.

Ryland protested again. "We put up more money. We should set the rules."

"Home team sets the rules. Fast pitch," said Oscar. "Now play ball."

Satchel pitched and Jasmine played short. We planned to switch them periodically to keep them fresh and to confuse the other team. Maisy caught. The three women were the best hitters, so Jasmine batted fourth, Maisy fifth and Satchel sixth. Bruce batted seventh and I batted ninth.

Out we jogged and took the field. I played third and Bruce played left field.

Satchel's first pitch whipped in. The Lion batter didn't swing, didn't even move. Strike one called the umpire.

Ryland went up to the umpire and said, "We will protest this game."

"Play ball," was the only reply.

Satchel struck out the side in order. She had a different arm angle for each batter.

When we came up to bat, we were surprised that the Lion pitcher was pitching much faster than in previous games. It was obvious he wasn't a trained fast pitch softball pitcher, but he'd pitched in enough games, and had enough force to get our first three batters out. We had one strike out, one ball hit back to the pitcher and one slowly hit to short. The pitcher was a bit wilder than in our previous game and we'd gotten to one full count. Not so bad, I thought. We had completed an inning and were still in the game, not like last time where we were down seven to zero after one inning.

Jasmine pitched the second inning. We didn't want The Lions to get used to either pitcher. The ball whipped by even faster than Satchel's, but with less variety. One player did hit the ball softly back to Jasmine, who threw the batter out.

In the bottom of the second, Jasmine was up first. She lined a clean single to right field. Maisy got up and lined a rocket to short right field. The Lions were very talented fielders and held the runners to first and second. Satchel walked on four pitches. We had bases loaded. The next two batters, including Bruce, struck out. I got to a full count, but I grounded very weakly to the pitcher, who threw me out. The score was still zero to zero.

There was no scoring until the sixth when Maisy hit a home run. We were up one to nothing.

In the seventh and final inning. Satchel struck the first two batters out. The next batter got to a full count, fouling off three pitches in a row. We changed pitchers and Jasmine whipped the ball in. It was inside for a walk. The batter went to first. The next batter was Ryland. The pitch came in fast. Ryland swung the bat like he'd swung the mace in his office and hit the ball so far it might still be traveling. It was a two home run. He pumped his fists as he circled the bases and was mobbed by his teammates when he scored. They were sure they'd beaten us. I was afraid they had too. I was wondering what it was like in a jail cell. The next batter grounded to me and I threw him out.

We were down two to one, with only three more outs. Our number three batter was up first and hit a single. Was the Lion's pitcher tiring? I hoped so. Jasmine singled, sending the runner to third. Maisy singled, scoring the first batter. It was now a tied game two to two.

We were going to get the money for earthquake relief, but for the game to end in a tie was as bad for me, as a loss because both teams would have to pay their charities. They'd try to cash my check, it would bounce and I'd go to jail. I was thinking of where I might hide.

But there was hope. We still had Satchel up. She hit the ball hard, but it was like a swinging bunt. The employee pitcher came off the mound, picked up the ball, looked Jasmine back to third, threw to first but was too late to get Satchel. It was bases loaded, no outs. The pitcher bore down. He struck out both Bruce and the next batter, going to two balls on the first and one on Bruce.

Then I came up. The first pitch was right over the plate. I swung and missed. The next ball was way inside, and I dove out of the way. The next pitch caught the inside corner of the plate. I didn't swing but now had two strikes against me. I was in a panic. I hadn't got a hit, not even hit the ball solidly; no one had except for Satchel, Maisy and Jasmine.

The count was one ball, two strikes. I didn't see any chance of getting a walk. If I struck out, I'd be finished. As I waited, time seemed to slow down. The next pitch was again inside. I jumped back quickly, and an image came into my head and, as my feet went back, I intentionally bent and leaned my body forward almost bending over. I heard a bang and felt pain. The ball hit me right in the helmet and I fell to the ground.

"Take your base," said the umpire. Jasmine was forced in. Bruce helped me up and I slowly walked to first.  We won three to two.

Our team and fans exploded in joy

My extended family and fans hugged me.

Oscar at WPIY called for order.

The Italian ambassador was at the game and a senior OH official presented him with a check for a million dollars.

WPIY interviewed Satchel. As I listened, I was horrified by what she said. "OH mistreats its consultants, keeping them in a slum within a beautifully appointed building." A media consultant from OH wanted to deny what Satchel said but the TV time had run out.

That night, our team had a team only party. Luigi was invited in because he had helped so much. We drank a lot. Bruce, Luigi and I were called over by Maisy, Jasmine and Satchel.

"I think I promised you a kiss if you got a hit," Satchel said to me. She kissed me long full on the lips.

"I think I promised you two if you got a hit," Jasmine said to Bruce.

"I didn't get a hit," he said.

Jasmine said, "No protests allowed" and kissed him twice full on the lips.

"And I think I promised you three," Maisy said to me, "but your cousin helped me so much and he's cute and hasn't had a kiss yet." She gave Luigi three deep kisses. Luigi looked to be in love.

"What's got into you three?" asked Bruce.

Satchel smiled. "A representative of the professional team was at the game. She told us in the sixth inning that we'd made her team."

"Is that why you complained to WPIY about the consultant's condition?" I asked Satchel.

"'I would have done that in any event," she said.

The team talked, danced and drank.

That was the last I ever talked to those three wonderful persons. They were on the Tampa Tigers, who were league champions three years in a row. I did hear that Satchel was invited to the 1983

All Star game and before the game challenged Gary Carter, Tim Raines, Dale Murphy, Jim Rice, Rod Carew and Dave Winfield to bat against her. She struck them all out. Maybe it's an urban legend but it wouldn't surprise me if it were true.

About two months later, "OH" started to re-decorate the area the consultants worked in. Satchel had shamed them into doing the right thing. A spokesman said the update was planned a long time ago but, in my mind, it was Satchel who made them do it.

I talked to Andrew on the telephone the next day. He congratulated me. I asked him how his plans were going but he only said, "Time will tell."

"So you figured it out."

"Maybe," he said.

About eight months passed. Andrew said nothing about his financial activities, but we continued to send him all the public information on IPOs that he requested. Luigi called me one morning and asked if I'd read the Long Island Investigator Newspaper? I hadn't. "Did you know that a church on Long Island just donated a little over a million dollars to Italian earthquake relief? "

"Was it Saint Paul's church?" I asked.

"Yes. How did you know?"

'Just a hunch," I said. Luigi was puzzled but I didn't enlighten him.

I called up Andrew to congratulate him. He didn't explain how he had done it.

A week later a police investigator came to my desk at work, took me to a conference room and questioned me. He said I could have a lawyer. I didn't want one. He asked if I was passing secret information to Andrew. I denied it. I told him how I had collected public published information and given it to Andrew. The investigator looked dubious but didn't arrest me.

That afternoon, Luigi called me to say he had been questioned also and had also denied giving any secret information to Andrew.

I got a call from Aunt Mary, who was frantic. A policeman had brought Andrew down to the station and they were searching the house. Andrew had requested that she call me to handle this problem.

Mary said that they took away all the reports Andrew had accumulated along with some notes and an Italian English dictionary.

Luigi and I went out to the house. It had taken this kind of crisis for him to break a promise to his parents never to go. We went with Mary to the station and waited for five hours. When they released Andrew, we went to a diner and he told us what happened.

"I insisted on being interviewed in Italian and used my thickest accent. I didn't want a lawyer. They asked me how in the world I could have made so many big winning trades in a row without insider information?"

They knew I had no known dealings with organized crime, so they ruled out that possibility. Then they started talking about you two must have given me insider information.

"So I told them how it really happened," Andrew said " I would read the IPO report, get down on my knees and pray for guidance, saying, Mary, Joseph, Jesus, please help me. If Mary or Jesus said something, I ignored them. They are the greatest of saints but not people interested in making money. But if, Saint Joseph answered my prayer and recommended a stock, I'd listen. He is both a great saint and a practical man. He had to find the money to keep his family together. The investigator looked at me as if I was a lunatic but they couldn't break that story because it is absolutely true. 100 percent true."

I was starting to think Andrew was cracked but I knew he'd only tell me what really happened if he were in the mood. About a month later, I was at the house, late at night. Everyone but Andrew and I were asleep.

Andrew began, "You looked at me like I was crazy. Let me tell you exactly what happened. I told the police the whole truth that

Saint Joseph had told me how to invest. They thought I was just an ignorant peasant. I'm not. Saint Joseph told me in a very special way and you're going to be the only person who hears it.

"I spent more than five hundred hours pouring over those stupid reports, trying to figure out what to do. I'd stay up late, smoke my pipe and looked at every word until I couldn't think any longer. I was going to give up and I said the old prayer, 'Jesus, Mary, Joseph, please help me.' I just sat there. No energy at all.

"Then I got a strong idea, almost an obsession to make a pot of coffee, relax, eat the very last of the Saint Joseph puffs. I put the other thoughts out of my mind and looked at the reports while eating the puffs. And there it was, once again, those words, 'indubitably,' and 'inevitable.' What do they mean really? I had thought of this a thousand times and never came up with an answer. What do they mean to you?" he asked me.

I answered that they both meant the same thing really. You're going to make money. A lot of it.

"That's what I kept thinking. I ate the last puff. Mary came in. I asked her if she was going to make more puffs soon.

"She smiled at me and said, 'As long as we're both alive, I'll inevitably make them for you.' She kissed me good night and went off to bed. I thought and thought. Would Mary have ever said indubitably? No, never. Neither in Italian or English. But she would have used the Italian expression for that word, which means, 'without a doubt.' 'Without a doubt' means absolutely yes, right now.

"But she had said 'inevitably.' What did it mean in this context? She wasn't going to make them now, but she would eventually. As long as she and I still lived, it was inevitable she'd make me some more of those glorious Saint Joseph puffs; sooner or later, just not now.

"I started to look again. On average, almost all the stocks eventually did about the same but the ones that Aaron said were inevitable often had very rocky starts and the ones that had indubitably usually did very well at first, fading a bit later. I had my answer. I bought all the new companies that Aaron said were "indubitably" going to go up and sold them right after the opening.

"And so, it really was Saint Joseph, and his mystical, magical puffs, that gave me the answer. So I just told the investigator it was Saint Joseph who had given me the answer. I would have confused him even more if I'd told him that Saint Joseph puffs had given me the answer."

I laughed.

"We both risked so much. Let's not do any betting for a long time," Andrew said.

I agreed.

The only thing left to tell about was how my bet with Luigi worked out. If you remember, the bet was that if the Red Sox won the pennant, I'd wear a Sox shirt for a week and, if the Yankees won, Luigi would wear a Yankees shirt for a week. The loser would also have to read the other's holy book.

You might remember that year that the Red Sox had a huge lead going into September and the Yankees caught up and there was a one game playoff in an afternoon game. Luigi and I took the afternoon off and watched the game from Ed's Bar and Grill. I had a Yankee Jersey in my briefcase, and I was sure Luigi had a Red Sox jersey in his, ready to make the other person wear it.

It was a close game. We'd cheer when our team did well and wince when the other team did better. It was tied and finally Bucky Dent hit a home run to win the game for the Yankees. I, and almost everyone else in the bar, started to cheer and jump around giving each other high fives. After a few minutes, I looked at Luigi, who looked to be repressing a tear from one eye.

"Give me that damn Yankee Jersey," he said, admitting defeat.

I took it out with pride. Then I thought of what Andrew always said, "Beat a man too much and collect and you might make an enemy for life. It's not worth it. Beat him and only collect a part and you'll make a friend."

Did I want Luigi to be my enemy or my friend? I wanted to rub it in, but I also remembered my promise to Andrew to make a friend of Luigi.

I took out the Yankee Jersey and started to hand it to Luigi. Then I took my hand back and put the jersey over my head.

"Let's forget about the first part of the bet. You can pay back that part by coming with me to visit Andrew. I brought you the Gospel of Matthew, you can read that, and I'll read whatever you brought. I handed him the Gospel."

He opened it, at random, and read out loud "Ask, and it will be given to you; seek and you will find; knock, and it will be opened to you."

"Pretty cool," said Luigi.

"Now let me read from yours," He handed me the Dhammapada. I opened to the first verse and read out loud, "You are what you think. All that you are arises from your thoughts. With your thoughts you make your world."

I looked at Luigi and said, "That's exactly what Andrew is always telling me."

Three weeks later, Luigi and I went to see Andrew. Aunt Mary brought in a huge plate of Saint Joseph puffs to celebrate the occasion.

Andrew joked with me, "So the inevitable has finally happened." Both Luigi and Mary looked at him quizzically, but I started to laugh.

Luigi ate a puff and said, "I love them. I've never tasted anything like them. Thank you for making them."

"Sure the hell beats brown rice and seaweed," I said.

"I like brown rice and seaweed," Luigi said.

"And I most heartily want to try it. Bring me some next time you come to visit," Andrew said.

"I'm not sure I should return. What will I tell my parents?" asked Luigi.

Andrew replied, "You'll have to figure out what to tell them. Maybe nothing at all but I'll tell both of you the secret to getting a girlfriend next time you come."

'Why not now?" I asked.

"It's been a long time since I was looking for one, so I'll need to review my notes and compress the knowledge to help you."

"You took notes?" asked Luigi.

"Of course," said Andrew. "Doesn't everyone take notes of their important discoveries?"

We both promised to come back.

"Don't forget to bring brown rice and seaweed. I want to try it," Andrew said.

"And next time, I'd like to try brijole," said Luigi.

"I don't often cook, but I'll make it myself," Andrew said.

"Maybe you'd better leave that to me," said Mary.

"Indubitably," said Andrew.

I fell to the floor laughing.

# MY TESTIMONY

Up until two months ago, I had never been in a police station. I was interrogated in a small drab office on the second floor, with a tiny barred window. The room smelled of sweat. The interrogation was much less dramatic than the police shows I sometimes watch because there was no background music playing. No, the drama was being created by what we were discussing, death, probably murder.

Now that I have your attention, I can introduce myself. My name is Margaret Ashley Gambina. I am going to write the truth. Since, I don't want to hurt anyone, I'll change the names of few of the people and institutions involved. Besides that, everything I write will be as true as I can describe it. I only have four days to write this testimony; so don't expect a perfectly told story.

I'll be long dead when you read this because this testimony will be placed in a time capsule in the Atlantic and Hudson Savings Bank in Brooklyn Heights for fifty years. I have only to finish typing this up and a dependable friend will deposit it without reading it. If you are reading this, I hope you gain something from it, as I intend to put all the wisdom and folly I've gained into it. I'll try not to bore you.

They'd left me alone in the interrogation room for over three hours. I thought maybe they thought if they kept me there long enough, waiting for food or a chance to pee that I'd confess. Eventually, in walked a short, squat man, with a flat face wearing a uniform and a tall, thin woman, with extremely short brown hair in civilian clothing. The interrogation began when Detective Joseph Jordan barked out, "The bottle of poison was found in your desk and your prints are on it. You gave Mr. Koshi a glass of whiskey, in front of twenty witnesses at the company party and he drank it. Traces of the poison were found in that glass. The glass had both yours and Mr. Koshi's fingerprints. You had a motive to kill Mr. Koshi. You hated him. Admit it. You killed him." His partner, Detective Adele Addison, sat silent.

It was two days after the office party at which Mr. Koshi had been poisoned.

"Of course I didn't do it," I said and laughed. "How could anyone believe something so absurd? Besides there were other fingerprints on that glass."

"How did you know?" asked Jordan.

"I was there. I have eyes. I can see."

"You're right. There were also the prints of Mr. Utsonameya. He was the one who put the glass aside when Mr. Koshi sat down and said he didn't feel well. Everyone saw you give Mr. Koshi the glass and ten people saw Mr. Utsonameya take the glass from Mr. Koshi. You hated him."

" Is that so?"

"What did you say? We know you hated him."

"Is that so? Can you read minds now?"

"Answer the question," demanded Jordan.

"I didn't like Mr. Koshi but neither did a lot of people. If everyone who was disliked by one person were murdered, there'd be no one left. You'd be a goner for sure. How could I get the poison? I don't even know what he died of."

"You're a Gambino. Of course you could get poison and I believe you're capable of it. Your whole family is criminal," said Jordan.

That was an absurd accusation. My father, Anthony, made it a point of pride to obey even insignificant laws. He'd never even jaywalked, something all New Yorkers do habitually. We never go near that distant end of the family, those who have an "O" at the end of their names instead of an "A" and who were often reported, sometimes falsely, to be involved in organized crime. For some reason, many people think that someone who has a name like mine has to be crooked.

"I'm not part of the Gambino's, I'm a Gambina. You must know that. Don't you check out any facts before you start accusing people?" I looked at Jordan as if he were an idiot.

Detective Adele Addison asked Detective Jordan to get us all coffee.

"Make it tea, good Japanese green tea if you have it," I said. Jordan shook his head. I knew I had made an impossible request and enjoyed it. I had to show them my strength. I knew he'd come back with coffee, which he eventually did.

Detective Adele Addison tried a different approach. She smiled at me as if we were friends.

"Jordan's a bull dog. He never believes what people tell him but I'll believe you. If you can give me a convincing explanation of how that vial got into your desk, I'd believe it."

I liked Addison. She listened and she was right in calling Jordan a bulldog and, to my mind, a simpleton. It felt good to be told that she'd believe me.

The truth was I could have gotten poison from some distant cousin. Fact was, both she and Jordan believed I had poisoned Mr. Koshi, Senior Vice President of the American branch of the powerful Japanese bank, The K. Industrial Bank, which had its main American office on Wall Street.

The poisoning had taken place at the bank's monthly staff party in the main conference room, converted to host a party. The long teak table was moved against one wall and covered with food, drink, glasses and plates. Folding chairs were put against the other wall, which had several very large, full-length mirrors on it. On one side of the room were windows with a few plants on the sills. There was an area where people could dance, which only began after people got completely loosened up.

No one ever explained to me why the company had these parties. In fact, working at a Japanese bank was difficult because nothing was ever explained; you were expected to already know. There are strict codes governing every aspects of Japanese life that the Japanese had absorbed while growing up and that I had no idea about. I always imagined the parties were designed to foster the idea that we are all comrades; all in this together, all essentially equal.

Yes, we were in it together but the idea that we were equal couldn't be further from the truth. Japanese society, especially banks have a strict hierarchical structure and the K. Bank was no exception. You knew exactly where you fit in the structure and being a relatively young America woman, I had three strikes against me. My status was so low that if I looked way up, I'd see one of the Japanese manager's ankles.

Why did I work at a job where I was so unimportant? My father had been a Japanese prisoner in World War Two and to say that he hated the Japanese with an undying passion wouldn't go far enough. To him, they were beasts, not human beings. I love my father and believed his stories of the horrors he had experienced but I felt there must be more to the Japanese culture than cruelty. I assumed they were flawed but human, much like myself, and I wanted to prove it to myself and possibly to him. Against his wishes, I joined the bank to try to find out the truth of the matter.

As I said, the bank was extremely formal. You might wonder how the Japanese blew off steam? At our bank, the answer was simple, they drank. Usually, not from nine to six but afterwards, they drank heavily and often. The Japanese men, at our bank, always drank The Famous Grouse whiskey. Many nights, when I stayed late, the bottle would come out and heavy drinking would begin. Things lightened up quickly. When they were drunk, underlings could insult their bosses and all they had to say the next day was that they were drunk, and they would be forgiven. But was all forgiven? I would have found it difficult to forgive if harsh words were directed at me but, not being Japanese, I was never sure if they truly forgave or not.

I don't know if you have ever been to one of these parties. If you're invited go, if you hear of one, beg an invitation. They were the most convivial parties I've ever attended. My rank was so low that I was almost invisible and I could do anything I wanted to.

I'm not embarrassed by what I did at the parties but I am surprised at my reaction as I write this. I worry you might think less of me. Silly isn't it? Will my admission make you doubt my story? I hope not but I'll be dead, so it really doesn't matter. Here goes.

I would look for one of the Japanese men sitting on a chair, say Mr. Haki. I'd go up and talk to him and then I would sit on his lap, one leg on either side of his legs, facing him and try to kiss him on the lips or at least rub my nose on his. He would frantically move his face from one side to the other to avoid my kiss and I would follow his lips, always trying to kiss him.

He couldn't kiss me because he, like all the male managers, was married and thus kissing me was improper. He couldn't shove me off either, because that would be rude and Japanese men, at these parties anyway, were never rude to the women employees. I thought that what I did was only fair. I was constantly in a position where I couldn't do anything right, so now I put the Japanese managers in exactly the same situation where they couldn't do anything right.

There were over twenty men in our computer department and I

was the only woman until Yuri (which means Lilly) Katanga joined our team fifteen months ago. She had recently graduated from college, joined the bank in Japan, and a few years later been assigned to the American branch.

Lilly was stunningly beautiful. Tall for a Japanese woman, with a small, slightly turned up nose, high cheekbones and fine, thin lips. She had long silky, straight, lustrous black hair, which she would wear, at work, formally up in a sort of bun. She and I would always be the first to dance at the parties. She'd let her hair down, shake her head and her beautiful hair flew this way and that.

The other employees treated me kindly but, when Lilly joined the team, she went out of her way to make me feel welcome and introduce me to her culture. I owe so much to her. Right before she arrived, I had been going through the most trying period of my life, having an operation and chemotherapy for ovarian cancer. I almost didn't feel like a woman any longer having lost so many of the opportunities I craved. My hair and eyebrows fell out and were slowly growing back. I must have looked like a monster when I was bald and sitting on the men's laps, trying to kiss them during that period of time. I was glad when my hair completely grew back. The nausea of the therapy had been awful and I'd lost weight, no longer being chronically overweight but now somewhat gaunt.

Other people tried to soothe me but I could hear pity in their voice and a hint of happiness that it had happened to me and not them and this irritated me. With Lilly there was naturalness to her response that was a balm to my wound. When I was with her, I felt that she treated me as she treated everyone else, each person equally valued, important and to be cherished. Cherished not because of our personal characteristics but because we existed. Plus for me, Lilly embodied the ability to move from the formal to the informal with perfect ease and knowledge of herself and the people around her. Perhaps, some of this was idol worship but I sincerely longed to be like her.

A few weeks after she arrived, she invited me and two other Japanese girls, her age, to participate in a tea ceremony. The three of them wore traditional clothing; I was in my regular clothes. Lilly said I was the most honored guest, being the oldest and therefore the most important and most respected.

The ceremony started by Lilly bowing to us followed by our bowing to her. She went through the formal steps of purifying the utensils and cups, putting the green tea powder into the china cups and pouring boiling water in and then using a whisk to whip the tea. It was so peaceful and formal, yet friendly. I felt something special, timeless.

I later learned that the ceremony was related to an inner spiritual experience of humility, simplicity. It was the beginning of my closer view of the more personal, intimate part of the Japanese as if what I had seen before was their brittle, prickly alabaster exterior that covered a hidden softer, warmer center.

Exploring further I discovered that the ceremony was related to the study of Zen Buddhism. There are two main schools, Soto and Rinzai. Rinzai is sometimes said to be for the Samurai's and Soto for the peasants. I thought of myself as a warrior so I chose Rinzai. I found a somewhat less formal Zendo and began to practice.

I learned the sitting meditation and the fast walking meditation. During sitting meditation, if one fell asleep or moved around, a designated person would hit you with a stick to wake you up. At first I thought this was humiliating but soon realized how much it helped me to concentrate. I began by counting and following the breath followed by studying Koans, those strange and mysteriously impossible puzzles. There are a great many of them, the most famous that everyone quotes is "What is the sound of one hand clapping?" That one, even though overused, was to have great meaning for me.

It is a tradition to be interviewed by the Roshi (teacher) and asked to repeat the Koan and your answer. To me, this seemed both immensely serious and incredibly silly. I had to give a serious answer to a seemingly impossible or gibberish question. Except the Koan's weren't gibberish or impossible, they just appeared to be. Thinking of the Koans reminded me of looking at myself. My life was serious, important, flawed and to many, including myself, often mysterious and sometimes funny.

I asked the Roshi's wife, named Suzzi, if she knew the answer to all the Koans? As I expected, she never answered my question. I teased her about not sleeping with Mr. Roshi, if he didn't tell her the secrets. When he travelled, she would conduct the interviews with students, so she obviously knew the answers. I had most of my interviews with her.

At the interview, I always gave her a funny answer first and then a serious one, the one I knew probably was wrong but might be going in the right direction. It wasn't until I said, "Let's just enjoy the day, good day to you" that she smiled and said we seemed to be getting someplace.

Almost every day, Lilly would spend a few minutes teaching me Japanese ways and the Japanese language so I could fit in better. We never discussed our personal lives but I felt a very deep bond between us.

Working at this Japanese bank was different than working at other American jobs. It wasn't true for American employees like me, but the Japanese employees got to work around 9 AM, put their heads on their desk and slept till around 3 PM. They then lifted their heads and started to work. They often worked until 1 or 2 AM, the next morning.

Over the years, when there were computer problems, I was there at 1 AM to see my Japanese colleagues, bow low and ask the boss, "May I please, go home now?" These requests were rarely refused. The employee would bow again and say, with humility, "Thank you Mr. Utsonameya," or whoever their particular boss' name was and leave very quietly. This both infuriated me and fascinated me. Why would they put up with this?

All this changed a year ago, when a Mr. Koshi came from Japan to become the highest-ranking manager in our area. He was very stocky and looked to be the strongest of the Japanese managers with thick arm and leg muscles apparent even when he wore a suit. His hair was very black for his age, only a few gray hairs showed. He had what looked to be a sabre cut on his right cheek and was missing the first digit of his left index finger.

He was different than the other managers. I never saw him give permission to go home on the first request. He'd make the requestor ask a second time and occasionally a third time, each time usually about a half hour later. His first name was Katashi, which means hard, and Mr. Katashi Koshi was very hard.

The first time I saw Mr. Koshi refuse to let someone go home, I tried to remember what my father had said about the prison camp. I remembered him talking of the cruelest guard, whose name was Katashi Koshi. The Mr. Koshi from the camp also had distinctive injuries. I clearly remembered that my father said many times that this guard had a thin, deep cut on his cheeks and was missing part of one finger but I couldn't remember which finger. I kept a diary when I was a teenager and thought I might have written down exactly what my father said about Mr. Koshi but I never got around to looking at it but I did start to closely watch my Mr. Koshi and wonder if he was the same man my father had met and hated.

Most of the Japanese men would surreptitiously watch the beautiful Lilly but Mr. Koshi, who was also married, openly stared, and talked to her every day. He didn't care who knew about it. I was sure he was making passes at her.

Did the men try to hide the passes they made at me? No! I can't remember a single pass made at me in my entire life. I am short; heavily on the plump side before chemo, have very curly disorganized hair that flares up in humidity like an erratic, unreliable fountain. Like my father, I have an extremely large nose. In my mind, my nose gives me distinction, like Jimmy Durante's whose Great Snozzola made him famous. My father would say to me "The two of us have great but non-famous snozzolas. Ours are just as fine as his."

A few weeks before the poisoning, my relationship with Lilly became more personal. We had just put in a major new system. The move was mostly successful and that morning all the programming staff gathered in a conference room to review the implementation. It was standing room only, the Japanese managers and important programmers sitting and the minor programmers, including Lilly and me, standing. Mr. Koshi was the senior manager and Mr. Fuji and Mr. Utsonameya were next under him.

"It is time to review the implementation," said Mr. Koshi.

"I am very proud of my team, our part of the system was moved to production and there was not a single error," said Mr. Utsonameya.

"Perhaps there were no errors because there has not been a single transaction against your programs so far. It may still fail," said Mr. Koshi.

"My programs were executed and we had only one small problem," said Mr. Fuji.

"Tell me about it and why your team failed," said Mr. Koshi.

'There was a change of requirements two days ago. We worked through the night but there was one small problem with the entries," said Mr. Fuji.

"No excuse. No excuse," said Mr. Koshi.

Mr. Koshi spoke English correctly and fairly quickly except when he said, "No excuse," which he always said twice. Mr. Koshi said it, with great emphasis numerous times every day. Sometimes I thought of him as Mister No Excuse, rather than Mr. Koshi.

Just to make it clear exactly how this one phrase sounded, it sounded like "Noo  X  KuSSS, Noo  X  KuSSS," with long pauses between each syllable. He liked to continue his remarks about the implementation failure but I won't try to write how it actually sounded to me but will simply write the gist of his comments.

"I do not accept excuses. Who made that change?" asked Mr. Koshi.

"It was Lilly. I take full responsibility for the failure," said Mr. Fuji.

"Yes, you are fully responsible but it was Lilly who made the mistake and I will not forgive Lilly's mistake."

For the very first time at one of these meetings, I spoke up. I pointed to my nose and said, "With such a huge snoozola, I can smell when something is wrong." Everyone looked my way. I continued, "Lilly did not make a mistake. She was given the wrong information. I know it. No blame can go to her."

To Mr. Koshi, it was as if I hadn't opened my mouth. He and the other Japanese managers continued talking among themselves, ignoring what I said. I avoided looking directly at Lilly but could feel her relief. No one ever directly contradicts Mr. Koshi and I had done it for her. I thought that maybe I had made it worse for her but I hoped not.

Later that morning, I walked into the ladies room and was startled to find that Lilly had one of the sleeves of her blouse rolled up and was in the process of rolling it down. There was a large black mark on her upper left arm.

"What happened?" I asked.

"Nothing happened."

"You have a bruise. Is someone hurting you?"

She changed the subject entirely, "Why don't you come with me to the Mets game tonight? They're the worst team ever but I like them."

"What about the bruise?"

"We'll leave at 5:30."

We went together to the game. My father and I had rooted for the Giants until they left town and I lost some of my interest in the sport. This was the first year for the Mets and they were awful but somehow Lilly had become a fanatic fan. She bought a program and kept score with the stub little pencil that came with it. From the first inning, she was like a different person than the one I knew in the office. It was as if a passion had taken hold of her, all the calm and dignity gave way to just having fun. She was like what she was at the parties, once she was drinking, only here she didn't drink. We ate hot dogs and I drank beer, too much beer.

Her scorecard was kept in English except for one corner, which was written in Japanese. It said, "Attended with" and then some Japanese words I didn't know. I knew the characters weren't for my name. I pointed to it and asked what she had written.

She didn't answer. She smiled and cheered as a Met got a hit.

I smiled and said, "What did you write in Japanese? Trying to keep something back from me?"

She changed the topic again and I looked her in the eye. "Tell me," I said.

"It says," and here she blushed and said something in Japanese, which I didn't understand.

"What does it mean in English?"

"Attended with the bird's beak."

"What does that mean?"

"I always write who I attend the game with on the scorecard. I also staple the tickets on it as a memento."

I ignored her. "What's the bird's beak?"

She hesitated.

"Tell me. Please."

"It's what the Japanese men call you. You're the bird's beak. You know when you sit on their knees and try to kiss them, they say, that you're like a bird, trying to peck them with your beak. I'm sorry."

"I'm proud of my beak actually. What else do they say?"

"That you are the rare Japanese Banker Bird. Exotic but to be feared and honored like a dragon princess spewing fire."

"You're making this up. To be feared? They don't honor me. They always ignore me."

"They ignore you because they don't know what to do with you. They mean it as an immense compliment."

It was almost the end of the game and the Mets were behind. Two Mets were on base. "They're going to lose again," said Lilly. "Not much hope now. " Up stepped Marvelous Marv Thronbury, who hit a triple to put the Mets up. Lily was shouting, "Yes, Yes, Yes. We beat them. Finally." A few seconds later, Thronbury was called out, on an appeal. It turned out, yes, he was on third base but he'd never touched first base as he ran by. The runs were taken off the scoreboard.

"Just like the Mets," she said. From that time, we became not close friends, but much closer.

Over the next ten days, I noticed that Lilly was sometimes sick, which had never happened before and she kept her arms completely covered. On the day before our monthly party, which would take place on Wednesday, she told me she had decided to go back to Japan on Saturday. She wouldn't tell me why.

About a half hour after the party started, I talked to Mr. Utsonameya, who was already swaying on his feet, well on his way to being drunk. Our alcoholic systems programmer was already falling down drunk. He was talking very loudly to Mr. Fuji. I thought he'd have to do a lot of apologizing in the morning because he'd always insult people when he was drunk. Most of the others were standing near the drinks table.

I saw Mr. Haki sitting on a chair in front of a mirror and walked over to him. At this point our systems programmer was lying on the floor kicking his legs in the air and singing a bawdy Scottish drinking song. He had a marvelous booming voice. Almost everyone was listening to him. A few were laughing at the suggestive words of the song. The Japanese are not prudes.

I sat on Mr. Haki's lap and tried to kiss him. While I was doing this, I noticed clearly, in the mirror behind Mr. Haki, that Lilly was in the back of the room, near the windows alone, with a drink in her hand. She took a small green glass vial from her purse and poured the contents into the glass and then put the vial back in her purse. No one paid the slightest attention to her. After she added the drops, Mr. Koshi came over and she offered him the drink. They went up to the window. It looked like he thanked her. He drank it straight down and put the glass down on the windowsill. I thought what happened between Mr. Koshi and Lilly was unusual.

After this, Lilly left the party. I got up off Mr. Haki's lap and followed her. She went into the lady's room and I found her kneeling over a toilet, vomiting.

"Let me hold your hair. You'll soil it, if I don't," I said.

Lilly continued to retch.

"Let me hold your purse, you're dragging it on the ground," I said.

I took her small black purse and put the strap over my shoulder. With one hand I held her hair and with the other I opened her purse, took out the vial and placed it in my bag. Lilly didn't notice.

"Tell me what's happening between you and Mr. Koshi. Do you love him or hate him?" I asked.

Lilly said something in Japanese that I didn't understand. I asked again and she said in English, "I'm not feeling well, I'm going home now." I felt sorry for her and did not want to find out more, so I asked no more questions. I gave her purse back and she left. I went back to the party.

I picked up the glass Mr. Koshi had used from the windowsill and wiped off the prints. Mr. Koshi looked as healthy as a rapidly charging bull. I asked the bartender to put whiskey in the glass and give me a glass of red wine. The systems programmer had stopped singing and stood up so I had a chance to dominate people's attention. Then I did something I had never done before.

I shouted that I was having a wonderful time. I went up to Mr. Koshi and thanked him sincerely for letting me come to this wonderful party and asked if he would share a drink with me. Everyone watched. It was his duty to accept but he seemed to do it gladly. I gave him his glass. We clinked glasses. He drank his straight down while I sipped mine. Mr. Koshi looked exactly the same as he had at the beginning of the party. I hoped that Lilly had given him a love drug. Ten minutes later, he started to sway on his feet. Maybe he was just drunk. He gave his glass to Mr. Utsonameya and sat down. I left.

I went to my desk, wiped Lilly's prints off the green vial and put my prints on it and put it in the back drawer. The next day, I learned that Mr. Koshi had been rushed to the hospital thirty minutes after I left. He died in the early morning.

I went to my apartment, took my teenage diary out of the closet to find exactly what my dad had said about his Mr. Koshi. I found the page but decided not to read it. I was already committed. This information could no longer help me but could make it much more difficult. I threw the diary down the apartment's trash bin. The building burns its trash every day. It would be gone soon.

When I was questioned on Friday, Detectives Jordan and Addison started gently, asking me what had happened at the party. They asked if I knew if Mr. Koshi had any enemies. I told them the truth that most people found him to be overbearing and that he treated people harshly by American standards but not brutal by Japanese standards. I didn't want to say too much because I didn't want to say anything about Lilly. If I could distract the police, she'd fly off soon, free.

Then they started to ask me about the drink I had given Mr. Koshi. Was that something I normally do? I told them no, it was just a spur of the moment idea I'd had. They said that they had the glass I gave him and were having it analyzed. I asked how they knew it was the glass I gave them and they said that both our fingerprints were on it.

It was then that Detective Jordan accused me as I wrote at the beginning of this testimony. I played for time thinking what I should do. Should I try to make it look like Mr. Utsonameya was involved? That wasn't going to work. I knew there was no evidence against him.

I had to protect Lilly but I'd play around with them first. That's when I'd asked for the tea. Time to think why I was doing what I had decided to do. In a few minutes I was positive what I would do and decided to let them have me.

When Detective Jordan got back I said, "You're right detective, I gave Mr. Koshi poison. I only wanted to hurt him; to pay him back for what he did to my family, not kill him but it was intentional. I planned it and I'm glad I did it. I'm proud actually," I smiled as I said it.

"Why did you do it?" asked Detective Addison.

"Let me tell you what I know about Mr. Koshi and why I tried to hurt him. This Mr. Katashi Koshi, was known as "Tiger Koshi" during the war before he went into banking. Tiger tried to leave his past behind him but I found out. He beheaded my two uncles during the Bataan death march. Later in camp, he was known for his cruelty, killing my father's best friend. Very proficient with the blade, he was. He took pride in his cruelty. His first name, "Katashi," means "hard" and Mr. Koshi was hard, in peace and in war."

"How do you know this is that same person?" asked Adele.

"Sometimes, when my father drank too much, he'd tell us about the march and the camp and Mr. Tiger Katashi Koshi. He said that Katashi Koshi had a scar on his right cheek that always reminded my father of Mr. Koshi's legendary long thin bladed sword and the first joint of his left index was missing just like my Mr. Koshi. Plus this Mr. Koshi is the right age, the right name, the right build and height. And he acts just like the Mr. Koshi my father described."

"Were you sure it was him?" asked Etective Jordan.

"Yes," I said. I had been very sad when my father died a year ago both because I loved him and because I had failed completely in my aim to convince him of the humanity of the Japanese. But with his death, the police couldn't ask him to verify what I said. I was glad that I destroyed my teenage diary. What if it contradicted my story? If there was any doubt they could widen the instigation and the crime would then be first-degree murder not revenge and manslaughter. To me, the absolute literal truth no longer mattered; I would save Lilly, whatever the cost.

I can hear you, the reader asking me was this the same Mr. Koshi? I'll be completely honest. I'm not one hundred percent certain but I am eighty-five percent sure. Was I sorry he had just died, even if he was the Mr. Koshi of the camp? Yes, very sorry.

I told the detectives that I was one hundred percent sure. They were quite happy to believe me. They probably didn't have any other leads or they thought, if it wasn't me, then who? There must be many others who hated Mr. Koshi. It would probably be harder making the charge stick against anyone else. But I may be defaming Jordan and Addison. I'm sure they believed I did it.

I told them a lot of the truth but not the whole truth. I didn't tell them I also had other motives for making my confession.

I'm not ashamed to write that I loved Lilly almost from the day she arrived at the bank.

The second was my father's passionate hatred of the Japanese and how it warped his otherwise kindly character. Hatred smashes the heart and health of the hater. The damage is obvious to others but not to the wrecked.

The third was that I fell in love with Zen practice and Zen stories.

I felt about the Koans, as I felt about life. Life is complex, confusing, mysterious and seemingly impossible to understand as are the Koans. Maybe it was crazy but I believed that if I could solve a Koan, I could understand life.

My fourth motive was that I was going to die soon. I hadn't told anyone yet but my cancer had returned, worse than before, having spread to too many places to operate on. Chemo wouldn't give much hope either. I couldn't go through that again for no gain. Not the most pleasant of news.

There is a story that before he became the Buddha of history, the proto-Buddha was incarnated as a hare. To save the life of starving yogis, he sacrificed himself by throwing himself into their fire so they could eat him. I could do something like that. I could save Lilly. My thinking was, why should Lilly die or go to prison? She has her whole life, a completely full life, in front of her. She has always made me feel at home and there must be some reason she did it. She was a good person to sacrifice for.

I was worried what people would think of me if I "admitted" my "guilt." Then I thought of another Zen story. A girl had a child out of wedlock and when asked who was the father, she did not want to name the real father. Instead she named a famous Zen master. When accused, the master only said "Is that so."

He lost his reputation and students but he took good care of the baby. A year later, the woman wanted her baby back and she told her parents the name of the real father. The parents apologized and took back the baby. The master's only words to the parents were, "Is that so."

"Is that so." Such an ambiguous but vigorous statement. I could say that to the police. What do I care about my reputation? I was proud of my decision.

In court, I "confessed" to manslaughter. No mention of Mr. Koshi's potential war crimes was made. I didn't want any accusation made against him.

As I sit in my prison cell, I'm reminded of the complaints some of my Manhattan friends have about the size of their apartments, calling them large closets. I'd tell them that your apartment is larger and more comfortable than my jail cell, which is bare of decoration and has bars. We have little diversion or fun and you can't go anywhere.

I miss my social life especially my sisters and cousins but I missed Lilly the most. My sisters and some cousins came to visit me but I never hear anything from Lilly. I didn't want to contact her because I didn't even want anyone to think there was any connection between us.

I kept my spirits up thinking what a wonderful prison this is compared to the camp my father had been at and by thinking about Lilly being free.

Prison is its own separate world, just like a Japanese bank is a world of its own, but I only have a little time to describe it. I shared my cell with a woman named Mildred, who is a small, gentle woman, convicted for murdering her husband. The way she described their relationship, I was surprised she hadn't done it years before. As I meet other inmates I began to believe that most of us were more victims of our circumstances than active doers of evil.

Mildred is a great, relentless, unending, continuous, fanatical talker. She seems petrified of silence. If you meet her once a week for coffee, she would have been a wonderful friend as many of the incidents she talks about are funny or interesting. Unfortunately for both of us, for long periods each day, she has no one to speak to except me and I have heard most of her stories many times over. You don't get many new stories sitting in a woman's prison. I know how much it hurts not to be listened to, so I spend a lot of time each day listening to her but it is never enough.

I wanted to get on with my meditation practice, so I'd ask her for three long silent periods each day. She said yes but, as I sat, if I even slightly nodded off or got restless, she would start talking to me. She was exactly like the person in the Zendo assigned to hit anyone who loses concentration in meditation. This did me a great service. I basically got to sit for hours every day, with someone making sure that I concentrated, all at the expense of New York State. I don't recommend you commit a crime so you can sit but to me it was a positive.

Every few weeks, Suzzi comes to check up on my progress.

I wanted to solve my Koan. My situation reminded me of the story of a man who spent years but couldn't solve his Koan. His teacher urged just two more intense weeks of practice and he'd succeed. That's the kind of advice Suzzi gave me. Seven months passed with what seemed to me very little results.

Finally the man's teacher told him to do one more intense week and, if he didn't succeed, he'd best kill himself. I saw my doctor again and he told me I had maybe a month or two left. I knew he was trying to be optimistic. I was just like the man in the story; we were both at the end of our possibilities. He broke through. I wasn't sure I could.

Sometimes I thought I got a glimpse of an answer. It's like looking at a picture with a million random dots. It is so confusing and then you see the pattern and wonder why you didn't see it immediately. The vision fades and it takes ages to come back. I went through that cycle many times. This time the vision stayed.

Suzzi came to see me. I sat in front of her and I stated my Koan. As was my practice, I first gave an answer to amuse her. Something that sounded funny and had that Zen ring to it. Today I stated my Koan and said, "The answer is eight slices of bread, four of them toasted, one buttered on the reverse side."

As always, Suzzi had no reaction. Then I gave Suzzi my real answer, the one I felt in my bones. Suzzi smiled, nodded, got up, hugged me and then calmly left. It was the happiest day of my life, so far.

Last week, I got a card from Lilly with a photograph of her, holding Jasmine, her baby girl, with her older looking husband beside her. On the back printed in Japanese was, "Welcome Jasmine to the world." Under that was written in Lilly's handwriting, in Japanese. " My gift from the bird's beak."

I cried, deep happy tears. Mildred asked what was wrong. I showed her the photograph and said, trying to choke back the emotions, "What an incredibly beautiful baby." Mildred nodded yes and asked what the baby's name was. I told her and Mildred began to tell me a story of her cousin's baby, who was also named Jasmine. I tried to pay attention but was too happy to notice much of what she said. She told me the story twice more that afternoon, so I didn't miss anything.

A few days after that, a friend told me of the time capsule and that the manuscript was due in four days. I wanted to leave something behind to possibly help mankind. My friend talked to the prison chaplain, who got me the use of a typewriter. First, I thought about what I wanted to say. The short deadline made it simpler to decide. You've now read most of it. I'll just add a brief wish for you.

I hope your life is as happy and as successful as mine. You may not be blessed with a giant snozzola, like mine, but I'm sure, if you really try, you can sniff out what you are supposed to be doing in this world. I'm not trying to tell you what to do. Everyone has their own way and tasks. I'm encouraging you to tackle the great seemingly unattainable mystery. It only seems unattainable.

It's late at night and this is due in a few hours. They were very kind and let me stay in the solitary cells so I could finish this and not disturb anyone with my typing.

As I type, the moon is rising. At night, they keep the lights turned down a bit. The window is high and small. The moonlight is faint but sublimely beautiful. I wish I could give you that beautiful moon but all I can give is this manuscript.

Fare thee well. Friend.

CPSIA information can be obtained
at www.ICGtesting.com
Printed in the USA
JSHW041620150122
21934JS00002B/5

9 781736 313442